Transparent Shadows

A Novel in three
Hilarious Episodes

M.V.S.Rao

PARTRIDGE
A Penguin Random House Company

For information and address : M.V.S.Rao,
Contact: mvsrao512@gmail or mvsrao512@yahoo.co.in

ISBN: Softcover   978-1-4828-1987-8
             Ebook   978-1-4828-1988-5

This Book is a work of fiction, People, Places, Events and situations are the products of Author's imagination. Any resemblance to actual persons, living or dead, or historical events, is purely coincidental.

Because of the dynamic nature of the Internet, any web addresses or links contained in this book may have changed since publication and may no longer be valid. The views expressed in this work are solely those of the author and do not necessarily reflect the views of the publisher, and the publisher hereby disclaims any responsibility for them.

To order additional copies of this book, contact
Partridge India
000 800 10062 62
www.partridgepublishing.com/india
orders.india@partridgepublishing.com

Dedicated to

Chalapati.
Sharada
Mahrookh

With Affection.

CONTENTS

Episode 3

SYNOPSIS

"All the world's a stage, and all the men and
women merely players; They have their exits
and their entrances!"
—William Shakespeare.

'Transparent Shadows' is a work of fiction, created
stories around two amateur professional actors,
who were depicted as popular stage artists, of Kolkata city
in India.

In spite long experience enacting various roles Shoilen
Dutta, finds that he could not get absorbed in real
professional careers to get lucrative chances in professional
stage, TV serials or film opportunities in Kolkata, due to
severe competition!. As he was getting past middle age
with meager income, he realizes the bleak future awaits
him. As he may have to quit or depend on others if he
becomes invalid or too old!. He, along with another a
younger amateur stage artist Lolit Sen, decide to make
better money by fooling the public by deception with their
clever acting in real life!. They make elaborate planning
in acts of deceit of different situations to somehow profit
from unsuspecting victims. Their grim ventures are

depicted in several episodes with touch of Hilarity. In each episode the duo deals with variety of characters different situations facing interesting twists and unexpected turns. It is in fact compilation of different stories in which the two play interesting key roles. When they unexpectedly face hard gutted dangerous criminals in their ventures they cleverly manipulate to expose them to the law without losing their own identities or motives.

This is purely a fiction and not at all based on real lives of any past or present stage actors.

The main hero Shoilen is created as a shrewd but a very jovial person with ready wit and tact. His supporting partner Lolit is equally good at acting and to convince persons, the falsehood as truth!. Each episode is created with variety of different situations and with different persons, with clever tackling of different problems. They almost succeed in their criminal ventures, keeping the readers also in good humor and interest. These two actors live by acting on stage to entertain the audience, to act in real life to fool the world!.

It is a crime novel with three hilarious Episodes.

M.V.S.Rao
Author.

PROLOGUE

Kolkata! . . . the magic city of India!, which has a respectable place for modern Indian living Arts! . . . . Culturally very nostalgic public encourage Art, Music, Dance and Drama with Passion. Kolkata's another great love as well devotion is for Durga Puja, especially during Dussehra festival. It is a great annual event when thousands of temporary structures known as Pendals come up all over Kolkata as well Bengal for mass worship of Durga by the public. More than life size colorful clay images of Goddess Durga and her concerts are placed with utmost Artistic ways. Goddess Durga is generally depicted in a dramatic way as if victoriously fighting demon king Mahishasura as mentioned in the Hindu epics. It is a joyful as well pious festival like Christmas. Novel feature of Durga puja, which is celebrated for 5 days, is interestingly tied up with cultural events held in make shift auditoriums with stages erect near most important Durga puja Pendals. The city becomes agog with public congregating to Pendals in thousands to worship as well witness cultural events like Music soirees, Dances and Theatrical performances held during that period. Many new talented artists come to limelight during these festival programs.

One particular year a Drama group with high reputation in the city was about to enact a play called 'Charulota' on 9 th day of Dushera which is penultimate day of the festivities as well last day for cultural programs. The temporary auditorium was part of an important Durga puja Pendal in the vicinity of Rashbehari Avenue, of Kolkata. Only dramas of high caliber theatre groups are arranged in that location. That day group's main organizer was a veteran stage artist Shoilen Datta, of Kolkata.

It was afternoon, and less than Four hours are left to start the play. All temporary cloth side-walls around the auditorium were closed or the public for preparation, decoration and illumination work by the drama group's volunteers and others connected workers in the stage as well auditorium. All were extremely busy with feverish activities on the stage and green rooms. The director and few important members including Shoilen Datta were sitting in the auditorium discussing the various issues connected with the drama.

At that very moment Shoilen's mobile ringing caused a minor deviation to that group. He pressed the button and revealed his name. He became stiff alert after hearing few seconds, there was a clear expression of shock of very serious news he heard. All others present were also tensed at his sudden reaction and staring at him with suspense. He was reacting in a serious way the caller's message and was questioning in a fast way with worried expression. Finally when the phone talking was over, his reaction was that a utter disbelief of what he heard!. He is noted for quick control of the situation however unexpected problems arose in drama activities!. This particular

Tele-message reflected a very disturbed reaction from him. He was speechless for few moments looked helpless covering his head with both hands, expressing his extreme anguish!, unable to react with his colleagues!. He then expressed with grave concern that day's play may have to be cancelled as Johnovi met with an accident and admitted in a Hospital!. The director as well all his colleagues were flabbergasted and too shocked at that unexpected turn of the tragic news. It was unthinkable to stage the play without her, their main heroine; as the pivotal role of the play was of her only. All were clueless, as no other lady was available to done that role, in in such a short period. There was heated discussion with no solution to the grave problem. All of them were too stunned as no one could find realistic solution to enact that play which was their most popular one, of their group. To cancel that play on the final day of Durga puja festival at the most prestigious location was unthinkable to the group. All were staring blankly to cope with the unexpected tragic news, with depressed mood.

All other actors and supporting characters were unaware of this serious situation; were all busy in their activities. At that juncture Shoilen saw Lolit Sen, their main anchorman for all the behind the screen activities of the play, being extremely busy with confident cool attitude organizing the set as well checking the props on the stage. At that time two female artists came to him and were bothering him about some act's details. He was thorough about this play as he was in charge of prompting and finer points of each and every actor's dialogues and entry and exit details in different sequences. He was expert in stage management. He is also very good in acting and doing different roles during rehearsals of any play during entire preparation period.

Physically he was slim and hardly Five feet two inches, but dynamic in his attitude. His fair skin turned red, due to hard work since morning. His long hair was in disheveled and unkempt way yet giving a dignified look to him!. Due to his short and slim figure, he couldn't aspire hero roles; he concentrated only on stage management activities. During his education years he was one of the good artists in amateur groups; but now his acting is restricted to do only minor supporting roles. Due to his friendly helpful attitude and pleasing personality he was the most sought after person with the entire group. Even Shoilen was his closest friend and used to take his advice for any play or connected infra-structure.

As Lolit went to the wings, chatting laughingly with the two female artists, Shoilen was staring at him at his figure of handsome stature but with height same as the females with him. Suddenly something came to his mind like a lightening!. He rose and told his friends to wait and went up the stage and walked towards the wings. He met Lolit with a hurried attitude and requested the female artists to meet him latter. He and Lolit went to a far off corner where he told him the serious situation their group facing in staging the show that evening. As an only alternate solution he spoke, in low voice, his sudden new idea. Lolit remained utterly speechless with the senior actor's unexpected request. He was trying to object by nodding his head with a negative attitude and pleading with a serious concern not to make that unrealistic proposal. After some fifteen minutes of heated close talk, Lolit understood Shoilen's sincere efforts to save their group losing their position of being top most drama group in the field. He seriously started considering whether he would able to do justice to that great new experiment!. But Shoilen seemed had his last word and made him agree to avert the catastrophe. He told with strong conviction, that Lolit has the potential to save the situation by doing that Charulota role, that evening, in a feminine make-up!. Lolit relented and accepted to try that experiment.

Shoilen immediately called the director to that place and put in his proposal with a sincere assurance. Director immediately agreed to Shoilen's unique idea as he had also full confidence that Lolit can only do the justification with in that limited period. They decided to keep that proposal within them and try a rehearsal immediately, without informing rest of the caste at that juncture. Shoilen called their well experienced makeup man, and informed the requirement. After a critically examining Lolit, the make-up man smiled happily and said he will be able to do his job with in 30 minutes.

Shoilen and the director had a close meeting as to how to introduce him as a female star with new name, as Kolkata audience would react with reservations, if it was revealed, that a male artist acted the heroine's role. There might jeer with mockery, which could unnerve Lolit, even if he tried his best to act as a female in a convincing way. They decided not to inform other artists of the play too. They wanted keep the secret till the rehearsals were enacted satisfactorily.

As the green room door opened a vivacious looking female star came out with full confidence!. Lolit with his slim figure with fair skin fitted well to act in a female role looking absolutely like a very well dressed lady from a noble family!. His big eyes added more glamour!. Long hair wig and artificial female curves added a sexy charm!.

Shoilen as well the director were really impressed with the transformation of handsome Lolit to vivaciously charming lady!.

All the main members of the cast were asked to congregate in the wing. All the female and male artistes as well as helping volunteers who assembled there were surprised at a new female star whom they did not see earlier. Most were staring at her as the face looked familiar but could not guess!. Shoilen introduced her to all stating her name as Miss Monjulota Mojumdaar, who also had acted as Charulotha for a different group.

"Unfortunately our main heroine Johnovi met with an accident and was admitted in a hospital and not in a position to move. We were shocked at her unfortunate absence, as it would lead to cancelation of that day's prestigious play. I was most worried as all of you know that so many days preparation to this play would have been wasted, if we don't be show our play in this venue, today. We made many contacts to face the situation with an alternate heroine as the only alternative. I got information about her and invited her to help our situation by donning Charulotha role. We are fortunate at her very kind gesture to help us in this critical time."

Some female artists smilingly went near Mojulota and thanked her profusely with greetings and shake hands. One or two ladies smilingly told that Monjulatha looked like sister of Lolit! They were searching for him in that assembled group. Then Shoilen smilingly informed the gathering they brought her only through his efforts. He requested all the artists to cooperate with the new entrant to make that day's important show a success. He informed a dress rehearsal would be first performed immediately with the new heroine.

All along Lolit remained serious with shy down cast looks. He behaved as if he was surrounded by unknown strangers, as all were staring at him with curiosity!. Even after accepting to do the female role he was inwardly very tense with a feeling of uncertainty. He knew thoroughly the heroine Charulota's dialogues yet an uncertain feeling was raging within him. He decided to face the situation with firm determination.

That attitude and continuous helpful suggestions from the director and Shoilen helped him to do that role. Main advantage was Shoilen was the hero in that day's play which also gave Lolit more confidence as he would acting with him only in most scenes.

All the artists were most helpful and encouraged Lolit, appreciating his talent in acting most convincingly during breaks. Within that four hours the team did two rehearsals to give flawless performance!. They were all set for the real show. Shoilen was very happy that Lolit gave the fillip in a satisfactory way even though it was his first big role that too in a female getup!.

When the rehearsal was concluded in almost in a realistic way, all the artists happily closeted Lolit to congratulate, He smilingly acknowledged and thanked them modestly. He treated all of them modestly with friendly gesture not revealing his true identity.

As soon the gates were opened, the auditorium quickly filled to the brim, with hundreds of spectators thronging on all three sides including part of the prayer space in front of the deities. All were eagerly waiting for that play to start. As the final gong rang, the show started.

It impressively began with background song, by a team of musicians started singing in a chorus. lead by a female singer. The well blended group song also started in low voice gradually rose to high pitch and again as back ground music!. The Key-board and Tabla instruments added more life to the song. The song was rendered, introducing the story background, in an attractive musical way as the deep Red front drop screen, gradually rose. The lighting also gradually became brighter depicting well designed interior of a wealthy home, on the stage. Lolit as Charulota looking like a beautiful lady with attractive make-up and dress entered from the left wing while Shoilen as the hero of the play entered from the right side wing. Charulota was adjusting a flower-vase singing within herself in a very low tone. The back ground music gradually faded with light instrumental sounds only, creating a very dramatic Audio effect matching with the opening of the first act scene very impressively.

Lolit first avoided looking at the audience lest they find him to be an imposter. First few seconds he felt nervousness and uttered his dialogue in low voice addressing Shoilen on stage who was the hero of the play. Shoilen understood his friend's stage freight and quickly came to his rescue as if it was part of the play he went closely to Lolit and held him affectionately and said:

"Oh! Charulota! . . . are you not feeling well? . . . . What happened to your voice dear! . . . I am unable to hear you?"

This was not part of the original dialogue but he tried to save the situation. Lolit understood his friend's trick. He immediately regained his posture and started uttering the dialogues gradually in a natural way with a louder voice; which helped him to lessen the initial fear. He observed that there was no negative reaction from the audience, which brought him confidence.

In few minutes Lolit understood that he was doing well; which brought more acting caliber on the stage with confidence!. He experimented a nice sounding style of speaking with a voluptuous feminine movements conveying a licentious body language also!. It hit the right chords in the minds of the male audience to give encouraging applause!. That gave full confidence to lose his earlier stage fright and acted freely. He virtually lived in that role and did full justice to that character. It looked as if he forgot that he was Lolit but became Charulota on the stage!

After the first act when the curtain dropped, Shoilen and other actors hugged him with happy emotion. All were impressed at his nice performance like a seasoned actor!. The show was a complete success. All the artists received a thunderous ovation from the audience at the end when they all stood on the stage after the final act, during the backstage anchor's announcing the names of each participant, as he announced Lolit's name as Miss Manjulota Mojumdar, all the spectators gave Lolit, in the Charulota makeup, a roaring standing ovation with continues clapping in appreciation of her acting. Lolit bowed respectfully with folded hands. The audience never had any least doubt that a male actor done that role with female make-up!.

When the show was over, Lolit became the star attraction to the group for not only saving their last show, but also doing full justice like an experienced actor in his first appearance in a major role on the stage!. Only after the rehearsals Shoilen announced to them with a mischievous smile that their own Lolit did the Charulota role. All the members roared merrily and hugged him with joyful show of appreciation. Shoilen cautioned the group never to reveal the truth about Monjulota Mojumdar!.

Unexpectedly there was a film producer, Chenchal Reddy, from Hyderabad, who witnessed the play. He was given complementary invitation by the Hotel management, who were the sponsors of that day's play. He was most impressed by the performance of Mojulota Mojumdar, who acted most dynamically the role of Charulota!, he decided to meet the charming artist to offer a role in his proposed new Telugu film.

*   *   *

EPISODE 1

Outline story

Shoilen Datta a veteran stage actor of Kolkata, was a very senior popular artist among the amateur drama circles. He was from a middle class family drawn to the stage acting, which became an addiction from young age neglecting the studies. He remained busy in that chosen profession, with dedication. His tall personality with booming voice well suited to the stage. Due to his stage activities of late hours working, he remained bachelor. To avoid disturbance to his family, he used to stay in a separate independent flat. He not only could act well on stage but in real life also he could impress every one with his presence. Besides being a shrewd actor, he had a ready wit and jocular imagination, to amuse unsuspecting strangers!. When he reached middle age, he started to realize his bleak future with dwindling income without savings. Due to high competition in Kolkata, he could not get absorbed in any professional acting jobs like TV serials or film line, which only offer lucrative careers for actors. His cunning-side started imagining to attempt risky unlawful methods to make high earnings!. He started to believe firmly to put use his known acting talent to exploit the foolish world around him, to earn better by deceit without looking from moral angle!.

Lolit Sen another amateur theater enthusiast like him was his close friend, even though much junior than him. Shoilen convinces Lolit to join illegal new venture. Lolit was an all-rounder in the stage mostly behind the screen in rehearsals acting, prompting and similar others. Lolit was also very handsome personality like Shoilen, but was slim and short. When an unexpected serious situation erupts he had to done the heroin's role to save their group's prestige show on their last day's important play. He acted most successfully and no one could know a male acted the heroine role!. He showed uncanny talent to act as a female, in a most convincing way. Shoilen felt Lolit's talent to act in female roles would give best advantage for his new crime plan!.

The duo decides to put into practice the new joint venture secretly and share the profits equally. Their first launching was a complete success, which they experimented on unsuspecting strangers in two trains, on the same day.

One of their victims was a professional Document Writer, Kalicharon Kundu, traveling as a passenger. They were flabbergasted to find unexpected huge haul of rich dividends, from his belongings.

(Part of 'TRANSPARENT SHADOWS'—A Fiction— written by the Author: M.V.S.Rao)

CHAPTER 1

*Shoilen Dutta wanted to entice Lolit
Sen in his new black venture!*

Kolkata, the oldest metropolitan city in India, retains
its rich Bengali culture. Our story starts in Shyam
Bazaar road which is hub of traditional Bengali theatre
activities of this busy city. It is also a unique place that
reflects the typical local citizens' outdoor life. Morning
to evening the place is generally bustling with different
type of persons from all walks of life. Women folk come
in small groups, in colorful hand woven local Saris
and traditional ornaments, chatting loudly their daily
happenings. The variety of crowd present reflects attractive
picture of colorful city life. The surrounding areas are
abundant with shops, entertainment centers, cinema
halls, cafes, drama theatres, dance and music training
institutions. Theatre and music are the average Kolkata
citizen's passion!. Many small eateries in that place also
cater as Addas.(loud chit chatting place for groups). That
is another popular pastime of local persons of all ages!.

Location of larger and smaller shops on the Main
avenue as well in the numerous by lanes bring hordes of

people from all walks of life for pleasant family shopping. With more than 100 years history the Shyam Bazar has developed into one of the most popular place in the city. With passing of years brought more traffic, crowds and noise yet the place always remained very popular with the locals!. Years have brought very little change in the life style and the typical urban Bengali flavor and culture, which is still the high point in this part of the city!.

On a particular day in the evening, amidst the busy noise and hustle bustle of the crowds, a tall dark Shoilen Dutta, was walking in a casual gait. He is a professional actor among amateur theatre groups. He was dressed in his usual western jeans and white Punjabee shirt (kurta). Even though past his prime, and approaching middle age, still walked like a youngish person. He is on his usual route of the pavement. He was so accustomed to walk in that place moving along unmindful of the surrounding crowds. He was going to meet his friend Lolit Sen. Even while walking his mind was busy thinking of the character role he has to play on the next day on the stage!. Sometimes rehearsing the dialogues little audibly causing stares from the close by crowd!.

Shoilen, a tall person with long broad face with befitting large nose and biggish eyes and forehead and having booming voice, was well suited to the stage. From school to college days he had high passion to act in Dramas. The theatre stage life always attracted him more than any higher education and jobs!. He had to discontinue studies without completing graduation because he preferred acting and avoided examinations!. Because of his aptitude and talent, to act any sort of role in dramas, made him a popular stage actor for the small amateur professional groups. Needless to say his middleclass family had to give up hopes to change his life style!. They had to accept his late arrivals or keeping busy whole day or absence for some days. Only his father who himself used be an amateur actor in his younger days had a soft corner for this son!. As a small boy Shoilen used to accompany his father many a time to rehearsals and dramas. At younger age the interesting life and joys of the drama life made a deep impression in him!. He also had an opportunity to do small child roles when he was twelve years old in two plays. It lasted hardly 15 minutes, but his happiness knew no bounds for the applause he got from the audience!. From that day theatre became his sole life ambition destination!.

He had his own two bed roomed flat at Monictola, away from his old ancestral house. He preferred his separate accommodation to avoid disturbance to the other family members for his untimely visits. Occasionally he used to go to the terrace of his old house to loudly rehearse his dialogues!. His family members and neighbors would sneak in to hear dialogues and solo acting. Being a professional he was unmindful of the onlookers. Everyone who knew him in the neighborhood of his old home would respect him and look towards him with awe at his talent.

Most days or nights his main avocation was to meet the co-artists, both men and women, of different ages in some old theatres or school halls, for serious preparation for stage plays. In such gatherings every individual would strive to give their best. They all had a common passion to make the drama a success!. Some days he was doing rehearsals for two groups at different times!.

Majority amateur actors and actresses were having some other jobs or other responsibilities. Some were only house wives. Most of them sought acting not for any financial gains but mainly for the irresistible thrill and passion to act on the stage!. They would all become closed knit group from initial preparation to final stage performance.

During the rehearsals time they gradually tend to become a fraternity group, sharing their joys and hardships, irrespective of their living backgrounds or social differences. Shoilen was popular and most sought after person of such groups due to his long association with theatre activities of that city.

Because of his reluctance to enter marital life he remained a bachelor in his family!. He would strictly avoid close contacts with unmarried women!. Many maidens would hang on closely to him during drama activities; he would evade them tactfully in friendly way. However he used to enjoy the company of married women calling them affectionately as Boudee (Elder brother's wife). Most family ladies would normally feel happy and give affection; which helped, to get good co-operation and sometimes more personal closeness!.

He used to be most busy before and during the annual 'Shorbo-Jonanee Utsab' celebrations,(Durga Puja or Dusshera festival of India) as a prominent actor. That annual event used to bring a big boost to Shoilen's performances. He used to get even invitations from other cities of India, from the outside state Bengali associations to enact in their drama shows.

He was a well accomplished actor, mastering variety of different characters on the stage be a hero or a villain or other supporting roles. His dedication was such; he virtually would live in any character in a realistic way.

In his real life also he was an expert in the art of mimicry to lecture like prominent politicians and other V.I.Ps and or others to his group or in small crowd, who would watch with awe, at his acting performances. Once during a dress rehearsal he went out with his friends to a restaurant. On that day he was dressed as a senior police officer for a particular play. The restaurant staff treated him with respect thinking him to be a real police officer. When he, intentionally for fun, he showed displeasure, in some food items, they pleaded to forgive and did not take the charges for the food!. He had other mischievous traits to fool unsuspecting persons with his acting talent and practical jokes causing bewilderment to them or he could also fool them with ease!. Many outsiders would be carried away by his concocted tales of his own creation with fragment of imagination, causing amusement to his close friends. He could tell with all seriousness giving least suspicion of any imaginative narrations. He enjoyed his chosen profession of acting whole heartedly. On the stage he could make anybody spellbound with his outstanding acting ability.

In spite of his busy life with full-fledged participation with dedication on the stage, his income was barely used to be sufficient even for his personal needs. He however could only a get a separate flat in Monictola, through one builder, who was his close friend in a theatre group. He allotted him at a minimum price out of respect.

His main ambition of becoming a successful professional actor was getting receded, as his age started showing!. He could not get foot hold in real commercial professional theatres, TV shows and film acting, because of the high competition!. That was generally the cherished desire, for most artists, as they are the main money spinners. With losing the prime age, he seriously started looking for opportunities, to earn better returns. Fear also started to haunt him that his acting career might tragically end if he becomes ill or if he met with an accident. He never wanted to be a burden to anyone. He had no big savings except his two-bed room apartment.

He seriously started to think of alternate ways of earning while still in good form. He knew without proper higher education he had very few opportunities in other fields to make better living. By nature he was a shrewd as well ruthless, could take hard decisions to achieve ambition; sometimes he would deceive his close unsuspecting associates also with least remorse. He found he could cheat many persons easily with lies by his acting ability!. His cunning-side started imagining to attempt risky unlawful methods to make high earnings!. He started to believe firmly to put use his known acting talent to exploit the foolish world around him, to earn by deceit without looking from moral angle!.

He started believing that was the only way left before he became too old. In the past he could easily convince or fool many persons in real life by his serious acting, many a times usually just for fun only!. He also strongly believed that he would require a very trustworthy partner to execute his venture successfully, as it wouldn't be practical to put into practice single handedly, He realized that for any such dark venture, a close partner is very essential to put his ideas to action.

He found only Lolit was his closest associate in his circle. Added to that he found Lolit also has an excellent acting ability. But he was bit skeptical about his cooperation as it involved criminal as well shrewd outlook in his proposed dangerous venture. For few months he was hesitant to seek his help, lest if he refuses his whole secret ambition would be exposed and get damaged. He started cunningly planning to become his closest friend than any other actor of his group. Lolit was most impressed and devoted to Shoilen for his versatility with practical way of organizing any play to minutest details, in addition to his outstanding acting. When Shoilen preferred his association than any other of the group, he felt elated and became his closest friend.

He felt proud to be his close confederate aid. Whatever plays Shoilen planned he sought his advice separately before revealing to others. They both used to preplan the discussions, and Shoilen would scheme some points to be voiced in group-meeting through him!. This added to his image and also made him an important member of Shoilen's drama group. There was much age difference as well acting experience between them yet he found Shoilen developed much confidence on him and openly used to express his sincere appreciation to Lolit before all the members. That made him to be more devoted with high respect towards Shoilen. He felt proud as their friendship getting closer. He found in spite of close friendship, Shoilen never took any advantage but always talked with sincerity and respect, never treating as a junior artiste. Of late they started meeting very regularly every day, discussing points of drama problems as well general chat. Never Lolit had any inkling that Shoilen was scheming to be his close associate with some ulterior motive. Shoilen built an absolute confidence that he felt sure that his protege could be now taken into his confidence to lay before him, his secret ambition. He worked for this day with utmost thoroughness. Shoilen found only little drawback in Lolit's outlook. He was attracted to young women artists in the group and found women members also liked him and sought his attention!. The real fact was Lolit joined the theatre group to move closely with women artists, as he felt it gave him also better opportunity to mingle with more forward type group of good looking young women!. But Shoilen felt this weakness would not be a serious minus point. He firmly decided to put into action to recruit him as a partner for his dangerous venture. He came well-rehearsed to brain wash him with his theory and he firmly believed that he would succeed in his attempts.

That evening he decided to open his secret criminal venture plan to Lolit in a discrete-way; starting with the frustrations he would face in his present conditions continue. He knew, Lolit, normally respected him and literally worshipped him as a true follower. He decided to take him as his only partner for the proposed venture!.

At about six pm Shoilen reached his friend Lolit Sen's work place, a big medical showroom with many counters, where he worked as a pharmacist.

Shoilen entered the large store and stood near a corner counter. A young sales woman was attending the customers there. He saw his friend Lolit in the interior busily checking some medicine packets. She addressed him courteously:

"Sir, what do you want please?"

He saw an innocent sincere saleswoman with thick rimmed glasses, asking him very seriously, when he realized that he never met her before, he wanted to confuse and upset her, as his usual trait with strangers just for fun.

"Miss I feel I had seen you some where! . . . yes I remember you are acting in Bangla TV serial 'Tapur-Tupur' is it not? How lucky to see you face to face! . . . your acting is great!"

She felt embarrassed, . . . felt shy at his mistake:

"No sir you got confused I never acted in any TV Serial. Sir which medicine you want please?"

"Oh maa! . . . how you look so great like a real TV star!"

"Sir please tell me about your requirement please?"

He asked changing the topic "Choti Di! (young sister) What is the departure time of Back Diamond Express? Does it start from Sealdah or from Howrah station?"

(Local Train and railway stations) He asked with innocent looks.

She stared at him and answered with a modest smile "Sorry sir I do not know the railway timings please tell me if any medicines are required"

"Young lady! . . . could you kindly tell me which is shorter route to Bangur Hospital junction via Alipore or Ballygunj by bus or tram? . . . I fear going by Metro".

"Sorry sir I am not very familiar with south Kolkata . . . . any medicines you require sir?"

She asked with little frown.

"Ok young lady I do not require any medicines, is there a watch repair section in this show room?"

"Sorry sir we don't repair watches here"

"Do you have a Gents' repellent scent to keep people away if applied?"

She stared with surprise at his silly requirement with disgusting look and tried to control her cool.

"No we don't sell such perfumes" She said with a frown.

"I didn't know that! . . . . OK. Pack me half kilo of 'Taalgur-Sondesh' and a pot of Mishti Doy give me cooled"

(A popular Bengali sweet and sweet curd) he asked her with all seriousness.)

She was astonished beyond belief at his requirements!. She thought he must be either a mental or making fun of her. The young lady, as it is was having a tough time, due to rush of customers since last 2 hours without respite. She was visibly shocked at this new customer's silly requests added to that he wanted to buy sweets in a Medical shop!. Her face became red with anger and she lost all her patience and growled loudly, in Bengali:

"kee moshay kee hosche!? Oushad dokhaner mishti kobe bikri korey?! shamne Mishti dokhan hosche otake jan . . . amar shamoy byardho koribenna !"

("Gentleman what happened to you!? How you expected sweets to be sold in this Medical shop! There is a sweets shop in this road go there! and don't' waste my time")

"kI bolchi shishtar kal ey dukhaner ami mishti kinichilam O badhralok amake diyeche tumi nutan asche kore shaper ki milibo janey na ! O bhadralok ko bulon . . . vo jaanchi"

(what sister! you do not know about your shop! . . . that gentleman there had sold sweets yesterday only, as you might be new to this shop please call him)

He said with a serious annoyed voice.

She became angry and lost her temper and shouted:

"kee chomotkar! Amaar Aushad dukhaaner apni mishti kinchen? ey dukaner bishoy ami bhallo janichi dayakore moshay turont beri jan amar shomay nashto koran na!"

("What a wonder! . . . you purchased sweets in our shop! . . . I know about this shop very well! Mister Please don't waste my time go out")

Adjoining few sales men noticed Shoilen but kept smiling, as most new his fun traits.

Pointing to Lolit who was busy in his job "That gentleman over there who acting busy doing no work has sold Rosogullas* yesterday in this shop . . . call him and he will help you"

The young lady was disgusted with his attitude and hurriedly went to Lolit frowning and showed him the silly customer and told him that he was asking for sweets in this shop and wasting her time by also asking other odd questions and requirements!.

Lolit who suddenly saw his friend broke into a big grin and greeted Shoilen and told the young lady that gentleman is his friend and not to mind his antics, that he is a most popular actor and has a habit of annoying some innocent strangers with such practical jokes just for fun!.

Handing over his duties he came out of the shop with Shoilen, still laughing at his friend's mischievous traits. He took his habitual pan from his silver box in his pocket, and put in his mouth. They both started towards their usual meeting place.

"The poor girl almost got fits with your irrelevant queries!"

"I was about to ask her whether ferry would be better or bus to reach Howrah railway station from Armenian ghat" . . . . but I thought she might burst-up or throw some thing on my face!" Lolit laughingly re-counted his antics with other salesmen earlier asking some medicines,

---

*   a popular sweet

with nonexistent Chinese names!. Another time for injectable rat poison with remote control mouse syringes!. With such light talks and jokes both walked towards a by-lane and entered into a small terrace restaurant located at first floor which is their favorite meeting place.

*   *   *

Chapter 2

'Crime Partners!'

Shoilen and Lolit got acquainted to each other in theatre circles only and both became very close friends. Like him Lolit was also a theatre addict. He was basically stage help than an actor, but his passion to theatre was as much as his friend. He was expert in prompting actors' dialogues during play and rehearsals helping arranging and erecting sets and props, before and in between, different acts. By constantly rehearsing as well prompting he developed an uncanny talent of remembering dialogues of main roles of the plays with ease.

Like his friend he was also a bachelor and spent more time in Drama activities after his work. He was mainly attracted to the stage for that thrill to work among the actors (specially Female) and dramatic circles!. His sincerity and good organizing capacity made him popular. He never preferred to act on stage, unless his services are required for minor roles only. Physically he was unlike Shoilen. He was very fair and a little short and slim with sharp facial features with big eyes and good personality. His voice was also soft but clear. Persons knowing him liked his mannerism and helpful attitude. His height was the main drawback for normal hero roles.

Every member in his theatre group liked him for his helping attitude. Lolit became shoilen's only closest friend. Both enjoyed and trusted each other's company, and they used to meet regularly. From past six months they became close to each other and he became sole confederate to Shoilen, compared to other actors of the group. This was mainly due Shoilen's secret agenda to rope him as a partner to his ambitious crime venture. He made him feel that he was only regarded as his Shoilen's only adviser as well closest friend. He used to narrate many times his personal problems as well stage affairs with utmost sincerity. Some times out of frustration the senior actor used to lament about his stagnant career and income in spite of so many hours of dedicated work.

Earlier he experimented to induce responsible acting career on Lolit under unexpected circumstance. When the heroine, of a play did not turn up, before a prestigious audience, the director and other artistes were in panicky situation at the unexpected catastrophe, as they would not able to stage the play without the heroine. No other lady was available on the stage to takeover temporarily. In a desperate resort Shoilen requested reluctant Lolit to do that female role, as he was well versed with the play and dialogues. At Shoilen's pleading Lolit reluctantly accepted to act the heroin's role as the director also fervently requested him. Shoilen firmly believed that only Lolit Could do justice and save that last day's show. That experiment became a success due to sincere efforts put up by Lolit.

He looked like a real lady after a good facial and body make-up. Added to that, his fair complexion also helped to give an attractive personality. He did full justice to that role also in that day's show. Even though he had no effeminate mannerisms in real life, but he could develop a real talent to imitate female way of acting on the stage, during the play!. The audience were not even were aware that the lady portion was done by a man in female attire!. All the group was very happy at the very good response from the audience!. From that day he had taken up to acting also on the stage occasionally.

As that was their last show the group went for a bash in a restaurant, as their usual convention. Lolit was the star attraction on that day for not only saving the last show, but also doing justice in his first appearance as an actor on the stage!. Every one praised him and congratulated him for his excellent performance. Some members hugged him on the back stage to express joyful appreciation. They all requested him to come with the makeup as Charulota (The Heroine's name) to the party!. Some even got photos taken holding him closely!. One such photo of a senior male actor created furor in his house as his wife saw the picture and thought her husband was embracing a lady in the green room!. He had to call Lolit to his house, to convince his wife.

(It was also a big joke as Lolit went to male toilet in the hotel, donning woman's attire; other men were shocked to see a charming lady in traditional rich dress entering the toilet with lighted cigarette in her hand!.) From that show Lolit became a good friend to Shoilen. Latter Shoilen relentlessly made efforts to make him his only close friend, with a sinister motive. He also understood the advantage of Lolit's excellent acting in a female role, in his ambitious scheme.

*   *   *

After the funny prelude in the evening at Lolit's medical show room, they both walked to their usual jaunt on the terrace garden of that eatery. They sat in a corner ordering their usual snacks and tea. After some general talk Shoilen laughingly informed that Mr. Reddy, the Telugu film producer, had sent an e-mail stating whether it would be possible for Miss Monjulota Mojumdar to reach Hyderabad after two months for preliminary talks. They both laughed and decided to keep him in suspense for more time.

After some more general talks Shoilen decided to raise the new topic for which he had made efforts for past few months with utmost patience.

"Lolit . . . as you are a pharmacist do you know of a safe drug which can make person lose consciousness within a very short period and not endangering the life?"

Shoilen asked in a low voice casually without any expression after making sure no other person was within hearing limits.

Lolit was first surprised with this sudden unexpected query from his friend. He stared at him with a smile "Of course there are few drugs . . . but why this sudden interest?! . . . . you asked quiet seriously! . . . Dada (Elder brother) for whom this drug is required?"

Without answering his curiosity he again asked seriously "Can such drug be administered to any person without their knowledge . . . It has to be given orally . . . well do you know of such . . . I mean medicine which has no odor or strong taste . . . . which may be procured easily?"

"Of course Dada! Such drugs are available. Even I can prepare it . . . . but you did not tell why you wanted this information?"

Before telling the reason for information for that drug, Shoilen, seriously opened his secretly scheming ideas to Lolit for the first time. Considering their ages and the bleak future awaiting them seriously he started narrating and unfolded his cherished plans to attempt to gain better profits from their acting talents. He expressed with frustration and reminded him that in another few years he would be losing his prime and that he may have to depend on others for living.

He expressed his ideas of not to go by morals but use their unique talents for survival with dignity by sophisticated fraudulency in exploiting the foolish public. He elaborated that if for few years if they lead a double life that is acting on stage for entertainment and acting in real life for monetary gains, they would be able to achieve a happy life before their old age. He elaborated the innumerable ways to fool the rich with sophisticated acting to achieve their goal. He explained with emotion he was seriously planning alternatives which may be illegal but could be put in action with a realistic imagination and thorough planning. In an almost whispered tone, his explained the object for knowing information about the drug. His idea was first experiment would be to use the harmless drug, on least suspected group, and narrated briefly the modus operandi. He also assured that the drug in question was proposed to be used not for all their schemes but only occasionally, but definitely in the first venture. He told the drug should be harmless, as he does not want to play with others' lives.

Lolit was shocked at his friend's dangerous adventure scheme and ambition. He remained silent for a longer time unable to digest at his respected friend's criminal plans. He seriously objected and cautioned about the dangers likely to be faced if their ventures turn out unsuccessful due to many risks. Shoilen heard his friend's advice calmly with full attention. He convinced him that they have potential and talent to attempt the new venture successfully if planned well. Shoilen was a master in convincing any opponent in arguments!. He spoke at length his plan of action and when and how to implement. He said without some risk one cannot expect high returns.

Finally he became emotional said in a sad tone if he doesn't join hands with him in this ventures he would prefer to leave the city and go to Benaras or Haridwar and spend his days taking Sanyas and live in an ashram than live as un-wanted person like a moron. He sincerely expressed that he would never think of making such plan with any other friend, if he doesn't wish to cooperate. He said dramatically that he never had such close friend as Lolit in his entire life. He firmly revealed that he wouldn't try to try the cherished venture without his participation.

Lolit felt most upset at his good friend's words of despair. He also understood his serious reason which motivated for his despair to venture the risky exploits. He also remembered how he himself personally could fool hundreds as Charulota!. The exciting new life in a way attracted him, as imagined by Shoilen, looked justified. His fear, about the negative aspects, was blurred and was drawn to the bright idea of the new challenging ventures. He felt like a mountaineer whose object was only to reach the summit forgetting the danger of falling to depths. He decided to accept his whole hearted cooperation to join hands with Shoilen without any wavering doubts, in a blind come what may folly!.

The senior actor uttered his great pleasure at Lolit's sincere attitude to full cooperation for the proposed new venture. He knew he would not be able to successfully implement without the support of a reliable partner with acting abilities. He did not feel like a spider attracting a victim to the web, but decided to knit webs jointly to attract other foolish victims!. Added advantage was Lalit's main aptitude to act convincingly in feminine roles also!. He whole heartedly thanked him in real emotional warmth. He also assured that no other actor would be roped in this new pursuit. Both decided that there should no secrets or misunderstandings in implementation of their new venture. Both also came to understanding to share the winnings equally. Lolit also accepted to stay in Shoilen's apartment, as their venture require daily contact.

Both friends came to a firm understanding and departed in the night.

From that day they started to plan and implement the first venture with utmost secrecy and dedication!. They made lot of trials, observed critically, all the difficult problems. They rehearsed their own roles with serious efforts including some visits to out stations. They took longer time for a methodical planning considering all the risks not forgetting even minor points, for their first venture!. Both started finding a new excitement of a challenge of real life acting in their carriers!.

The closest friends became partners of sophisticated crimes.

*   *   *

CHAPTER 3

'A timid bride becomes a nagging wife!'

One day in the evening, as the Kalka Mail train was about to leave from a platform of Howrah station (Main railway station of Kolkata), a newly wedded Bengali couple entered a two tier A.C.Sleeper coach just few minutes before the departure. The bride has completely covered her face with new wedding sari and shyly followed her husband with attractive jingling sound of her bangles and anklets. Both were still having typical make-up of bride and groom. They continued to stand near the door as if bidding farewell to their relatives and friends on the platform. As the train started they finally got to their reserved seats in the compartment. As the train moved faster the bride was weeping profusely unable to leave her people. The compartment was full with mostly Bengali families. Many persons sitting near the newly married couple, were moved by the continued sobs and tears of the bride seeing the fast departing platform and out skirts of Kolkata. She was it seems first time leaving her parents and could not bear the separation and looked with fear and timidity she was weeping profusely. The

Husband was trying his best to console her and assuring her not to worry. He looked like an unpolished simpleton with mild manners in his talk. He was showing utmost courtesy to speak to her with kind words not showing any annoyance! He looked worried as it was his first experience to talk with his bride separately. In spite of his pleading persuasion she could not control her deep hysterical emotions and demanding to accept her request. Men as well women seated in close proximity were deeply moved by that scene. The husband was much upset and did not know how to divert her attention. As the scene continued for some more time reaching to a high pitch yet in low voices, few by standers took initiative and asked him what the matter was. He told them they were married previous day only and the girl had never traveled anywhere without her parents or known relatives before marriage. As he had no leave he had to start journey on that day only to join his duties at Delhi. Even though she agreed to travel with him after the wedding but now she is upset with fright once train started moving. She was traveling first time in her life to such long distance. She is very much unnerved and crying to take her back to Kolkata. She is insisting that they should get down next station to stay some more days with her parents!. He was at the wits ends for not able to convince her of his problem to return back to Kolkata. He was assuring her that within a month he would bring her back to her parents. She is insisting that she would come to Delhi next month only after staying with parents till then. While he was narrating in low voice with restraint she was sobbing with tears, in spite of her veil all could see her timidity and agony!.

Every person especially the ladies were very much moved by the girl's bursting sorrowful mood. The groom started getting unnerved seeing her uncontrolled louder grief. He was at wit's end at her obstinacy; desperately he sought the help of some women to persuade her to continue the journey. He was utterly shocked at his bride's unexpected display of panic!. As she was a stranger to him before the wedding he was not aware of her timidity and unreasonable attitude!. He was trying to control his annoyance not to create discord between them. Quickly this touching story reached the adjoining sub compartments also of that bogey; women from there also came to her to console the newly married girl. In India, married women volunteer to help ladies especially brides, in-distress even if they are complete strangers.

Elderly as well younger ladies gradually formed a group of sympathizers!. They came very close to her, as the girl's husband made way for the ladies sit near her to advise her. Some even holding or touching sympathetically requesting her to understand the reality of a woman's life. At some day every girl has to accept a new life with husband after marriage. She continued weep hysterically requesting them to tell her husband to take her back to Kolkata!.

Only after some continued persuasion by many ladies, slowly she started to gain little courage seeing so many ladies talking with her in a helpful way explaining patiently the reality. Her fear reduced, and her hysterical attitude gradually calmed. Some good reasoning by elderly men also acted to pacify her mood. It looked she was convinced that all of them were sincerely trying to help her and advising her to accept a good wife's responsibility. They could change her outlook with their efforts, her mood to understand to reason. She became silent for some time and gradually started to listen still with fear and tearful eyes. She shyly embraced some elderly ladies and cried like a child keeping her head on their shoulders. All the ladies embraced the new bride with affection and advised her to accept the new life bravely. She was telling them she felt really panicky when the train started leaving her parents and relatives.

She gradually realized her foolishness. All were satisfied that at their success in able to save the serious situation!. Gradually she started to treat all the ladies like friends. To their quarries she told them her back ground and gradually with shy smiles she started to find about the north whether fish and rice would be available or not similar such domestic queries. She told her name as Baijoyanthi and she lived in a Village called Debirpara of Hooghly district and studied in high school there.

She rose and touched the feet of all the ladies and elderly men for their blessings. Finally after solving her problem, the ladies retuned back to their seats happy to see the groom's gratitude. Everyone felt relieved and happy that their effort had succeeded to bring harmony to the newly married couple. They started to talk each other in whispering voices and gradually became intimate. But she insisted her husband that they must come back in a month's time. He pleadingly assured her with oath on Kalee Maa (Mother Goddess Kalee).

When the dinner time approached after an hour the newly married were over whelmed with joy by the affection shown by most, in offering food, fruits and sweets in spite of their request to kindly excuse. One elderly lady came to her and affectionately put a sweet in her mouth. After almost all had meals and started to make arrangements for making their beds; the newly wedded couple wanted to get the blessings of all the persons in that compartment as an acknowledgement to all for their kindness.

They wore the wedding symbols like the head gear of the groom and the special dress of decorations of the bride. They went to every person and each separately touched their feet bowing before them. To every man they visited, the groom took out a Shondesh (a popular Bengali sweet) from his bag and put in his mouth with all reverence and affection!. Many passengers who were seeing them first time were also happy to see a newly wedded couple seeking their blessings I the train!. As it is a general custom for the newlyweds to offer sweets to all elders and youngsters by hand, to show respectful courtesy!. Similarly the bride put separately into the lips of ladies, exhibiting coy shyness after getting their blessings. She touched feet of all the elders with respect. All the persons ate the sweets happily blessing the couple with sincerity for their nice gesture.

After an hour the train reached Asansole junction. Mysteriously the newly married couple hurriedly got down with their heavy suite cases, from the train even though they informed all that they are going to Delhi!. The bride earlier took out the sounding ornaments. They did not bid farewell to their new friends. Surprisingly the passengers of the entire compartment were fast asleep and it was almost dark as lights were all switched off expect the light blue night lamps in the corridor. It was nearing eight 830 pm only. The groom cunningly locked the vestibule doors earlier.

The couple quickly got down other side stealthily and quickly reached parallel platform without looking back crossing the risky rail-track; they rushed to the distant waiting room there. As soon the train left, they happily but silently expressed their joy for the success of their errand by shaking hands with happiness. The pretending newly married couple was successfully able to serve Shondesh sweets laced with drug to all the passengers. When all of them became unconscious the two quickly robbed all the valuables, jewelry, ornaments, watches, purses, cell-phones, ladies' hand bags from the unconscious passengers and made a clean sweep. They put them in their almost empty suitcases and got down!.

They had also taken a brand new leatherette travel bag from the last passenger in the lower berth. It looked attractive with a bright yellow color.

They went into the waiting room toilets and returned with retouched makeup not as groom and bride but in different appearances and clothes, as married couple!. He put on a beard and new hair wig. He was walking with one foot dragging as it was bent. The wife looked visibly pregnant walking slowly holding her husband's hand. They reached another platform where the Punjab mail to Howrah, was to arrive. When the train reached the plat form they entered into a two tiered AC compartment where they had reservations.

Both settled in their seats keeping the suit cases carefully. The compartment was full of passengers all busy in their companies, lot of noise and lot of merriment. Suddenly there was as a commotion as the newly entered couple stared to argue with each other with anther false story!. Most passengers in the vicinity, surprisingly saw, the slightly dumb headed husband looked with disgusting way, as his wife was arguing nastily with him. His loud mouthed wife talking fast way in her East Bengali type rough dialect in a most unreasonable way!. All the passengers who were near about were all staring at them enjoying the silly dialogue. The husband was found to be slow in telling with terrible stammer, in his West Bengali soft dialect. His jerking with repeated shouts due to stammer looked pitiable and many tried to suppress their laughter. He looked miserable; yet he was not yielding to her but replying loudly in crude jarring stammer. His condition seemed pitiable!. They gradually started louder verbal accusations denouncing each other, unmindful of the fellow passengers!. The quarrel gradually reached louder with verbal attacks in a most crude way. Both telling his or her point of views only, not listening to other, which turned to be show of disturbing nuisance!. Other passengers were shocked to see husband and wife carrying loudly domestic quarrel unashamedly before public in a train compartment!. Some looked with a grin laughing within, some witnessed with disgust. Almost majority were listening to them with suppressed mirth. Gradually the argument turned to more louder exchange of meaningless shouts!. It looked both lost their cool and started telling the onlookers about each other's negative points!. Subject was almost a trivial family affair.

Argument was concerning the naming for the new born and later where to go whether to her mother's place or his house, and other petty matters!. But it became a prestigious issue to yield each to other. The woman was seemed short-tempered shouting shamelessly before all the passengers in a shrieking voice!. She was crying hysterically in a dragging squeaky way to accept her proposals only, while her husband was only looking with deep annoyance but was replying with equally loudly trying to find words to express his anguish! As he was getting angrier, his stammer also increased giving a miserable appearance to others. Disgustingly the woman tried to reply him with imitating his stammer ridiculing with contempt; the husband enraged at his wife's bad manners in mocking him before others. In a fit of rage he gave her a sound slap!. All the passengers were dumb-struck at that violent turn family quarrel as the husband hitting her roughly in the train!. Suddenly with loud screams his anguished wife rushed to the door shouting that she would rather die than staying with him!. As she opened the door and was about to attempt to jump from train, her husband and co-passengers became panicky rushed to control her, and forcibly held her and closed the door and bolted. They almost had to drag her all the way to her seat!. Everyone was too stunned at the turn of unexpected climax. All started pacifying the enraged lady with soothing words at the same time other ladies were holding her giving some kindly advice for restraint. Everyone was pacifying her with kind words referring to her advanced pregnancy. All were advising she should never attempt such dangerous steps considering her condition. To every ones astonishment, the husband sat on the floor holding her feet, addressing her name 'Madhobi' and started weeping and pleading to excuse him and forgive him for slapping her. He started to bang his head with shame on the seat!. He was repeatedly telling her to excuse him with more stammer due to his mental emotion. He looked very much embarrassed in a pitiable state. He was shocked at the dangerous step she took. He was worried with guilt he would have lost his wife and first child due to his foolish anger and losing control of his senses and by slapping her. Other men pacified him and lifted to his seat. That area became crowded at the dangerous turn of events. As curious passengers from all over the compartment reached there and crowded around them; nearby sitting persons telling in subdued voice the dangerous act attempted by the pregnant woman!. Most others who did not witness the family fight felt pity on her advising the husband to treat his wife with an understanding tolerance. Every one even after moving away still discussing with each other at the way some husbands even show cruelty towards even pregnant wives!. Some thought him to be a drunkard with least feelings towards his wife.

The lady by then completely became quiet crying with shameful feeling even started to plead that it was very wrong on her part to attempt in fit of anger; she requested her husband pitiably with choked voice to forgive her. The husband also took her closely and pacified her with tearful sentiments, calling her dearly addressing Madhobi. After good advice to both of them, passengers started to return to their seats. All were happy and heaved a sigh that nothing untoward happened due to their timely intervention. She slowly bent her head with humility. The shaken husband meekly accepted her and begged her never to resort to such dangerous foolishness. They were touched by their story and her serious emotional outburst. Persons who witnessed took pity on the husband. All were discussing in hushed tone giggling at the pair who made laughing stock of themselves which was about to turn tragic.

Finally the lady felt ashamed and greeted all of them with folded hands, her reddish eyes brimming with tears, to kindly forgive her and thanked all. As the train was in motion the second attempt of fooling the onlookers by the actors successfully completed. Nobody had least doubt or motive about the silly couple's exhibition of a domestic quarrel in the train. Every one again accepted gleefully the Shondesh sweet offered by the husband and wife as a way of expressing their gratitude for saving her and their yet to be born baby. They got blessings and advises to not to make their life miserable with quarrels. She was still whispering to some on way complaining to them that her husband though a good person but spoiled by his mother.

Needless to say that all the passengers least suspected that it was a just an acting, by two veterans!. They all ate the sweets, talking among themselves, joking how such crazy persons exist in the world!.

As the sweets were laced with drug all of them fell asleep within 15 minutes. Within thirty minutes the husband and wife started to quickly rob them also as they did earlier in the Kalka mail!. Before their final errand act, the woman conveniently took off a cotton pillow pad inside her dress which made her look as a pregnant woman!. As the train reached Durgapur station they quickly got down from the compartment from the rear door and made their way to waiting room on the other side platform. There were hardly anyone to notice a pretty lady with a bag entering into gents toilet!. After ten minutes a smiling smart young man with long fashionable hair, in jeans and T-shirt holding the same bag came out!. Feminine symbols of padded Bra and hips padding were also taken out to look like a normal man again!. The person who acted as husband also changed to another dress and makeup with a French beard this time with normal gait. They both came out and went separately to another platform each holding suitcases separately, one of them was holding a bright yellow bag, in addition to his suitcase.

There Garib-Rath train from Patna was expected to Howrah. They acted as strangers to each other and boarded the train separately and occupied their berths at different compartments. Both immediately went to sleep after securely locking their luggage. The train reached Howrah in the early hours.

*   *   *

CHAPTER 4

A Document writer's Diary

Shoilen and Lolit were in a happy mood after the first venture succeeded and everything went as planned by them. They went into minute details for almost three months before their final action. Even the drug which was mixed in the sweets was tested discretely on friends and strangers. They even tested on themselves to find time of losing consciousness and for the recovery.

There were lot of reports in the Newspapers and TV news coverage on the two railway robberies taking place on the same night and many reports reflected suspicion that both were done by the same woman and the man with a cunning deceit. But as the robberies took place within few hours some thought some group of four or more persons working in league to fool some passengers to rob them by offering sweets mixed with drug to make them loose consciousness.

Contrary to the reality the majority of the co-passengers were of the view that the whole robbery was planned by the cunning women in the disguise of wives only; acted as an innocent timid bride or uncouth loud mouthed nagging-house wife! They were of the opinion the groom was clumsy and unintelligent!. In the second robbery also the co-passengers observed that the wife dominated all the time and the husband was just made to obey her command!. Not a single report suspected the woman could be a man in disguise. When these actors put up make believe scenes which no one suspected at their clever act of deceit. None could see the face of the timid and foolish bride due to her veil over her head, in the first act. The second role as a stubborn unreasonable wife made the fellow passengers abhor at her undignified wordy duel at her husband in spite of the being a pregnant woman!. They avoided seeing her face and were feeling sympathetic to the husband and his pathetic attitude towards his wife like a virtual slave. His eyes were always down caste and exhibiting a hurt feeling ashamed to show his face to fellow travelers. All of them were looking at him most of the time and hating the aggressive attitude of the unreasonable wife, making a vulgar display of her overbearing personality belittling her husband before others. Whatever the wife wanted him to do he was obeying timidly as he appeared to in a shocked state seeing her un-thoughtful action. He was virtuously shivering with fright at the thought of her serious attempt to jump from the fast running train. She would have been dead and every one would point at him for that tragedy; he shuddered at the thought of his future life. He was really fortunate that fellow passengers' timely help in stopping her. Both of them could fool the fellow travelers in a convincing acting, and achieved their objective!.

Both had a big laugh reading the reports. It was really Sholen's good planning and acting guidance creating such realistic scenes, which made all the passengers believed to be true happening between husband and wife. After they found to be a cleverly planned train robberies then only they realized that a well-hatched trickery was played on them with hoodwinking with clever make believe acting by the pairs. Shoilen intentionally kept a low key for his role. His helpless husband's role did not reveal his professional stamp!. He wanted to avoid too much dramatization of both, as people would likely to suspect their real background.

Before leaving the compartment in their first robbery, they took away new leatherette travel bag of a lone passenger. It looked new and nice with bright yellow colour. They carried it along with their two empty suitcases which they filled with all the looted valuables from the passengers. That last passenger looked like a shady character with his beard and long hair; He was a short person with shifty mannerisms. They found him to a greedy as he wanted to grab as many sweets as possible from them, when others accepted only one sweet and didn't expect another sweet. When Lolit was giving a sweet to a lady near his seat, he went near her and stretched his hand requesting for a sweet; after receiving one he requested for a second and ate that also. Latter he took two sweets from Shoilen. He ate four sweets. Shoilen was worried about his consuming four sweets, but Lolit assured him that the drug would not cause any serious danger but he is liable to sleep for long hours. It really happened that way and he was unconscious for a very long time and he was taken to a hospital for medical treatment, under police custody. (Which Shoilen and Lolit came to know on the third day about him and his name and back ground)

In the media report the total loss was put to about twenty to Thirty Lakh Rupees. Both of them were amused at exaggerated figure of their loss given by the passengers who lost the valuables. They found out they could hardly make few Lakh rupees only from the jewelry and cash. They could purchase few thousands' worth clothes other accessories and few house-hold gadgets on the next day morning from the stolen credit cards, visiting large show rooms at far off places in the city, using the names mentioned in the cards. Most men had few hundreds only in their purses, but had credit cards and expensive mobile phones. Many handbags of ladies contained more cash and ornaments and mobile phones. Lolit collected variety of perfumes, lipsticks and makeup creams.

When they reached home they carefully stashed the cash and ornaments carefully after listing. They decided to get the Gold ornaments melted in some different goldsmiths' small work places, to convert ornaments to into solid gold pieces and cash them latter in stages spreading a long period.

When they were engaged in a discussion on some matter in their room; there was a muffled but clear ringing sound of a cell phone audible very close to them. After seeing all sides Lolit found it was from the Yellow bag. They found the passenger had nothing in his pockets except a pen and train ticket. They decided to carry that bag as they could not open that in hurry for their hasty departure.

They laughed at his greedy way he took sweets from them almost grabbing! While leaving the compartment they took out his bag and dumped near him and below his berth, six other passengers' bags filled them with some various passengers' cheap quality wrist watches, few ladies hand bags after removing the costly contents. Similarly they intentionally put some men's purses also after removing the money and bank cards, under his pillow. They were sure the police would suspect him to be one of the members of the robbing gang and case will be diverted away from them. They put few extra sweets in his pocket also.

Suddenly from that same bag a different type of ringing sound from another mobile was heard. Both looked around and found the source. They ignored that ringing also. Again after few minutes still another different type of the ringing sound with a Bangla-Filmi song was audible from the same bag!. Both became curious and opened that yellow bag; they were surprised to find three mobile phones on the top. When they checked, the caller's number was same in all the three phones. Each phone had small pasted strips on the back side of each instrument, with separate written names and phone numbers. The three names were Gobindo Laha, Kalicharon Kundu and Gadhador Kar. They just ignored the mobiles and looked into the other contents of that bag. Rest were ordinary clothes and a small bag with personal items like toothbrush etc., There was also another small pouch with a false hair toupee for gents wearing. On that a label was affixed stating a name of Gobindo Laha. Being actors they laughed at the false wig he was carrying while travelling!. They assumed that he might be sometimes disguising as Gobindo Laha with a completely different hair style!. Shoilen felt, that passenger with beard and long hair was also might be false identity. They were surprised and surmised that he might be also acting like them to cheat or may be escaping from being caught by the police in some illegal transaction. They also found a men's hand bag containing 10,000/-rupees all in 500 notes. They were happy at that cash which also they did not expect from him!. Inside they saw a red covered pocket note book. On the front page name and address was mentioned as

Kalichaoran Kundu,

41A Chakradhar Mukhopadhyay street,

Medhinipur-3,

West Medhinipur district.

Now they realized the name of the yellow-bag's owner was Kalicharon Kundu. Inside the small book on the next page itself a left-luggage receipt was pinned. It was a typical thin yellow colored paper railway receipt voucher stating received one box to be kept in left luggage room, signed by the in-charge luggage room, of Howrah station of Eastern Railway. It was having date of three days earlier. To keep the receipt in position, he fixed that to the second page with a safety pin; which attracted their attention.

"Lolit we have to immediately collect his box or bag kept in the station. Since it was deposited before the start of the journey means it might be having some important or valuables items inside. Normally no one leaves a luggage in the cloak room before starting a journey; persons who come to change to another train, if they go to city during the break normally leave their luggage for safety. Let us both go fast to the railway station and collect it before the owner comes back."

They quickly reached the large Howrah station went to Left Luggage cloak room; Lolit went in to the in-charge clerk and handed the receipt. The counter clerk examined the receipt and informed him that extra charges have to be paid after each 12 hours. Lolit paid the extra amount as required. The porter went inside and dragged out a large old trunk box, as it looked bit heavy. It was a large ordinary sheet iron trunk box painted black, with a heavy pad lock. A bold name in white letters name was painted on the top as Kalicharon Kundu. Lolit didn't show any surprise and collected it as if it belonged to him. He signed the register as Kalicharon and proceeded outside; he engaged a porter to carry it to his vehicle. He proceeded towards the exit without looking back. Shoilen joined him and both came out of the station to the parked Maruti car of Lolit. While driving, he stopped at a road side locksmith and got the heavy lock opened, stating that his key was lost.

After reaching the flat, they opened the box; both were surprised at the contents. There were six thick box-file covers; each containing copies of non-judicial stamp paper documents in bunches, all listed. They took out top document just to see. The document was of a property near Shova-Bazar, of Kolkata. It was a coloured Xerox copy. It was a sale deed written more than 70 years ago, in which vendor's name and Vendee's names were given, written in Bengali flowing script as commonly used in document writing without giving little space between words.

They kept back the document and put aside the files. Below them was a leather office bag with zip closure. When they opened they were startled to see it was fully packed with currency note bundles of 1000 Rupees and 500 Rupees. They could guess it had few Lakhs of Rupees!. They least expected such a big fortune from that unimpressive bearded short man. It also contained a leather bound diary like book, in which he wrote the back ground and details and dates of various document deeds he prepared. Below that bag were few packets of blank stamp papers of different denominations. There were also bundles of blank white papers, with variety of pens with different nibs. There were many stationery items like pencils, nib-pens, erasers, coquille pens and drafting ink-pens rubber stamps, inkpads, large clip board, magnifying glass with illumination etc., all kept in separate card board boxes. They thought he kept his important personal office documents and equipment that box and securely deposited in the cloak room of the station!. They presumed that he came from Medhinipur with his personal documents and taken up an unexpected trip to Delhi or somewhere. They still were puzzled at his three names. When they emptied all the contents from the box, a copy of 'Anand Bazar Patrka' newspaper was spread at the bottom. Lolit was surprised to find that the bottom was about 4" above the floor level. He removed the paper, and examined the bottom board. The bottom was also painted black. When Lolit tapped it sounded like a thin ply wood board!. He made a check with his fingers all round that board. He found there was a very narrow gap on all sides of the board. It had hinges on one side and a small knob at other end. He held knob and lifted the board. It opened like a hinged cover.

Below that shutter a folded woolen shawl was spread. Below the shawl the entire space was filled with small silken bags tightly tied with silk string for each one. Shoilen took out one of the bag and opened the string. It was filled with glittering gold coins or gold Mohurs each of the size of a bigger rupee coin, weighing about a tola (10 Grams). There were about 9 bags kept tightly with cotton around to reduce the movement of the bags, while the box taken out!. Each must be containing about Eight to Ten coins. Both poured all the coins on the newspaper and were flabbergasted at their unexpected find of shining heap of the gold coins!. They were shocked beyond belief of their discovery of new valuable booty!. Both were nonplussed and dumb struck!. The amount of fortune they could collect on their first attempt of their new career made them most unbelievable!. Both bowed with humble adulation to Goddess Kali's framed picture on the wall, to respectfully thank the Goddess for bestowing with valuable fortune to them.

They realized that collecting the Steel Trunk, belonging to Kalicharon Kundu, a document writer of Medhinipur, from the left luggage room was their very wisest decision. They were over whelmed at the unexpected find of large treasure from a most unsuspected traveler!.

They decided to go through his diary for getting information from the mysterious Kaliichron Kundu who also seemed to impersonate in two more names—Gobindo Laha, and Gadhador Kar.!. The three mystery names and the huge amount made them curious to get more details from his written diary. After carefully stacking the valuables and cash they sat and started to go through Kalicharon Kundu's diary with much inquisitiveness. They were also curious about the identity of the caller to all the three phones, who might have close relationship with Kalicharon.

*   *   *

EPISODE 2

OUTLINE STORY

Kalicharon Kundu, of Medinipur, a large town near Kolkata, was a licensed professional Document Writer of properties. He was a crook with no remorse or sentiments. He mercilessly deserted his innocent, mentally retarded young wife, to retain the wedding dowry. He dumped his own widowed aunt, in an Ashram in Brindavan, to take over her landed property. He was a greedy and deceitful person. He developed uncanny craft to create false documents with forgeries. He kept not only copies of the documents he wrote, he also used to write a diary of all the persons and events connected with each documents. Shoilen and Lolit, who came across his belongings, got a lot of information regarding Kalicharon's illegal involvement in creating false documents. They decide to take advantage of Kalicharon's escapades with a cunning motive to get advantage from his crooked deeds.

Kalicharon was much benefitted in preparing a false Will-Document, which he made to write, for a very rich property belonging to late Romakant Choudhary of Medinipur, in the name of Chandramoni Debi, his concubine. He was enticed by her and her uncle Durjoy, to write that Will. The Will was done with back date, after

47

brutal murder of Romakanto. Kalicharon was astonished at his power of his forgery, which could give big fortune to Chandramoni Debi. Later he was involved forging a signature, on another false Will got made by another Medinipur residents, Chandon and his wife Ruma, to get maximum benefit of division of properties of late Malothi Debi Ghosal. Kalicharon was unhappy at the paltry amount given to his effort. He double crossed Chandon and exposed that crooked deed, to other two sisters of Ruma, who were deceived. He made money by exposing the forged Will. Kalicharon was critically punished by Chandon, for his deceit, which made him to flee from Medinipur to work under Durjoy, at Kolkata. His first job in the city was to make fake originals of old property Documents, of Kolkata, for Durjoy, who was a tycoon and a leader of a Maphia gang in red light area of the city's Sona-Gachi locality. The original Documents of a property were cleverly smuggled from a bank, through an officer of that Bank. The owner of the property had pledged his originals and got a loan from the bank; which were replaced with fake documents by Durjoy's gang. He planned to sell that property with the original documents, for high monetary gains. The bank officer who was involved was murdered, to remove his link with Durjoy. Kalicharon was frightened seeing the news of murder.

On the same day he was ordered by Durjoy to go to Allahabad. Kalicharon became nervous apprehending that Durjoy planned the trip to eliminate him also. He boldly decides to expose Durjoy through a secret anonymous letter to the police head-quarters; and planned to run away from Kolkata. But on knowing that, he was being sent on request from Chandramoni Debi, whom he passionately adorned, he decides to travel to meet her. He did not post his letter to the police. He kept that in his document files, to take action after returning back to Kolkata.

While he was traveling in Kalka mail, he falls prey to the make-believe drama enacted by Shoilen and Lolit. They happen to see his documents file in his possessions. They were shocked to learn about Durjoy's dangerous criminal activities, from Kalicharon's secret un-posted letter to the Police. The acting duo, cleverly fool Durjoy and make a big monetary gain. Latter decide to go to Allahabad to meet Chandramoni Debi alias Mononmoni Debi to blackmail her to make profit.

(Part of 'TRANSPARENT SHADOWS'—A Fiction. Author: M.V.S.Rao)

Chapter 1

Story of Kalicharon Kundu,
A document writer from Medinipur

On the day Shoilen dutta and Lolit Sen, started their first experiment of their criminal adventure, on Kalka Mail train; one of their victim passengers was Kalicharon Kundu. He was travelling under the name of Gadhadar Kar. He was originally a native of Medinipur of West Medinipur district of west Bengal. His father was a class four employee of the state government service; he could educate him up to matriculation in a local school. He was never a bright in studies but developed a knack of cheating and 'stealing from his younger days. Many a times he was beaten whenever he was caught in his misdeeds by his teachers and students in the school. His one good quality was he was exceptionally good in hand writing. He developed to write in neat uniform way both in Bengali and English scripts. He had also a fascination to imitate his class friends and teachers' hand writing as well signatures very effectively. He didn't know that art of copying signatures was known as forgery!.

Due to his negligence in studies he failed in school in thrice in various classes. He could never complete his Matriculation examination. His father got fed up and put him as an attender job in a bank, through his known colleagues. During probation period itself he was caught stealing some wad of notes from a the cash counter!. The manager dismissed him after a sound thrashing!; without reporting to police seeing his young age. He tried to do little jobs in shops, cafes and others but nowhere he could stick longer time due to his dishonesty.

He never had any good friends in the school also, due to his insincere ways. He was mostly a loner. In the home his father's widowed younger sister used to look after him, as his mother died when he was young. She was an innocent affectionate woman with little education. She had inherited some few acres of land in the nearby village, through her marriage. Her brother gave to local farmers on lease and she used to get annually some income. She used to look after Kalicharon, her nephew, as her own son.

Once he happened to see his aunt's old registered document in aged brownish paper with print on top like in currency notes. Till then he never seen a stamp paper used for writing property documents for registration. He was fascinated to see that writing in black ink, The script was such all Bengali words with letters were connected to each other as in English in a particular style!. This type of style in writing registration documents was developed during British rule. Closed script was adopted to avoid any insertions of new words or figures by any unauthorized persons, in the sentences.

Seeing that script with curiosity he copied almost exactly on a white paper. His father was much impressed with his son's talent. Till then Kalicharon never heard about document writer job. That day his father brought few old copies of documents, to house, to practice copying by his aptitude. His son copied them with a pen with all sincerity and keen observation almost as in originals!. His father understood his son had an inborn talent in document writing script. It normally takes few years hard practice for most; he found without any guidance his son could grasp this art. His father, who used to work in revenue department, could get him introduced to the Sub-registrar of Assurances, through his influence. Seeing his document script the officer arranged an apprentice job for him under a Licensed Document writer by name Jogesh Maity. On his first job when he was asked to copy a document, he not only written that very successfully he copied the signature also of some person which was at the bottom!. He was more stunned at Kalicharon's dangerous talent of signature forgery!. The senior copy writer laughed loudly at his unknowingly performing a forgery. He mildly warned him never to try such things that as it is considered as a criminal deed. In few months he got the license of a Document writer given by Government of west Bengal.

Gradually he grasped the innovative craft of making documents with legal wordings. He learnt drafting preparation of documents for registration of properties, affidavits, promissory notes, transfer deeds, partition deeds, gift deeds, 'Will' preparation, exchange of property deeds and other such requirements. His employer was in much demand by senior lawyers and staff of Registration office, touts who hang around such offices getting new clients. Kalicharon's ability was also spread among them; he used to write some documents in his house after regular hours without the knowledge of his employer.

Being a person with crooked ideas, he quickly understood that there are lots of opportunities of wrongful deeds in documents pertaining to property matters. He gradually understood that his employer was much in demand for creating false property papers by illegally using his old dated stamp papers, for making back-dated documents. He understood that litigant matters arise mostly on property documents!.

His first chance to create a false document came unexpectedly to him directly. One day a prominent rich local businessman of Medinipur, Romakanto Choudhari, died in an accident. He was a middle aged person with lot of property. He was a tough type of person whom other relatives and colleagues feared to interfere in his personal affairs.

The death of Romakanto was the hottest topic in that town. On that same night at about nine, a stout man with rough bearings came to meet Kalicharon, in his residence. He covered his face to disguise his identity. He informed in a hushed tone that a respectful lady wanted to talk urgently to him privately regarding property documents; he kept two 500 rupee notes in his hand. He informed that he came to take him on his bike. He warned him not to tell any other person about that meeting. Kalicharon accepted to come; he hurriedly dressed and came out and accompanied the stranger. He took him to his motorbike kept at a distance from the house. He drove rapidly in the night to the out skirts of the town. They finally reached to a narrow road leading to a gated private property. He stopped his vehicle near the gate and took him inside through a drive way to an isolated old mansion amid lot of large trees. On their arrival two huge dogs, chained near the gate barked ferociously seeing him. With one sharp warning from the person who brought him, made the beasts kept quiet still mildly growling. Kalicharon was frightened by the dogs and that eerie surrounding. On the way he was informed briefly that he was summoned urgently for some private advice. He talked to him in a low voice even though that place looked deserted.

"Kalicharon babu!. Did you hear about death of Seth Romakanto Choudhari?"

"Yes . . . I heard he lost control and while driving on the highway and hit a tree and died on way to hospital . . . very sad news!"

"This old mansion, named as 'Kedargowri' belongs to Chandramoni Debi, second wife of Seth Romakant, She is my sister's daughter. Due to her husband's sudden death she was sobbing uncontrollably. Being second wife she lives in this house as per husband's wish. The family did not allow her to stay even for few minutes in his house when she went to see the body, . . . the dirty family were against her, as Romakanto used love her more than his first wife. She cried appealing them to see her husband's body, but they did not show any sympathy . . . and forced her to leave that place immediately!. She had to return crying silently all the way helplessly!. In what way she was responsible when he died in an accident!. His house was full with his first wife's children and relatives and lot of friends who gathered there to prepare for the taking the body to the cremation ground. They all hated her for Ramakanto's closeness to her. Since morning she refused to take any food or water!. She requires a very urgent help or assistance from you, as she would not expect any one else to help her now, we will pay you well for any services. Please keep this meeting strictly secret"

Kalicharon was nonplussed at this strange request as he hardly knew anybody or acquainted with any of Romakant's relatives. He remembered a year back, he scripted the registered document of 'Kedargowri', belonging to late Ramakanto Choudary, when he purchased that property. But he silently nodded his head and told in low tone he would render any help possible.

The house was big with old type of furniture. It looked less lighted reflecting a gloomy atmosphere; the family seemed to be in mourning. Very few lights were put on in the main drawing room. One elderly lady and a young woman were sitting on a sofa waiting for him. A table lamp close to them shed light on the two persons with dark background of the hall. He was impressed by the young woman's astounding beauty!. In spite of no makeup and ruffled sari, she looked very charming with distinguished personality. Amid the gloominess in that hall, she was glowing with a provocative feminine glamour!. Her delicate ivory colour skin, her red lips, large eyes with shapely lashes and long loose curly hair, added to her charm.

On seeing him the young lady held her mother and started to cry showing her emotional feeling. Her mother put her hand on her head and was trying to say words to sooth her. He greeted her and touched her mother's feet with respect. He sat with uneasy outlook as he didn't know how to impress them; he was also surprised how they could know him. Her uncle also sat.

She gently hinted to her mother and uncle to allow her to speak alone. He was surprised that in spite of deep sorrowful mood, she was well composed to take situation in her hand and talk the matter personally. She requested him to follow her and took him to a bed room, and switched on the lights. The door was closed by an automatic door closure. He was amazed at the huge bed and colourful sheets, pillows and covers. A mild fresh perfumed was air made the room made the room very pleasant. The room had a rich ambiance with carpeted floor and decorative ceiling. All the walls were covered with light coloured printed wall paper with carved broad framed paintings and photos. There were few photos of her with her late husband in very compromising poses!. The room had large window with heavy curtains, huge mirrors were on the wall on two sides, a glass shuttered almirah was stacked with wine and foreign liquor bottles. A large TV was hung on opposite wall. Kalicharon was amazed at the luxury of that bed room!.

Suddenly she held his hand with a warm tender feeling. Her delicate hands were very graceful with long figure nails shining with dark brown colour!. He observed with her short sleeved blouse having only strings at the back, made her exposed back and arms attractively gleaming!. Her holding his hand and her closeness made him pleasantly embarrassed as he never had such experience with a very beautiful woman. With every movement of her hands and feet, the bangles and silver anklets were making soft musical sound!. Her slim body with round hips and shapely thighs moved with grace!. Her close presence made him joyfully restless!. She spoke softly with a sweet voice, to feel at home as a younger bother to her husband. He immediately understood that she required some guidance in some property matters. He decided to take advantage of her, and exploit the situation. With a false modesty he respectfully addressed her as Boudee (elder Brother's wife) and tried to touch her feet. She raised him smiling within. She could understand her close presence roused his passion and was eager to touch her body, in some pretext!. She was in fact wanted to tame him and follow her command. She encouraged by coming closer and patting his shoulder with her hand, as if impressed with his sincerity to cooperate with her. The enchanting perfume of her body and her touch really worked magic on his senses. She had that feminine talent to control the males with little effort!. She virtually mesmerized him to follow whatever she would say.

She made him sit on a two-seater sofa and she sat next to him almost touching. She told him her husband had purchased that house last year and promised to give it in her name; but before he could do that he left this world and made her as helpless woman. She was his second wife, married more than three years back. She said he was looking after her well, to have comfortable life. She asked him demurely how to hold that house in her position as his first wife may claim it, and throw her out.

He said in a sheepish way that since she was also his wife she would automatically can claim this property as her share, since the building was in her possession. He assured her that she may not have any problem.

She held his hand showing affection and telling with a whispering way, like a happy secret, that she hoped what he said could happen truly. She informed him that they became friends at Kolkata and married her in a temple, and requested her to stay in that house after he purchased. She said that most evenings he used spend time with her only. Prior to coming to Medinipur she was staying in Kolkata, where she had a separate house in Bhowanipore. He used to visit her very frequently. She informed with regret that, had she purchased the mansion directly in her name it would not have been a problem. She sold her property at Bhowanipore. He died suddenly before writing it in her name.

Kalicharon immediately understood that she was legally not married to him; as such she had to surrender that property to the family. He knew that he had to do some illegal method to help her, but decided first a negative approach to scare her, and make her to desperately seek his advice.

She suddenly rose and brought the original registered document. He knew it since it was drafted by him as per his employer's instruction. He said gravely it would be not possible to claim the property even if the document was with her. They can get another authenticated copy through the court.

Suddenly she became bold and asked him with low sweet voice, whether he could create a Will with back date as if made by her husband that she had gifted that property to her!.

He was flabbergasted at her direct bold approach, without any formal discussion, to make him commit an illegal deed!. He knew he could make with little effort, including a forged signature and required documentation on a non-judicial stamp paper. Even if it was an unregistered document still court would give cognizance to such a Will in case of sudden death. He was amazed at her direct approach without mincing words!.

However he wanted to show his cunningness by movement of head and a sympathetic facial expression, to express the negative reply. He gravely told her it was impossible to make such document without the owner's signature and minimum two unrelated witnesses' signatures.

She heard him without giving any hint of disappointment but looked at him with a sly smile as if not bothered at his advice!. She deliberately took out a prepared sweet scented Paan (Beetle leaf) put her in her mouth with a slow attractive movement. In that process she did not even put back her sari which had slipped exposing her voluptuous body shape under her blouse!. She casually told him:

"my dear young man . . . dont show your negative response when Goddess Lakshmi knocks at your door brining a fortune to you!, I got from a reliable information that you are very good in copying signatures . . . If you refuse I cannot force you to do my work . . . I can always get some expert from Kolkata to do my job, my uncle who stays in Kolkata knows many who can do this minor job. It is up to you if decide to accept my request . . . I am prepared to pay you a good amount which you might not have earned so far . . . I don't beg or bargain with your terms . . . My uncle would drop you back immediately. But I am sure you will do this justifiable service to me . . . otherwise you will regret latter . . . if you refuse"

Her voice even though in a low tone but said with sharp and hard way!. She lifted the slipped sari back on her body, and looked at him a minute with harsh gleaming stare. Then she turned her face toward another side, as if she lost interest in him. Kalicharon was astonished at that lady's sudden change from grieving mood to forceful shrewd attitude. He thought he could play little tough way with an upper hand and bring her to his terms. But suddenly he developed cold feet at her unexpected aggressive attitude!. He suddenly felt as if sitting next to a beautiful wild beast that can devour him. He was literally shaken hearing her commanding words and confident outlook. Earlier he was attracted by her real feminine charm at close quarter. He developed a strong male desire of joy!. He could see that she was not very strict in morals. He thought once he would agree to do her dangerous job, he dreamt he would exploit her to get money as well her intimacy in exchange. He realized she was much above his class!. His emotions had evaporated and he started seeing the reality!. He understood her ruthlessness even with few words, he also realized it would more dangerous if he refused!.

He decided to accept her terms with some little bargaining to do that risky job!. Being still inexperienced he must accept that job with much caution to develop confidence to implement in future to execute such unlawful commitments. She got up from the seat to hear his final answer . . . she looked in a determined way to throw him out. In real fact she was acting to impress him that he has of no importance to her, and not that much dependent on him. But she was successful in covering her real feelings, ruthlessly concealing her desperation!.

Kalicharon yet tried to control his guts to do some hard bargaining. He said "Boudee! . . . Iam willing to help you but as it is a very risky job I must be paid a good amount and this must be kept very secret . . . . please never mention to anyone including your lawyer, about my service. That is my sincere request."

Chandramoni observed him keenly, she could easily understand that he fell to her gamble as well her charms and also visibly shaken at her attitude. She laughed loudly hearing his caution, as if hearing a joke!. She told him to she wouldn't risk telling anyone outside this family. She told sincerely:

"I will harp that the gift document was done by my husband almost six months earlier and nothing else, I would tell that she had no idea as to who prepared that will for him. He lovingly gave that along with the registered document of the property".

"Ok madam!. That is very nice reason . . . . let me ask some information . . . . Please remember some exact dates at least six months earlier, when you both were together at Kolkata, with proof if required in future . . . ."

"Kaleecharon! . . . . that is not difficult to prove . . . we generally used to stay in some luxury hotels most times at Kenilworth Hotel near park street . . . I don't know why he had a liking to stay there mostly when visiting that city. I will give you dates as I always used to mark on a calendar our visits . . . he always used to book in his name, sometimes I used to reach earlier and book in my name, as I am very familiar with that city . . . . to have time for rest and get some make up and relaxation at their excellent beauty salon with spa."

"Madam Could you get any real proof of your stay in Kolkata with him any date?"

She thought over for a minute and suddenly like a flash she remembered an incident shared with her husband.

"Listen . . . it so happened we met a retired former famous football player of Mohunbagan team in the hotel lounge. Romakant was his ardent fan. He was very happy to see him in person so close!. He introduced himself and requested that player to have a photo taken with him as a token of joyful proud remembrance. He agreed with a smile and we had that snap taken by a staff member of the front office, at our request."

She brought an album from a cupboard and shown him a photo of Romakant and herself with the player. The player was in the center with Romakant and Chandramoni on either side. The player was closer to her holding her with his hand on her shoulder touching her body boldly!. The photo had an in-built date and time of the camera printed at the bottom."

"Excellent proof! . . . . of your stay on that day at Kolkata!"

Kalicharon mused noting the date in his small book, with satisfaction. He checked the date in his small notebook calendar, and found that was not a Sunday.

He was now eager to get that document to be done at the earliest.

"I can manage to get 1000 rupee value non judicial stamp paper with date-stamp of that date which is about seven months earlier. It is best to get a non-judicial stamp paper as if he himself purchased . . . . it gives some authenticity, as even plain paper will also accepted after death . . . . I suggest tomorrow early morning I will go with your uncle in a taxi to Kolkata, Please try to arrange taxi from Kharagpore, instead of your personal car. I will accompany your uncle to purchase stamp papers of more than 6 months old and I will take in Romakant sab's name and address, and I will sign his signature. I got address of a vendor of stamp papers in Alipore, Kolkata. He normally charges much higher price for a thousand Rupee non-judicial stamp paper, such papers are very difficult to get from any stamp vendor to sell with older date stamp. Witnesses should not be your relatives and they should give their residential address. Witnesses were supposed to be present when the deed was signed in front of them."

"Kalicharon! . . . Now I understand you have good professional eye with practical planning . . . I appreciate you volunteered to accompany my uncle to get the stamp papers. I am very thankful to you! . . . . If the required stamp papers are brought tomorrow, you stay here and complete the task of writing the Will here itself. I can arrange to get the witnesses signatures at Kolkata, my uncle will manage that . . . . excellent ideas you told . . ."

She found him to be quite smart the way he quickly thought a plan of action, even though he had an unimpressive short personality with shifty eyes!. She decided to pay a decent amount for his services. To express her satisfaction she went very close to him once more put her hand behind his shoulder with a friendly tap in an affectionate way!. She knew any man would fall for her if she exhibits her little tricks!. He was too impressed and felt joyful at her intimate expression!. He almost missed a heartbeat at the close touch of her voluptuous body!.

Kalicharon decided not to ask about the fees, . . . he was expecting a high amount and he was not sure how that cunning lady will react. She would surely give him a decent payment, as she would be inheriting a valuable property!. Yet he felt he must give her hint. The property seemed to be very large estate with orchard.

"Madam you have a good knowledge . . . you are an intelligent person . . . please pay me which you feel good for this risky venture involving costly value of this property"

She smiled happily and put her hand in a friendly way. She told him her uncle would pick him at a place close to his residence to avoid prying eyes.

When he returned home it was past 11 in the night. He did not tell his father or aunt about his new risky job.

He requested permission to be absent from duties. In the night he practiced to forge signature of Seth Romakant, which he took from the madam. He never had scruples to bother as he was a born crook.

Next day he started journey by a taxi to Kolkata, with her uncle Durjoy at a very early morning when it was still dark. He went the stamp vendor and achieved what he aimed, without much hurdle. They decided to reach Medinipur only after dark, to avoid to be seen with her uncle in the town. He developed a closer intimacy with Durjoy Basak, due to his continuous stay with him that day. He observed most of his acquaintances looked shady characters and talked with fearful respect. He was surprised that he took him to Sona-Gachi locality of Kolkata when they had free time after completion of his job; where he took him to his a flat. He just informed that it was his friend's place. He didn't show surprise when he opened with his keys and the flat was in condition as if being frequently used. He was asked to prepare the draft gift deed in a front room, where he stayed whole day. Durjoy gave the points to make a convincing reason to gift the Kedargouri mansion in appreciation of Chandramoni's faithful help in his business. Kalichron made the draft of the Will as dictated by him constantly correcting sentences. He realized acquaintance with such persons would be helpful in future for his career. By eight at night they returned to Chandramoni's residence.

She was waiting for them; she greeted Kalcharon in a friendly way taking them both to a study room. She was in colourful sleeveless thin silken nighty, with black innerwear, with hair tied loosely with a ribbon, the hair ends forming a thick pony tail hanging in the front. She looked aristocratic in her informal dress. For Kalicharon, it became problem to stop gazing at her attractive appealing appearance!. She had no makeup yet her clear skin was glowing tenderly smooth!.

There he carefully wrote that Will on the stamp paper, he got from Kolkata. He deliberately used a different type of script type instead of his normal style, to avoid suspicion on him. He did exact forgery of late Seth Romakanto Choudhari's signature. It was a perfect job. No hand writing expert could find any flaw!. He wasn't aware that he was being video graphed all along secretly when he was writing the document and explaining to keenly watching Chandramoni. A framed photo of Romakant with her was on the table which was also became part of the Video. He was telling her husband if alive on that day would also believe that it was his signature!

After the job was completed, she spoke laughingly with a pun, that she was thankful to him for coming forward on his own and suggesting the idea of that Will and doing that job taking personal interest. He was stunned as well confused at her joke but covering his feelings he laughed with her:

"Madam . . . you are a great respectable lady . . . . I sincerely felt to do any service to you itself a privilege . . . . you deserve this help, I would be always at your service, Seth Romakant must have blessed me from heaven and made me to do this job for you!"

He told sheepishly, unaware that was also recorded in the video!. She felt happy at his words. She was still in the mourning appearance yet looked jovial. When he was about to depart, she praised him for his true help and mildly touched his hand, showing her gratitude.

She handed over a flat leather bag with a thick wad of currency notes. When he tried to tell he would always help her for any such future jobs, she smiled sheepishly at his fool-hardy sentiment.

Her uncle dropped him very close to his house, at a lonely place. He sternly advised him not to put all the money in a bank, convert to gold and keep it safely . . . . never tell anyone including his close relatives. He saw all around and took out a pistol; pointing at him in a vicious way with a mean voice he gave a final warning "Dont you ever try to contact my niece never and ever in your life, forget her existence! Dont ever try to meet even in future we don't know each other . . . . understood . . . now get back to your house, . . . but remember if you ever pass this information . . . your dead body will be on the railway tracks near Kharagpur or hung from a tree . . . . Remember you will go like Seth Romakant . . . . to hell or heaven! . . . That bastard started cheating my niece for another woman . . . . he paid for his foolishness! . . . . that is my final warning to you . . . in fact Chandramoni instructed me to eliminate you also after your job was completed . . . But I only cautioned a second murder next day might cause problem to us . . . . But if any suspicion is aroused from your movements . . . . no one can stop your death . . . remember . . . but if you behave as told I may contact you in future as I found you to be useful!"

He was about to start his bike, Kalicharon quickly went close to him and touched his feet with respect and meekly told "Moshaay!. (Gentleman) I am lucky to be acquainted to you . . . You can be rest assured if I make wrong move against madam . . . I will be the victim . . . I am very happy to be some service to your family . . . . I rather seek your help in future please allow me to contact you only and never will I try to meet or contact the madam. I am telling you truthfully" Durjoy saw him and could feel he looked real sincere . . . He realised that he could use his services in future and he could read that he was a clearly crooked in his sneaky way but no guts to face to strong opponents!.

He advised him that with his expertise if he made footing in Kolkata he would have a better success than a small place like Medinipur. He would try to help him if in future if he ever decides to start work in the city. He shook his hand and smilingly he gave an encouraged look and quickly drove away on his bike.

That way Kalicharon started criminal escapades of making false documents.

*   *   *

CHAPTER 2

*Ruma and Chandon's false
separation for property gain!*

Kalicharon Kundu remained staring at Durjoy's last warning! . . . He realized that he was involved neck deep for the false Will with forgery and also might be involved as one of the co accused in the murder of Romakant!. She would not hesitate to involve him if truth comes out!. For a moment he literally shuddered at the danger he got into, he cannot escape if caught by the law!. He was aghast to hear that dangerous lady's plan to eliminate him . . . . He was really shaken by her ruthless thought after showing coquettish acting in her house after getting his sincere help!. But he was too impressed with her charm and boldness, She did not take his uncle also while discussing with him. Her beauty and her body scent still lingered in his thoughts. He thought it might be 'Durjoy's creation to scare him. He really became a slave of her!. Smilingly he reached home. But Strangely he felt elated at the first successful errand of the wrong side of the law!. He was very satisfied at his ability and never felt any fear or regret. He felt happy to hold the heavy bag!.

He was also happy to be closer to Durjoy, he knew for his career such persons are assets!. Once inside his home he was in his normal dull expression. He went to his room and secretly counted the money . . . . he was really surprised to find large amount much more than what he was trying to ask or expected. He kept that in a secret place. Latter He made few trips to Kolkata and exchanged money for Gold coins.

He came to know that Romakant's concubine left the city, he mused she must be baiting for some other big fish!. He never tried to contact Durjoy, remembering his warning.

Romakanto's lawyer was surprised to see that he did not execute any Will of his property but gifted through a Will, only the valuable old mansion he purchased one year back. He could not find any flaw when he tried to pry its background!. Police also could not prove any foul play in the accident!.

Kalicharon's first criminal job was a grand success!.

*   *   *

When his father tried to arrange an alliance for him, he could not get any good match. One marriage broker got a match for him from a village near Bankura. The girl looked' very charming in the photo. They also offered a good dowry, which mainly attracted him. When they went with Baraat, no female relative went with them. After the marriage the girl was brought alone to Medinipur. On that night he found to his horror that girl acted like child and found to be mentally retarded!.

Within a week his enraged father went to girl's parents' house to talk about the deception they made in performing that wedding. He came to know that they had gone on pilgrimage. But bride's father's close acquaintance took him aside and advised him not to get into trouble as he might report to the police that you are harassing his daughter and asking more Dowry, and may get you arrested. His father could do nothing but fuming at the girl's parents and the marriage broker for their wrongful act. He wanted to send back the girl with the dowry they gave, when her parents return after two weeks!. But Kalicharon had a different sinister plan. He never wanted to return the Three Lakhs dowry, and ornaments. He told his father not to do anything in hurry, the girl might improve latter.

One late night he silently cut her long tresses in her sleep. He took care to see no cut hair pieces were left on the cot or floor. He carefully put them in a plastic cover. Few days earlier he bought young boy's shirt, and pant, to fit her body. In the night he removed her sari and petty coat and put on the boy's dress. She looked like a teenage boy. He booked a taxi earlier and kept it waiting. He selected a Telugu speaking taxi driver, at Kharagpur railway station.

In the night he woke her and gently said he would take her to her parents. She was very happy at his words, he gave her favorite sweet to eat, and gently he took her outside with maximum care not make any sound. He warned her that others would stop her to see her parents if they were found. His father and aunt were in deep sleep. He put off the main switch and made the house dark. He gently closed his door and came out of the house silently, keeping a hand on her mouth lest she would make any

talk or make childish prattle. He took her to the Taxi and
asked the driver to take to Kharagpur railway station. The
driver thought a young boy was accompanying him, who
was giggling and talking little; as he was continuously
eating some sweets without any concern. As Kalicharon
was talking in Bengali in a soft voice to the boy the
driver didn't take any interest of their talks. He paid the
taxi driver whatever he demanded, when he reached the
station.

The girl somehow was happy that she would go to
her parents. She was happily obeying him whenever he
gave sweets. On the way he covered his body with a sheet
and put on a woolen face cap, which covered his face and
head. He also put on dark glasses. He put a sheet around
her also. He came to the platform and waited. An express
train to south India, from Howrah came to halt on the
platform, he took her and entered a sleeper compartment
when some passengers opened the door and got out. The
compartment was almost dark with few night lamps. He
took her to the corridor, and spread a folded sheet on
the floor and made her sit. She rested on the sheet and
innocently went to sleep quickly, as it was late night. He
gently came out and stood at a distance outside in shadow.
Some passengers came into that compartment closed the
door, as the train started to move within no time it was
out of sight. He quietly came out least bothering about
that innocent girl's fate, as the train took her away to some
unknown destination. He knew she doesn't have any idea
of his name or the place; he also knew that no one can
understand her gibberish innocent baby talk!. He went
back to his house which was still dark. He put on the
main switch and quietly entered his room and closed. He
had thrown out the plastic bag with her hair on way, while

on move in the taxi. He hoped that he would not face any problem. He slept with least feeling of regret!. Next day he got up late and casually enquired about his bride, saying she went out of the room before he woke up. While returning from station he left the front door open. Whole family and friends made a desperate search for her and started to look in various places of the city and outskirts asking all known persons.

He reported to police after three days, not informing her mental state. He gave the police her photo taken with him after the wedding. She looked very good looking and jovial with bridal makeup!. After writing the F.I.R., he sought an interview with the Inspector. He went to his room and started silently crying with uncontrollable emotion. The Inspector was moved by his false show of sorrow. He assured him that they would thoroughly make search for her and send copies of her photo to other stations also. Kalicharon feebly requested him that he had some secret to convey. He requested to listen alone. He bowed his head without seeing him at his eyes as if he was ashamed to convey what he had in mind!. He then slowly informed him, that his wife was not happy with him, that she and detested him. He told with utmost shame that he was nowhere in front of her beauty and she used hate him from the first night as was not that type of romantic or able to please her.

"I was very repulsive to her and she never allowed sleeping with her. She never took initiative to live normally in the house. She had some occasional calls from someone and used to speak secretly. After she ran away, next day morning she phoned from some long distance from a public booth, stating that she will not come back to me as she had decided to live with some other person whom she loved. She warned me that in case if I reported to police she would rather die than come back. She threatened she would commit suicide and write badly about me to see that no me that no other woman would marry me in future. And that I was ill treating her . . . sir I am forced to accept the reality. Sir please tell me what to do . . . I did not inform my father or her parents, what she did . . . I am feeling ashamed to tell anyone that my wife ran away from me to live with some other person, I am very much upset and don't know what to do . . . I'm making this confession to you and seek your sincere guidance,. I or she would be never happy if you find her and bring her back forcibly."

He started to silently cry, continuously clearing his eyes with a kerchief. The Inspector was also stunned on hearing his story. He felt real sympathetic to him. Finally he said that he understood the seriousness of the situation and some rogue women trouble the men this way. He assured him secretly that he would consult his senior and try to do not much effort to trace her . . . he asked him why he gave a police report knowing the consequences. He also warned that if his story proved to be false that he would face very serious consequences. Kalicharon old pitiably he had no alternative due to pressure from his family and her parents, and that he had no guts to tell the real truth, which would make things still worse. He folded his hands and told that if his story proved to be false he would face any punishment. He said that he would write and sign his version for confidential police record.

With his false story the police did not take serious action to search her. His father wrote letter to her parents informing that he girl ran away from the house. He assured them that they complained to the police. In a month's time the families gave up hope and prayed for her safety. Kalicharon was certain that if other state police happened to question her, dressed as a boy the girl would not be able to communicate anything.

His aunt had a slight suspicion that Kalicharon must have left her somewhere. She was awoke, when he returned in the night. But she did not bother to ask at that time. When he heard talking to her father he was enraged at her and shouted that he doesn't know anything about her Disappearance. Latter the family forgot about her. After few months his father died.

In another few months he took his ailing aunt on the pretext of taking her to pilgrimage. He took her to Brindavan and got her admitted in an ashram, without her knowledge. He knew she would lose her voice and would not be able to communicate after few days as per the doctor's warning. He came to know it would be very costly to get her treated. He made her sign, a document as if she gifted her property. He got neighbors signatures as witnesses. He bluffed her that was done as per some government order.

He paid the Ashram, paying a year's deposit for her staying there (without her knowledge!). The amount was not much. He gave the Ashram all false information about him, his name, his place etc. He told them that he was a distant relative and that he had some personal domestic problems to keep her. Yet taking a humanitarian view she was trying to help that poor widow to have a peaceful life in the Ashram. He promised to send amount every year. He requested them with a choked voice with emotion, to look after her well.

To her he said, that urgently his presence is required for few days at Medinipur and tenderly told after few days they would go to other temples of pilgrimage when he returns, as she would be very comfortable in that ladies Ashram, till then. He quietly left to his home town.

He sold his father's small house and shifted to a rented house in a different locality far from his old house, without informing to neighbors. He sold all his aunt's lands which were gifted in his name. With least regret he erased from memory about her and left to her fate in a Ashram without informing her!. He never felt any sort of remorse towards her for all the service she rendered to him looked all along like a mother and gave all affection and love. He never had sentiments for any. That is his type of life.

He became bolder with his successes in crooked deeds, which gave satisfaction to him.

*   *   *

With some years of working under Jogesh Maity, he developed complete confidence in writing various types of deeds. His employer always kept final draft copies of different documents, he submitted for registration and other jobs. He was sure his employer's work would be completely would be taken by him, and constantly used to look for some loop holes in them. He followed his example and started keeping copies of all documents he made in privacy in his home. He also used to write separately in a diary giving few details of all the back ground of the documents, for latter remembrance if required, and also to see loopholes if any, for future action.

Kalicharon used to secretly pry into his master's secret copies of documents pertaining to transfer of properties. He suddenly found out that his employer had changed the distribution of the landed property deliberately not following the Will of a deceased person, while making individual documents. He did not follow the real contents of property division. He understood that his employer must be hand-in-glove with the new benefactor in the sinister deed. After serious prying, he unearthed his secret plot to a draft of an un-authorized duplicate Will.

Medinipur's one of propertied person was late Pramod Chandro Ghosal. He had landed properties and houses located some in West and East Medinipore districts; he had acquired the properties consisting of lands, houses and a rice mill, when it was one district, before division. He had only three daughters in whose names he divided the properties, which were to be transferred only after demise of his wife Malothi Debi.

After Promod Chandra's death, she requested her son-in-law, Chandon and daughter Ruma, to stay in her house to assist the running of family property affairs. Ruma was her second daughter. Malothi Debi was too weak and ailing. Chandon had his own business and separate house in Medinipur, but he accepted the additional responsibilities. The other two daughters were living in distant places with their husbands.

Chandon was upset when he came to know the contents of his late father in law's Will through his lawyer, who was his close friend. His wife's share was lesser compared to the value of other two sisters' shares of the property, because of type of lands and location. Most of the high yielding good agricultural lands were to go to the first and third daughters, including the urban properties while sub-urban properties and more dryer lands has gone to Ruma, the second daughter; even though their father tried to divide the properties by equity basis on area wise.

Cunningly he decided to deceive his wife's sisters, to get maximum benefit to his wife in the property distribution. He hatched a crooked plan to make a show of serious situation of sharp differences with his wife. His wife Ruma, feared immediate consequences of their false drama in real life, but agreed to play her role as she would be highly benefitted, to gain a big property!. They started their acting in a realistic way.

Chandon and Ruma started to argue in bad temper as if both were unhappy with each other and situation had come to a serious state in few months. Both would exchange loud arguments almost in their daily family life. However they used secretly plan in their bed room to make dramatic way of serious rift in their relationship!.

Her ailing mother was much distressed at her daughter's family life and tried her best to restore peace between them. In spite of her intervention there was no respite in her daughter's family life. She used to cry before her in his absence, telling that her husband was cheating her taking her own money and ornaments regularly to another woman, that he was beating her in drunken condition!. Her mother was much upset and tried to interfere in their lives, to restore normalcy. Ruma and Chandon started to fight each other before her with loud hysterical verbal arguments blaming each other. Finally her son in law angrily threatened before her and other relatives that he decided to leave her and live separately. He left the house as if he was unable to live with her. Malothi Debi was too distressed at her daughter's life. She desperately called her other two daughters and their husbands to restore her second daughter's miserable family life. Within few days they arrived, to seriously try to restore normalcy in Ruma's relationship with her husband. But the situation suddenly changed into a tragic anti-climax.

Malothi Debi's condition became worse and became seriously ill; she suddenly went into a coma, and died in few days!.

Chandon and Ruma enacted that drama, to make Malothi Debi to feel pity on her second daughter's miserable family life!. He got made a separate Will as if made by his seriously sick Mother in law.

The lawyer and the document writer Jogesh helped him in devising the new Will. The transcript was in such a way that the second daughter would get maximum share and best part of the property. The Will was secretly made through an understanding by which the lawyer and Jogesh Maiti were to be also benefitted. Before he could get his mother in law's signature, through Ruma, she became too serious and half conscious. He wasn't prepared such situation would come so suddenly!.

Jogesh hinted to Chandon to get her signature forged by Kalicharon in the newly prepared Will; he avoided telling directly to his own employee. Kalicharon bargained for more than what was offered by Chandon, when he visited his house in the night secretly to get the forgery done. He realized the stake of high benefit as per the new will. Chandon forced him to accept his offer by indirectly threatening of consequences if he refused. Kalicharon knew of Chandon's influence in Medinipur and his capability of making his life miserable. Keeping his anger within him, he accepted to do that job; intentionally he didn't do a good job while copying her original signature. He signed all pages as required. Chandon managed to get two witnesses signatures also, who were his known persons. After the death of Malothi Debi, the forged will was read by her lawyer to the family. The other two sisters were very much upset as they got much lesser shares of the property compared to their second sister. Their husbands have also felt that injustice was done by their mother-in-law, taking pity of her second daughter's misery.

Kalicharon decided to exploit this secret and make a good profit by exposing the crooked plan hatched by Chandon. He secretly met the eldest and third sons in law and conveyed to them that he had proofs that their co-brother Chandon hatched a plot to gain maximum of the property of late Pramod Chandro Ghosal, to his wife. He conveyed that it was a forged signature on a Will supposed to have been made by Malothi Debi. He would inform the secret with proofs of the foul play, if he gets proper reward, on his terms. He explained how cunningly Chandon made the Will in such a way that best part of rich property went to his wife. He promised his secret would help to get justified shares to their wives. He wanted some advance payment and balance when they win the case. He convinced them that he knew the culprits. They were convinced that as he was working under their family lawyer's organization, he must be having knowledge of some sinister plot. He assured that he would give the proofs to file a criminal case against Chandon and his wife for the fraud they committed to gain maximum. He showed a part of the original partition and the extent of damage in the forged Will.

After seeing the part of the original Will the two sisters and their husbands discussed among themselves and decided to accept the terms of Kalicharon without involving him. They too suspected some sinister mystery in so much improper distribution of the property. They paid him two lakh each and promised two pay other two lakhs when they would win. He advised them not to hire local lawyers but a reputed advocate from Kolkata. He gave them the copy of the original Will of Pramod Chandro Ghosal and the date of signing of second Will by late Malothi Debi. In fact there was a condition laid by late Pamod Chandro that his wife has no right sell or transfer any part of the property and no right to change the division of the property as decided by him. His own daughters were not aware of their father's conditions laid in his original will!.

When F.I.R of a criminal case was lodged against Chandon and his wife Ruma, the police arrested them on court orders. Chandon's lawyer got immediate bail very next day informing that he was not living with his wife and late mother in law; being a lady Ruma was also came out of the prison within two days. Both were let out on bail, while the police making further investigation against them through the public prosecutor, as the proceedings were yet to be finalized for formal charge sheet.

Chandon knew his co-brothers were not that smart in legal matters, and was surprised at their getting deep into his well hatched plan!. He was a very shrewd man and he got strong suspicion that his secret came to lime light only through Kalicharon. He sent for him and bluffed that he got information that he divulged the distorted facts about his mother in law's Will. He charged him in angry tone that the case was initiated through his instigation. Kalicharon was struck with fear knowing the notorious reputation of Chandon in Medinipur. He kept a blank face like a mask showing surprised innocence; he begged him to believe that being a timid person could never dare to go against him. Chandon was not convinced about his reply and decided to watch him secretly.

He first faced a taste of his ire, when he was summoned by some unknown farmers from a nearby village, and requested for meeting their head. He was taken out of town in an isolated place and beaten very badly, and left him lying on the road with major injuries. He was rescued by some passers-by and was admitted in a hospital. He could not attend his professional work for more than three months. He could guess who was behind that attack. He also knew that if he reported to the police he could never prove his involvement. He decided to leave Medinipur till the court takes action on Chandon for his involvement of the case of false Will. He understood the reality that he would have bleak future if he remained in small town. He also found it may also become civil case when he learnt that Ruma contested with counter challenge that her mother had right to alter the will of her late father if family circumstances call for a change, as she was deserted by her husband. He knew civil case means the property division would remain stagnant till court decides. Such cases run years for final settlement or arrive at a Compromise—within the parties. He recognized that he would hardly get few cases to prove his expertise and talent in creating false documents in both Medinipur districts. His master also might throw him out on Chandon's orders.

When he was in a depressed mood, suddenly he got a call from Durjoy asking him to see him at Kolkata next day. He thought it was a good omen with a promise to have a new venture with change of place. He felt, Durjoy, calling him for new job probably for an illegal job. He was happy as that would make him to play with upper hand and take his help to start work at Kolkata. He actually wanted to contact Durjoy to request him to help to move to Kolkata. He went to that city next day to meet him at an address told by him.

* * *

CHAPTER 3

Durjoy makes Kalicharon his Slave!

He went to meet Durjoy at Kolkata, at an address he informed. It was a dilapidated old building named as 'Jyotsna Bhvan' located on Gaurab Sanyal lane off Dhani Ghosh Sarani (part Beadon steet). Ground floor had some shops, and saloon, beauty parlor and an eatery. It was a not a very big building. All the four floors above had balconies, on road side, where some ladies were standing and watching the street. The entrance had one staircase and an old lift which was out of order. As he entered the building and was climbing the stairs to reach the fourth floor, he felt that he came to a wrong address. At different levels and corridors he was exposed to a different type of living areas. He didn't feel it was a building with different families; instead he saw clumsily dressed and crudely talking majority women of different ages.

He asked an elder lady whether the building is Jyotsna Bhawan, she stared at him in surprised way and bluntly said she doesn't know and left him. He asked a younger woman . . . standing close by. She as wearing a thin

Lehnga Sari holding the Pallu in her hand . . . . she giggled and said:

"Mama! . . . you should ask that before entering this building! . . . yes it is Jyotsnaa Bhowon . . . . whom do you want to meet?"

"I wanted to meet Durjoy mohaashoy . . . . do you know him?"

She put blank face . . . as if she never heard such person . . . she inquired which floor . . . When he informed fourth floor . . . . She again laughed . . . . with laughter she said that he is at second floor.

"Debjani stays in second floor. But if you want to go above . . . that is your desire!"

He was confused. He asked innocently "who is Debjani?!"

She again laughed and said mirthfully:

"Queen of this floor! . . . ami! (me)" and quickly left him, giggling and pointing a door in that floor with a mischievous look. He was perplexed and climbed another floor and seeing the same type of unpleasing scenario he stood wondering he was about to call him on mobile, Suddenly He heard Durjoy calling him from fourth. He saw him laughing and waiting for him. He asked him to come up. He invited him happily and took to his room in that floor.

He hurriedly went above, unable to forget her joyful talk. As he reached third floor, Durjoy called him from above looking at him happily. He took towards his room, giving welcome nod.

After a long time he was meeting Durjoy, but there was hardly much difference, he was looking active with jolly mirthful face yet giving a dangerous appearance which doesn't permit anyone to take him lightly. He was wearing dark glasses giving a sinister outlook.

He was looking heftier with an increased waist line, with air of roguish aggressive attitude. He was sitting in front of a large table with one visitor chair; there was also a separate sofa at the opposite side. There was a door to the balcony in the back. The room was fairly big with an attached bath room. A large painting with frame was on one side near his table. He made him wait in his room in a corner as he was busy with his own work, and least cared to talk to him immediately. Kalicharon could not guess how he came out to call him. Latter he found he had a small video screen near his table showing movements of persons at the entrance to that building. He couldn't understand what business he does. But he was busy talking in a coded language giving instructions and ordering some to do different jobs all with secrecy. He suddenly sent him to an adjoining room to wait, as two ladies came inside to talk with him. It was not air-conditioned but had a fan. That room had a long narrow table and two chairs. He surprised to see he kept his office in an old building, mostly occupied it looked by sex workers. His followers looked they would obey whatever their master ordered irrespective of consequences.

After about thirty minutes others have all left, he called him. He told the guard outside the closed door not to allow any person till he tells. He then called Kalicharon and asked him to sit on a chair opposite to him. He was bit disappointed at his attitude towards him.

After very short general light talk Durjoy told discretely that he requires his services to prepare a fake copy of a property document, to appear like the original. He informed the basic information only. That original, which is still in the file, would be smuggled out from a bank by next week end. That document has to be made into a duplicate copy by manual work, necessary counterfeit blank stamp papers similar to originals and required rubber stamps were already arranged. He told another fake originals have to be created copying exact way as the original documents, to be replaced in the bank. He informed that color-scanned copies, of the original documents, are already with him to start the work. The work has to be completed by next Sunday night as that fake one would have to be taken back to the bank by Monday morning to be replaced as original one. He informed him that the owner of an old independent two storied building with some open land in that neighbored had pledged the original documents recently with a bank, for a large amount of loan. He said that the loan was sanctioned and drawn by the owner, after completion of the legal proceedings. That person working in America and would go back within a month. He informed that the owner would not come back to Kolkata under normal circumstances till three years.

"Even if he comes back he doesn't stay in that old building. He gave that building on lease to some lady. This was one of the old original buildings of that locality. The present owner would not know even if the property is sold, as he got rents for one year in addition to six months' rent as returnable deposit, as the usual conditions in most buildings and flats here. He might try to contact the tenant who would not be traceable as the property might be rented to a different tenant or get it demolished to construct a bigger building with more floors, after two years by a new owner. I do not care what might happen in future after a new owner buys the property legally.

Once it is sold the present owner would have only the fake document in the bank records!."

He laughed and continued:

"I made arrangement to get that original documents on Friday and have to be replaced by Monday. You come back after two or three days and come prepared to stay here till next Monday. You have to start practicing from the Xerox copies. The new copied document should be ready by Sunday. Even if the work requires late hours work . . . . it has to be completed without fail before Monday morning . . . Once we get confirmation of the owner's departure to America, we start the main work to sell that property, you are to make a new sale deed with the original document, as the property would be sold by a person who would impersonate as the owner and sell that to another customer through new registration."

Kalicharon understood his requirement and accepted to do the job staying in Kolkata.

He took that opportunity to take help from Durjoy, to settle in Kolkata and leave Medinipur for good. He briefly explained the dangerous situation arose due to false suspicion on him by a local influential person who made his life miserable and his staying had become unsafe there. He informed his ambition to start work in Kolkata. He desired to work under him and latter look for other jobs. He pleaded for help and guidance to work in the city. Then he made a self-boast to remind him as how he made a false Will for the benefit of Chandramoni Debi, that secret was so far never suspected by any one in Medinipur.

This crude reminder from Kalicharon looked like a veiled threat to Durjoy. He quickly understood that he must have been forced to leave his hometown as he must have been caught double crossing a client in an illegal job. He was upset and very furious for his foolish prattle to remind him his last job entrusted. He didn't show his irritation and anger but showed a smiling exterior. He made up his mind to permanently eliminate him after getting his services for the new job. He heartily laughed as if he said that as a joke covering his anger.

"kalicharon! . . . I am happy that you decided to shift to Kolkata, brother you would be like my close friend . . . . I will give whatever help you need to settle here . . . my little request never utter the name of my niece at any time in the future. What about your family will they also come here?"

Kalicharon bowed him with high reverence and expressed his gratitude:

"That is a very great help sir! . . . I humbly fall at your feet for your great benevolence . . . I am greatly relieved at your kindness . . . . I am alone at Medinipur . . . unfortunately all are dead . . . I will shift to this city immediately . . . . Sir I am struggling to live there under threat from a local goonda . . . no other person is with me to help. I promise you to do whatever entrusted to me with sincere devotion . . . . sorry for my mistake of reminding that past little service to you"

Durjoy was relieved to hear him say that he was all alone and facing enmity locally . . . . which was the main reason shift to the city.

"Kalicharon . . . do not worry now as I would protect you from any danger from there . . . . You quietly shift here never reveal your address to anyone at Medinipur . . . as you should not underestimate any enemy . . . you come with your things and work here, I will arrange some accommodation also close by . . . .

I have some work for an hour, in the meantime you go through these documents and also make a list for your work requirements, sit in that room where you waited earlier, adjoining to my office you have to do that work there only"

He gave him the colored Xerox copies of the documents and similar old blank counterfeit stamp papers. Kalicharon started to study the document pages; they were made about more than 70 years back on old pattern British Government stamp papers. Plan of the site giving location was also made on one of the stamp papers giving the names of the surrounding land marks then existed. The ageing of the old document with fold marks and was reflected in the colored Xerox prints!. The documents were written in typical Bengali manuscript, describing sale deed and original owner's name etc., in normal standard way. The owner's fingerprints and witnesses signature and registered in 24 Paraganas district sub-registrar's office. Along with that a copy of a gift deed of the property by the owner to his son, the gift deed was vetted in the court, as the rightful owner succeeding the original vendee; that document was also more than 30 years old.

When Durjoy returned, Kalicharon told him:

"Sir, creating a fake document of this is not one day's job but it may take about five days . . . as the new document papers are to be artificially aged to look like old documents, that takes more time . . . than writing"

"How can that be possible? we can manage to get the original documents for two days only. That also with a great risk . . ."

"No sir . . . I don't require original documents . . . I can prepare the similar documents from these colored prints. They are very clear to make exact copies Sir . . . your new blank counterfeit printed stamp would look suspicious as they are crisp new papers. They should also look old and faded."

"Then how that would be possible!. How to make them look old . . . . why you require five days to make copies of them?"

"See sir . . . these new papers are to made to look like old and authentic . . . that requires artificial aging to each paper separately, that is a bit slow process."

"Oh God . . . you are a genius to think of that . . . but how do you make new papers to look like old papers?

"Sir . . . I will do new papers to appear like more than fifty years old, even hundred years . . . which I learnt; I will do them before you. I made a list of the articles required"

He handed him a paper with a list of following odd items. It contained a Tea Making Kettle, two deep glass trays, any brand strong ordinary tea powder, an electric hair dryer, a simple baking Owen, thick round make up brush, Indian Ink. laminate clip boards to fix stamp papers, block sponge, in addition to two thick candles, two fresh lemons etc.,.

Durjoy was surprised at the list, but he appreciated Kalicharon for his sincere attitude, to make some real efforts. Without asking he explained the process he is going to adopt "Sir, each paper to be made separately processed dipped carefully in the cool tea liquor in a tray, after which they are to be baked in low temperature in an oven which changes to paper to giving old paper look. After papers dried they will look like old papers with dark pale yellow color. I will write copying the old documents in the same style, including various signatures on those aged document papers. Writing to be made with nib pen dipping the nib in black ink mixed with few drops of lemon juice. After writing, each sheet is to be exposed to candle light heat, which will give faded old look to newly written script".

Durjoy understood the process and decided to video tape the process for future such jobs. He was surprised that the dull looking Kalicharon is quite sharp in work and intelligent. He knew such people can be very manipulative and untrustworthy. But once more he expressed great joy by flattering briefly.

He informed him that he had arranged a lone single room flat in fifth floor of a building at a walking distance from there. That he can reach the fifth floor by back stairs which are not used by outsiders and that he should not become friendly with other occupants in that building, as no one would be trustworthy. Kalicharon was happy to learn that an accommodation was arranged. He decided to shift within three days with his bags and baggage.

Suddenly Durjoy became serious and informed him as master tells his slave.

"Kalicharon . . . you must become a new person with a new name once you join my organization to work for me. You will have a new name as Gobindo Laha and not as Kalicharon Kundu . . . Another thing is whenever you travel on my work outside this locality which I would be informing . . . . you have to impersonate as another person . . . . by the name of Gadhador Kar. I will arrange two different hair wigs for each name in addition you have to wear a false beard also for Gadhador, that will completely alter your face . . . When you come back I will arrange those wigs and also you will be given two separate mobile phones, one for each name"

Kalicharon was nonplussed at his strange orders. He could not imagine anyone could live as a separate person!. He is not escaping from any police hunt to hide with different name and different face!. He felt miserable and mildly tried to tell his views:

"Sir! . . . How can I suddenly change to new names since childhood I am accustomed only to my own name . . . my document writer license also in my name only!"

"Don't worry I will arrange another license for your Gobindo Laha name . . . You don't require for Gadhador Kar any license. Since nobody knows you here it hardly matters to you if work under different name. I have my own reasons for you to be called in different names. Also it will protect from your present enemies Who would not be able your new identity!. If you have reservations to obey my order . . . . you need not return back to me"

He said in a hard way. Kalicharon with a bowed head understood he has no other alternative except to accept his command. He knew he was helpless. But as he was a cunning person by nature he decided to act humbly and learn his weak points and exploit to his advantage latter, so far he was getting upper hand in his private life . . . he could not understand why a drama is being played with him as an actor!. He decided to wait and watch to escape from his clutches, once he develops a footing in the city. He also felt may it was necessary in that way in a big city while attempting to commit a big fraud!.

He told meekly accepted to obey his orders. He went and saw the lone flat at fifth floor level escorted by Durjoy's assistant. He found it to be a small one room accommodation with a bath and kitchen. It was empty and the walls were all dull grey as it wasn't painted for some years it looked.

He went to Medinipur and resigned his job and after working two days and stolen some more stamp papers etc. As they were illegally kept, he knew that his master cannot report against him even if he finds the loss. He had a steel box wherein he kept all his saved money, as most of it was earned by deceit!. He converted maximum amount to Gold Mohurs (Gold coins of 10 grams weight each). He also kept his Diary and copies of documents he prepared and some old original document stamp papers, including secret illegal deeds in preparation of some documents. He had kept record with details. But mainly he never had any bank account and all his earnings and sale of properties were stacked in that box only.

When he reached the new flat after returning to Kolkata, he went straight to the small one roomed flat, key of which was given by Durjoy. First thing he noticed was the name plate on the top of the door, with his new name as Gobindo Laha, Document writer. He was surprised to find that it wasn't painted newly but it looked like an old name plate painted much earlier!. He felt a doubt whether it was another person by that name who also was a document writer!. He set aside his doubts and thoughts. It reminded him that from that day he as to start life with his new name!. He opened the door and found to be cleaned and kept ready. There was a cot, a table and two chairs. On the top of the table there was a very good quality new leather bag, with bright yellow color. A slip with the name of Gobindo Laha was tagged on the bag. He understood that bag was gifted to him for out station tours. He brought only few personal items—his steel box, a suitcase with clothes and some other household utensils and cooking pans. He disposed other old items in Medinipur Itself. No one came to see him off when he sat in the train, as he did not inform any known person.

After closing the door he opened the new bag on the table. Inside there were two pouches with name tags one with name Gobindo Laha and other with Gadhador Kundu. Each had a separate hair wig to wear to change his outlook!. He first tried Gadhadar's wig and false beard, when he saw his face he himself could not control laugh at the complete transformation of his face, with long hair and a beard. Even he looked different with the wig of Gobindo Laha!. He accepted his fate to live few weeks or months with the new avatars. He could not understand reason of his strange orders. There were also two cell phones with new names pasted on each. Suddenly Kalicharon realized that his flat has a duplicate key with Durjoy!. He felt upset at that unexpected problem.

He understood there is no security to his personal items, especially his steel trunk wherein he kept all his lifetime earnings he made so far, amounting to more than 20 Lakhs. He got made special compartment inside to secretly keep his gold coins, in addition to currency notes. He never put his money in a bank. He felt utterly restless with fear that if he would lose his hard earned money and become a pauper. Added to that his flat was isolated single flat on the fifth floor, rest was a terrace only. He didn't know whether the flat or whole building was under the control of Durjoy. He became nervous as he had no alternative but to live there, as he had determined to leave Medhinipore for some years. He decided to have a new lock to his room and additional lock to his personal steel trunk. He came out of the room with Gobindo makeup. He decided throughout the day he must wear it as per

Durjoy's strict instructions. When he came out there were few ladies all collecting the washed clothes dried on the terrace, all looked at him with surprise and fear. One lady even dared to address him as Mama (uncle) to enquire whether he had taken that flat. He replied with least interest and quickly climbed down the flat to the street. He purchased two big strong locks, in a nearby shop; he also purchased an iron chain with a lock to tie his box to the cot.

When he reached his flat, getting his things, he placed in some order. He tried to conceal his big iron box, under the cot with double lock, and covered with a bed sheets.

Suddenly he got a ring in his new phone, and as his old habit told Kalicharon speaking. Other side it was Durjoy,

"Gobindo how are you? . . . I am keenly waiting for your arrival . . . are you settled well in the flat?"

"Yes sir!. It is very nice I have just arrived in the evening . . . I find it to be quite comfortable. Thank you for the nice bag you gave sir!"

"Very good, . . . If you have any problem or you require any thing you tell me . . . let us start our work and complete this week. Today you go and have food and rest . . . there are restaurants close by"

Next day he met Durjoy and started the work on the new document, in an adjoining room. After working two days he meekly expressed his insecure feeling in his new flat, and he was unable to sleep well fearing somebody might intrude into his isolated room. Durjoy laughed and said he will tell some guards of that area to look after him. He said casually that no one will dare to disturb him, as they know the consequences. He took a revolver casually from his table drawer and told in joking way they know how dangerous if any one disobeys his orders in that building. Kalicharon was stunned beyond belief. He literally was shaken. He was utterly confused why for such a minor problem he was showing a gun!. He could never understand Durjoy's thinking and his surprising actions. He felt a real fear to stay near his very presence itself. He felt a shiver inside reflecting deep dread for accepting to work with him!. He felt it was a wrong decision to accept to work with him.

Next few days he worked hard and completed the fake property documents which looked more than Seventy years old. It looked as good as the original. He made them look genuinely old by artificial aging process. Durjoy arranged to get the duplicate rubber stamps same type as used in the original. The fake documents were given on Saturday to the Bank officer and who removed the originals from the file on Friday evening and handed over to Durjoy's representative. The officer was astounded at the expertize. He felt some expert has done the reproductions as well signatures in exact way. The bank officer was on transfer orders and got hefty reward from Durjoy. Since he knew the old records are not likely to be checked as all the formalities were completed, and the documents would go into a locker in a strong room.

*   *   *

CHAPTER 4

Joyful boat-ride in Hooghly River!

That Bank officer-officer was much impressed when he saw the forged signatures, in the fake documents. He was looking secretly for the services of a forger; he was planning another deceit act from that bank before getting relief from that branch. He secretly explained his requirement to his secret contact who conveyed to Durjoy. He spoke with him directly on phone and both planned the time and place for doing that job. Till then he never spoke or seen Nilesh Sanyal, the bank officer in charge of the loan transaction to Gnanendra Guha on his property.

Next day Durjoy took Kalicharon in his car, on that day he asked him to come as Gadhador Kar. He sat in front seat next to the driver. He was surprised to find Durjoy also in a false appearance; he nicely dressed as a Punjabi Sardar with a turban and false beard!. He was astonished at his complete transformation!. He had warned him earlier that he would also be coming dressed as a Sardar, hinted not to show any surprise.

They went into a large hotel compound and parked the car. Durjoy went inside that hotel, telling him to wait for his phone call. He met the bank officer in one of the exclusive restaurants.

Both never met earlier and got acquainted. Durjoy got his dangerous work using the bank officer through a common known contact person. The bank officer sent this unusual request for the services of an expert forger; which he accepted to do his job and arranged that hotel meeting. Both talked in a friendly way and the officer was impressed at seeing the Sardar Durjoy Singh, talking Bengali fluently. Durjoy found him to be equally overbearing and looked cunningly self-esteemed and ambitious. He secretly felt to be an unreliable partner to be cautious.

A little time latter, Nilesh later he gave him an envelope in which there were three personal blank cheques of a proprietor of a very large construction company, with name printed on each leaf, issued by the bank. He also brought out a Xerox copy of a used cheque of the same person. The officer had intentionally removed carefully three blank cheques in a cunning manner selecting at random from between pages of the new book ten days earlier; when he issued new book to him. He did it with a crooked motive, to cash them for his personal benefit!. He detected easy way of pilfering some amount from the contractor's account, as many times such large transactions took place in the privacy of his cubicle. He said in a whispering voice that those cheques were to be signed and filled by his signature copier.

Kalicharon was sitting nervously waiting for a call from Durjoy. Surprisingly He got a good payment for his services, for the fake document preparation; which made him, feel more secure to work with him to do sincerely his jobs. When he got the call, he told the driver and went into the Hotel; one waiter was waiting to receive him near the entrance, who took him to the private dining area of a restaurant. It was a posh restaurant, where he found high dignitaries were having drinks and lunch talking in low voices. When he reached the private Partitioned dining area a smartly dressed lady host was taking the orders. She looked once at him and didn't take much interest. After she left Durjoy introduced him as Gadhador Kar document writer. He did not tell the name but simply introduced him as a senior officer of a bank. He made him sit on a vacant seat at another table close by which had no plates for food service.

He handed him a copy of the cheque which had printed name as Benugopal Sur and a signature was above. Kalicharon found that he signed like a less educated person. There were twists and turns in English letters in a crude way showing less knowledge in writing!. He was first asked to do practice that signature on a blank white paper. Kalicharon became deeply engrossed as the two were having drinks and chit chatting general topics. While doing his work with concentration, he was listening intently their conversation also. He suddenly heard Durjoy asking the officer, if he is ever tried an exclusive boat ride with nice company on the Hooghly river. He said he can arrange pleasure journey with food and drinks with entertaining company, with complete privacy. He said he will arrange as a compliment to show his gratitude to his most friendly help.

He said that the river boating in Hooghly is very pleasant in the evening after darkness. He also informed that he has a nice boat with cosy private bed cum lounge suite at upper deck, with complete privacy. He assured that they would return within two to three hours. He said he would be accompanied by two of his guards, who will stay with the boat driver.

The officer showed interest and accepted his offer, with gleeful mood.

Durjoy next asked whether he would like to look at a beautiful parrot that was collected recently by him from a private aviary just fresh from Mainamar jungles. The officer asked with suppressed mirth with keen interest.

"Is that a wild or tamed? . . . . I heard Burmese birdies especially wild Arakanese look very cute!"

When suddenly, they found, Kalicharon was also listening to their conversation keenly. They stopped the topic and asked him how the trials were going. He took that paper where he made more than thirty almost similar signatures. Last few were really looking authentic. The officer felt his happiness looking at the masterly forger's work. He then asked him to sign in the same way on three blank cheques, and gave details of each to whom to be written with dates and amount. All were to be paid to same material supply firm. Kalicharon remembered the amounts, to be all slightly less or more than three Lakhs in each and total was Eight Lakhs Fifty thousand Rupees. He completed that small job within five minutes and handed the three cheques.

At that time one of the waiters came to their table and asked whether the food can be brought. Durjoy requested Kalicharon to wait in the car and if required to have lunch in any close by eateries. The officer suddenly rose and shook hands with him and kept four 500 rupee notes as a good will gesture. He accepted and left to the parked car. He went for lunch with the driver. During his lunch while he was talking general topics he inquired the driver whether his saab (boss) was having an big cage for nice parrots. The driver laughed and said saab never kept parrots; but suddenly in a humorous way he said he has variety of birds who dress in Saris!. He again said not to tell what he told as he was just joking!. But Kalicharon understood.

After a week after that he was having breakfast in a small café near his building, Kalicharon suddenly found a news item with photo in a local newspaper, on his table. The face of a man in the photo attracted him and he felt it looked vaguely familiar, but swollen in a hideous way. He read the news and was stunned. The police have found a dead body which was floating in Hooghly; most places flesh was eaten by fish in the river. The body was found north of Panihati ferry ghat. In report it was mentioned that It looked definitely as a planned murder as the body's legs were tied to a boulder before dropping in the water. In postmortem report, it was found that he was drugged, before death. The murder must have taken place two days back and the body came up as it was swollen and floated caught in a river bank net, in a vertical way; only his head was above the water. In his torn clothes his purse and ID card were found, he was recognized as Nilesh Sanyal, an officer of a bank who was earlier reported missing by his family. He was transferred few days earlier to Durgapur branch; he was yet to be relieved. They found mysteriously some signed unpaid cheques with past dates of a big customer of the bank in his table drawer; police are investigating about them as details were not disclosed. The police announced that if anyone has some knowledge or suspicion about that murder to contact to the police headquarters and assured their names would be kept confidentially. They mentioned the contact phone number and the address.

Kalicharan was aghast seeing that news and became nervous with fright. He carefully picked up that newspaper and kept in his bag. He reached his room and out lined the news and cut portion with photo and kept in his personal papers. He shuddered at the cold blooded murder, of the same officer who had smuggled the original documents from the bank and replaced with fake documents in their place. His service to forge signatures in three blank cheques was still fresh. He remembered Durjoy's invitation to that person for an evening entertainment in a boat ride! Now he could understand it was an invitation to that officer to his death!. He used that officer and disposed him to avoid future problems. Kalicharon realized that he might be involved as an accomplice to the crime. He knew the Kolkata police C.I.D section is very efficient in investigating crimes. He feared immensely but decided to remain ignorant about this affair. He also decided not to discuss that incident and show complete blank face to any one if they discuss about that murder. He suddenly got a phone call from Durjoy, who ordered him to do a short trip for him outside Kolkata. He indicated that he has to travel that day, to Allahabad as Gadhador Kar to find about details of a private property, and check the documents. He said he arranged a ticket in Howrah Delhi Kalka mail. He ordered him to come and meet him immediately.

Kalicharon suddenly felt a sudden trembling fear and realized that something dangerous might happen to him. He suspected that the train journey was a guise to eliminate him. He sweated inside trembling!. He felt a cold rage to destroy Durjoy to save himself. He thought over some time and decided to take some action. He quickly wrote something in his diary and also wrote a letter in Bengali with a clear script for easy reading. He addressed to Kolkata police and signed 'anonymous'. He put one of the copies in a postal envelope and he kept both of them in a file and put them in his steel box. He decided to run away from his clutches and wrote the letter exposing Durjoy's two crimes, one of bribing the bank officer to secretly smuggle the original property document from bank records, and latter meeting him in a hotel inviting him to a boat ride in Hooghly, where he must have committed that murder. He mentioned the date and time, name of the restaurant and the hotel, and his disguising as a Punjabi Sardar. He also described his past crime of killing Romakanto Choudhary at Medinipur, to take over a huge property by a false will to his niece Chandramoni Debi.

He decided to post that letter and also speak on phone without revealing his name from a public phone booth, after collecting the train ticket and come back from his office. He planned to run away to Medinipur instead of going to Allahabad and with his important personal items. He quickly came out and walked to Durjoy's den, which took him fifteen minutes. When he met him, he found him to be in a very relaxed and in a good mood. That made Kalicharan to feel slightly at ease. Unexpectedly he asked him to be seated in a chair opposite, which he never offered except on the first day's meeting. He made sure no other person was present.

"Kalicharon! . . . . I got an unexpected message from Chandromoni that she wishes to talk to you, when I told her that you are working with me. She now resides at Allahabad. I do not know the reason, and told me nothing to worry but just wants to talk to you about some property documents urgently. You have to go to Allahabad immediately to meet her. On her request I booked berth for you under Tatkal quota to travel to that city. I told her your present name as Gadhdor Kar, but she said that she had registered in your original name, a room in hotel Yatrik of that city. You don't have to go to her house, but she will meet you in the hotel."

Kalicharon was much relieved to know the purpose of his visit to go to Allahabad. He felt very happy to meet Chandramoni Debi after a long time. Her beautiful figure came back to his mind, brought pleasant memory of her sweet personality. But he did not show any feelings as he was fearful that he may not like his joyful eagerness to meet Chandramoni Debi.

"I will go to Allahabad as required sir . . . I will stay in that hotel and I will phone you after I reach there and you may inform the madam about my arrival sir"

"Ok take the travel bag I gave you for travel to stay two or three days and see the city after you complete your job . . . if required by her you may stay longer . . . she will tell about your return journey . . . you may go now and have your lunch and prepare to go to Howrah as early as possible to avoid traffic jams"

He handed him the ticket and some money for travel expense. He returned to his room in a very happier mood, he was really felt joyful to meet Chandramoni Debi. He remembered the large payment he had received from her; such amount he never received so far from any other job. He decided to take his valuable steel box and deposit under for safe custody in Howrah station left luggage room; as he was not sure of its safety in his absence for few days in his present flat.

He decided not to be in hurry to post his letter to police, and would think about that after his return, as his mind became free of tension and fear, which the news of the murder of the bank officer made him. He went to his the Kalka mail train compartment after safely depositing his steel box in left luggage room of Howrah station and occupied his lower berth. As the train started he was reading a co passenger's newspaper. Suddenly he was attracted by many ladies gossiping with pity about a bride traveling in the same compartment who was crying. He did not take any interest.

Latter as he was about to go to bed, he saw a groom and bride were distributing sweets in a happy gesture to all passengers and getting their blessings. He eagerly awaited their arrival. When a well-dressed bride came and putting a Sondesh (a tasty sweet of Bengal made in the shape of a thick soft round biscuit) in the mouth of a lady with a joyful way and taking her blessings, he suddenly went close to her and stretched his hand requested for a sweet, with a smile. The bride smiled and gave him one sweet. He put in his mouth and asked for another. The bride first felt undecided but she gave another sweet and quickly left fearing he might ask more. He ate that second sweet also. Finding them to be very tasty he thought to take those sweets from the groom also, who was following the bride to offer sweets to men. The groom put another Sondesh sweet in his mouth with respect and happiness and touched his feet. Kalicharon happily blessed him and requested him also for another sweet. Shoilen acting as a groom, was about to give, but was warned by Lolit dressed as the bride, who just reached in time to stop. But by that time he grabbed the second Sondesh from him and put that also in his mouth!. Both Shoilen and Lolit could not control laughing at his greedy behavior. They quickly went back to their seats. Thus he quickly ate four sweets which acted very fast on his body and in few minutes he felt sleepy immediately and fell into a deep sleep in his berth. He was unaware what happened to him for next twenty hours as high dose of a strong sleeping drug entered his body system.

When some persons got up after three hours and finding the compartment in darkness and most persons in fast asleep they thought it was late hour and tried to get back to sleep; suddenly one lady got up and shrieked loudly and shouting she was robbed of her gold ornaments. Immediately lights were switched on most persons of nearby berths got up to investigate. Within minutes most other ladies also discovered the loss of their valuables and jewelry including handbags, and started loudly shouting at their loss. Men found with horror their purses and mobile phones were missing from their pockets. Every passenger's glasses were also taken away to make them inconvenient to read or tread. All the passengers woke up due that big hullaballoo, and found out their own loss also and joined the chorus. Somebody pulled the chain and the train guard came and latter the train duty railway police. All understood the grim situation amid the angry shouting of the passengers.

They all found out that the newly married couple were missing from the berths and only one passenger was still fast asleep!. Some passengers found that their bags and ladies purses were on his berth some below his berth. Every one tried to wake him but he did open his eyes and continued snoring loudly in a deep sleep!. While the railway police handling him, they found the hair wig and false beard got loose and came out!. In spite of slapping he did not open his eyes!.

The train resumed the journey and stopped longer time at Dehri-on Sone station, in early hours. Where the Railway police had taken reports from all the passengers and their losses and taken Kalicharon out on a stretcher to the platform, they could not find any of his personal luggage.

The Railway protection police inspector, collected the list of names of the passengers of that compartment from the ticket collector. Most passengers gave a list of their losses, and mobile phone numbers of the cell phones. The inspector dialed some numbers and found them to be switched off.

(Shoilen and Lolit managed to switch them off all the stolen mobiles much before, in the waiting room after getting from the train except the three phones in kalicharon's locked bag)

When the train left the passengers saw Kalicharan lying on the railway platform on a stretcher still unconscious; most of them cursing him as a member of a robbing gang. While most continued heated discussion on the notorious pair in the disguise as newly married couple, each giving theory but no one suspected it was done by two popular actors of Kolkata!.

*   *   *

CHAPTER 5

Railway-Police officer confused with Kalicharon's Prattle!

Kalicharon was living in dream world for almost more than 18 hours!. By the time he got up he was feeling extremely week and unable even to open his eyes. He suddenly got sensation of getting from a nice sleep. He could slightly open his eyes but still in dull sleepy mood. He could understand that he was lying in a strange place. He tried to fully open his eyes and looked around he saw two police men were guarding him. He found that his bed had one foot high guard railing around. He found his body had numb feeling and could not move. A glucose liquid drip was being injected a thin tube through his left hand veins from a bottle tied at top. An oxygen mask was covered on his mouth and nose. He was alone in a small single room. When one of the police saw him waking up with body movement and open eyes he hurriedly went out to call his officer. A nurse came there and saw him staring and trying to talk. She went to call the doctor. A young lady doctor saw him with surprised look and he first checked his Blood pressure and pulse, then she removed the oxygen mask. Kalicharon thought that she was Chandramoni Debi and felt happy . . . he feebly spoke:

"Nomashkaar Bowdee . . . . I came to help you I will see your documents . . . . but I am unable to remember how I came to your house!"

The lady doctor looked puzzled and thought he was still not come out of delirium.

Doctor spoke in Hindi:

"you are in a hospital Don't worry you are alright now."

Kalicharan could not grasp her reply and again closed his eyes with weakness. He again to open and asked feebly How he came there. Before the doctor answered a police officer entered the room and asked the doctor about the condition of the patient.

"He seemed alright now except very week and just now he seemed got senses and was trying to talk. He seemed still out of bearings and still in little delirium"

The Police officer asked whether he can talk to the patient. The doctor said "You may question him for some time. The nurse will stay here and glucose drip has to be continued. If he feels too week allow him some rest to resume your interrogation"

After she left the Inspector sat on the chair and holding a batten, he asked him in a soft voice with a smile,

"What is your name?"

Kalicharon to remember and said in a low voice:

"Gobindo Laha"

"Tell me your real name?"

He felt that something wrong happened and they are investigating. He remembered that he must tell his real name.

"Kalicharon Kundu"

"What? You said your name is 'Gobindo Laha earlier! What is your real name?"

"What is this place? Where is Chandramoni Debi ?

"You were left by your Chandramoni Debi and man with her?"

"I don't know whom she married again after she got her husband Romakantho was murdered! . . . . why you are asking me?"

Inspector became serious as he found that the prisoner was involved in a murder case also. He gave a serious stare at him and took out his small voice recorder and switched on.

"What is your real name?'

"I told you my . . . . my . . . . name" . . . . He faltered and said "Kalicharon Kundu"

Officer became a bit annoyed and hit his batten on the arm of his chair to bring fear to the patient he asked angrily:

"But You were travelling under the name Gadhador Kar! . . . . are you having three names?"

Kalicharan still was unable to remember he got really confused. He was still half conscious as he was living in dreams of past life!. He still did not fully come out of the dreaming world for last few hours . . . . when he suddenly got up and still confused what was happening to him. Then he thought that he was talking to the Medinipur police inspector!. He was trying to control his fear!. He blurted:

"Sir I have not cut my wife's hair and put in the train . . . it is false allegation that she was mentally deranged! . . . she ran away"

The officer could not make anything from his talk! . . . He understood the prisoner was in a fearing mood of his past deeds.

"No . . . I am sure you are bluffing you only cut her hair"

Kalcharan was shaken and trying to defend himself . . .

"No sir either my father or my aunt must have cut her hair and put in the train . . . I am telling the truth."

and he started crying.

"Where do you live? . . . . tell me your address we will contact your family"

"Sir I am now not married again . . . please sir . . . as I told you earlier my wife ran away with her lover . . . I never took three lakhs dowry"

The officer laughed at his whimsical reply was annoyed at his hysterical ramblings . . . but he thought that unknowingly telling some truths. He must have taken dowry, on that itself he can be booked.

"First tell me your name and family address to contact"

Kalicharon's vision became too blurred and again went back to his dream world . . . started telling "Sir my father used take bribes . . . . he only asked dowry . . . . but I am honest . . . . My wife admitted me in widows' ashram in Brindaban . . . . my aunt ran away with her lover in a train to south"

He was looking half conscious.Every one present in the room could not control laugh.

Officer became serious.

"I see . . . you ran away from Brindaban . . . . Why were you having a false beard and wig?"

He was again came to reality and did not know what to say:

"The beard grown in Ashram"

"A false beard and false hair grown on you!?"

He just slightly hit him on his cheeks to bring him to reality.

Kali Charon tried to touch his face surprised to see no beard . . . but unshaven face!

"I don't know sir I am Gobindo . . . when I travel . . . I was wearing beard to change my looks to Gadhador Kar . . ."

"I see while travel you go as different person!"

"I am not at all involved in Nilesh Sanyal's murder . . . or Ramakanto's death . . . his Will was not prepared by me . . . ask her"

"Ask this nurse?!"

"No . . . Chandromoni Debi . . . owner of Kedargowri mansion"

The officer was aghast at the dangerous criminal deeds he was talking and the strange names.

"Who is Nilesh Sanyal . . . . tell me the truth?"

"I don't know him . . . . He likes wild parrots from Mainamar . . . . he was telling to Durjoy"

"Who is Durjoy?"

"Durjoy! . . . . Yes . . . . he is uncle of Chandramoni Debi . . . . a beautiful woman!" . . . .

Kalicharan smiled remembering her name and again repeated,

"She is most beautiful woman . . . . very charming and tactful than Durjoy!"

"I see . . . you love her?!

He laughed . . .

"No sir! . . . . I worship her . . . . I cannot afford her!.".

He looked around with a feeling of fear that Durjoy might be watching!

"Durjoy Moshay ordered I should not talk with her"

"Do you know Where Durjoy stays?"

"Debjani does not know!"

"I see! . . . . Who is Debjani?"

"Queen of Jyotsna Bhawan"

The officer found either he was trying to be funny or telling some truths and some meaningless prattle!. He found he has doubtful manners with his shifty eyes and not looking straight . . . always turning another side while answering. He knew that is the way criminals' look.

He stood up to resume interrogation after the prisoner is more conscious. He was fully convinced that he was from that train robbing gang, with a shady back ground, also definitely involved in murders and other illegal activities. He felt that he was unknowingly blabbering some truths of the past crimes!.

He thought that this prisoner should be guarded safely as his accomplices might either kill him or take him away cunningly, as he might tell the truths latter . . . He told his duty guards to be very vigilant and informed them that he would arrange two more guards as any attempt might be made by his gang to kill him or kidnap him. He ordered the guards to be very vigilant and ordered not to allow any intruders to meet him without his permission. Also asked them to observe and note whatever he talks or names he utters. He gave his small voice recording instrument to one of the guards and instructed him to record if he continue to talk. He decided to postpone the session seeing his meaningless chatter. He went back to his office with an excited mood, as a key witness of a foul gang was in his custody. On the way he requested the in charge doctor that his condition be reported to him as he seemed still blabbering without reality.

He immediately sent a coded message to Railway protection force headquarters at Howrah. He informed that the prisoner goes by three different names, Gadhadar Kar, Kalchoran Kundu and Gobind Laha and travels as Gadhador with a false beard. He mentioned the three names as uttered by the prisoner, seem connected in the crime. The Male accomplice seemed to be a person named Durjoy and other two women to be Chandramani Devi, and Debjani. That first Lady told to be the owner of a mansion called 'Kedargowri'. The second lady quoted as queen of Jyotsna Bhawan. He felt one of those two might have been dressed as a bride, to fool the passengers. Durjoy might have acted as the groom. They distributed drugged sweets to passengers and robbed them. It seemed from the talk that Chandramani is most beautiful cunning woman whom the prisoner liked passionately. From his talk it seemed Chandramoni might be very high priced prostitute.

He informed the prisoner seemed from Kolkata speaking Bengali. He also informed that these three might be involved in murder of two different persons whose names seemed to be Nilesh Sanyal and Ramakanto Choudary. He also Informed that Nilesh sanyal might be having aviary with parrots from Mynamar. He added the murder information may be passed to Kolkata police. He seemed involved in also in forcibly putting a woman in a train after cutting her hair, may be after making her unconscious or admitted her in an ashram in Brindavan. It looks he might have married her for dowry and abandoned in some ashram in Brindavan. He informed that he would pass further information after resuming the interrogation.

Kalicharon felt very weak and started realizing that he was talking irrelevantly, and telling some secrets without any control on his thoughts!. He realized that he was not able to think normally. He couldn't understand what happened to him and why he was in that state. He didn't know since how many hours or days he was lying. When the guards sat at a distance he saw around, and called the nurse.

He weekly asked her why he was brought here and what happened to him. He asked in Bengali . . . the nurse who was from Kerala knew little Hindi . . . She could not understand his language; she called another local nurse who asked him in Hindi.

"Kyaa chaahte hain aap?"

He repeated his question in Hindi.

"You were brought from the railway station; you were lying in a compartment of a train in unconscious state . . . . The police brought you to the hospital as you were in a coma . . . do you now remember your name and address?"

He suddenly remembered his journey in Kalka mail and he was going to Allahabad to see Chandramoni Debi. Then he saw all around and asked where his bag was. He suddenly became nervous that his bag must have been lost!. He continued searching all sides for his bag. He remembered that he kept the Left luggage room receipt in that bag . . . any one could claim . . . bastards may rob all my earnings! . . . he was muttering and cursing within himself.

The nurse called the police and told them that he was enquiring about his bag. The police again switched on the recorder and asked him he asked very roughly in Hindi "You remembered that you were traveling? . . . what is your name?"

Kalicharan stared at him and decided to tell some truth "my name is Gadhador Kar . . . from Kolkata . . . . I was traveling to go to Allahabad . . . . Where is my bag?. It is a bright yellow colored travel bag . . . . new leather bag with zip . . . . Personal things are in them"

"You tell my officer . . . may be in the police station . . . . I was not there when they arrested you . . . You ask him a when he comes latter."

He suddenly realized something happened to him during journey . . . but why was he arrested! . . . He was slightly relieved to know his bag was in the police station. He was trying to remember everything he went to sleep in the train and when he got up he was in the hospital. He could not remember anything else. He got into coma during sleep? . . . He remembered the happy newly married couple offering him sweets . . . . He started thinking that making him unconscious might be Durjoy's work secretly. His man must be travelling with him and given an injection, to kill him, somehow he was rescued by the police . . . and doctors saved him . . . . but why arrest him . . . . he was getting confused and started worrying.

An hour later the same police inspector came and sat near him and asked him the first question.

"What is your real name?"

Kalicharon meekly replied "Gadhador Kar"

"Address?"

"sir . . . I have forgotten my address can you please get my personal leather bag, it has bright yellow colour . . . . I will open and show you my address somewhere in Sona-Gachi in Kolkata . . . . my cellphone was also inside my bag"

The officer became alert hearing the famous Red light area of Kolkata as his location . . . he felt he was definitely a rogue from some dangerous underworld!.

"We didn't find any leather bag near you, you had only others' bags near you along with stolen watches, purses, and other valuables . . . who was behind that train robbery . . . all were taken by the owners your co-passengers . . . . tell me truth who else are there in this robbery? . . . . we will be lenient to you . . . tell me Gadadhar what is your cell phone number!"

Kalicharon was stunned beyond belief . . . .

"I don't know anything about the robbery . . . I was a passenger going to allahabad please return my bag?"

"Silly idiot! We never found any bag with you . . . You are telling lies"

"Wwhaaat! . . . . my bag is really not with you!? . . . then where is it?"

"No I am telling you the truth we did not find any bag as you described in your berth . . . There was no luggage in your berth or below"

"Let me go back I have urgent work in Howrah station . . . please send me back immediately"

Inspector lost his cool for his irrational behavior. He shouted "Dirty Rascal . . . tell first details of your gang . . . don't try to fool us with your dirty tricks . . . . you never had any bag you were after others' bags . . . bloody train robber!"

Kalicharon was not hearing his accusations. His mind started whirling at the loss of his bag with that his left luggage receipt! . . . . he would lose his life's entire earnings and money from sale of his properties as well . . . . more than 25 Lakhs! . . . he was feeling desperate the loss of his steel trunk box was unthinkable and lost mental balance unable to face the loss of his huge personal money, a big fortune . . . . he was becoming nervous and . . . that loss triggered his anxiety . . . he was shaking unable to control his emotions and mental agony . . . oh my God! I lost everything . . . . Large amount including gold Mohurs! . . . all due to the police and Durjoy! . . . Durjoy's man must have taken away the yellow bag after injecting me with a lethal drug. He suspected that Durjoy presented him a bright yellow bag, which was an unusual colour . . . to be picked up easily by his man. He started crying loudly and violently tried to get free . . . he became uncontrollable . . . he lost everything his lifelong hard work more than 25 lakhs cash and gold . . . . He lost his normal thinking and started crying and shouting and got up throwing the tubes and he spat at the inspector with all contempt . . . he became really lost his reasoning and lost his normal thinking he was unable to control his emotions! . . . . He started to cry hysterically loudly then he started to laugh loudly . . . He was cursing Durjoy in most dirty slangs and shouting loudly! . . . telling him as murderer and dirty pimp and other vulgar names!. He tried to get himself free and jumped out of the railing and fell on the floor hitting his head to some steel table. He smashed many instruments!. Was shaking and fainted as complete blackness engulfed him and became still.

In the meantime the police and the inspector tried their best to control him the hospital ward boys also came rushing to the scene. Doctors came running. They finally controlled him and lifted him to his bed; they first thought of giving heavy sedative but decided against it as might go back to coma again. They tried to pacify him to and tied him to the bed.

Vexed Inspector went out wrote a long report stating some crimes and other silly talk he did earlier. The Inspector was in an angry mood. He felt sure that the prisoner was involved many dangerous crimes. He decided to send another message to the Howrah head-quarters, briefly mentioning the present status and only adding that the prisoner seemed to reside in Sona-Gachi area of Kolkata. He also mentioned that his real name as Gadhadar Kar. He seemed to be carrying large amount cash and gold in his new yellow bag . . . it is getting mystifying whether he was shocked and disturbed or acting. His behavior looked to be a dangerous crook. Travelling but might not be involved in that train robbery case but in some other serious crimes. He mentioned to the headquarters to give wider publicity about him in the media to get his known accomplices.

The inspector was puzzled as the prisoner's distress seemed genuine for his lost bag. He decided to use third degree methods to get the truth out of him once he gets discharged and sent to the police station. He also thought that man was acting as mad, and was creating just a drama. He decided to keep a strict watch on him.

*   *   *

The real fact was, Kalicharan had an unexpected severe mental shock due to his complete loss of life's all personal wealth. He lost his huge life savings which he earned by crooked ways and now a pauper with nothing. He became insane due to that shock!. All his savings just evaporated like a mist. Weak minded Kalicharon could not take that reality. He was staring blankly, as his mind also became blank and behaving with no understanding about his surroundings. He really went into a coma!.

The crooked Document writer of Medinipur was destined to become a long time prisoner with mysterious past and unknown future!.

*   *   *

CHAPTER 6

Ujwolita Keen to meet Chandramoni
Debi alias Manonmoni Debi!

As Shoilen and Lolit were in a discussion, suddenly the cell phone, with name of Gadhador Kar suddenly rang again from Kalicharon's yellow bag. Now they were more informative about his back ground and dark activities seeing his Diary, in his steel trunk box. They ignored the call, but noted the caller's number. Both became alert, looking at a different ringing sound from the phone of Gobindo Laha. As that phone stopped, Shoilen noted the caller's mobile number. After few minutes sound came from the phone of Kalicharon Kundu with a Bengali song as part of ringing!. They ignored the call again and noted the caller was same to all the phones!. They both decided to get some information from the unknown caller, who must be connected to Kalicharon. They wanted to contact him through some trickery!. Shoilen made a phone call to that number after ten minutes from one of the other passengers' stolen mobiles, out of curiosity. The other person answered little doubtfully seeing an unknown caller's phone.

"Durjoy speaking"

Shoilen gave the phone to Lolit with wink, to talk as they planned earlier!.

"Namaskar Moshai ami Rupali of 'Shundar Bonita' Beauty parlor bolchi (talking) . . . can you kindly listen few seconds?"

"Tell me what you want . . . . how you got my number? Do I know you!?"

"Kshoma korun Moshai (Excuse me gentleman) . . . . Sir! . . . . my company gave some numbers to call as public relation campaign can you give me few minutes of your valuable time sir?

"Sir Our company has a most modern Beauty salon in park street We are celebrating our second anniversary by giving fifty per cent reduction only for a week to all our services as a goodwill to our valued clients . . . I can call to your house to explain your ladies our special package . . . we can send also our girls to do facials and pedicure and other services right at your home which of course would cost twenty five percentage less than normal"

Lolit talked imitating in a female voice in an attracting way.

Durjoy interrupted "My ladies may not be interested . . . however I will contact you latter . . . . after talking to my wife . . . Madam is your parlor located in Park street?"

"Yes Moshay . . . . ours is a very modern one all with foreign trained ladies"

"Is it . . . very interesting. Rupaalee! are you one of the Beauticians?"

"No Sir! . . . I am from Public relations section head . . . . I was a hostess in Singapore Airlines joined 'Sundar Bonita' a month back . . . we may start a separate wing for mens' beauty salon . . . next month which would also will have only lady hair and massage specilists . . . Thail girls trained for gents! . . . There you are to welcome after inauguration . . . . of course I would invite you on the first day itself"

"Oh so nice of you miss Rupalee! . . . that I will avail . . . . I will contact you after talking with my wife . . . . you are very sweet to talk!"

He switched off. Lolit could understand the owner's gruff voice now telling which mellowed way with courteously!. He could guess that other person looked curiously attracted by his way of talking in a more pleasant way. He was sure he would call latter. He informed the same to Shoilen, who was listening with grin.

They realized the same person named Durjoy was very anxious to talk to Kalicharon.

They took out the Diary like bound book, to see what information it may contain. On the first page, it was written Personal and private diary belonging to:

Kalicharon Kundu,

Document writer,

41A, Chakradhar Mukhopadhyay street,

Medinipur-3, West Medinipur district.

They found that there was some other address written earlier, and struck with a pen, cancelling that and the present address was written in Red-ink. It seemed he wrote a diary of some or all of the various documents he prepared, giving dates back ground and purpose of each document with details of the clients. First few pages were dull recording of various documents he wrote and consisting of properties, lands, gift deeds, sale deeds etc. Suddenly a loose newspaper cutting was pinned to page 26, drew their attention. Anther news-paper cutting was pinned was located on another page which seemed the latest one seeing the condition of the paper. It was connected to the last entry. They found one neat hand written letter and a sealed cover addressed to the officer in charge Hooghly river crime branch of Police Head Quarter Lal bazar Kolkota, in his latest entry.

Out of curiosity they first wanted to see the first paper cutting news pasted on 26 th page. A pen line border was made around the news item. It was a news item from Medinipur about accidental death of a prominent businessman, Romakantho Choudhary, of that town. He died while driving, in a country side narrow road. It is learnt that he hit a tree to save collision with a speeding truck coming opposite. The truck could not be traced as the driver drove away fast. Before his body was taken to the hospital by an ambulance, there was a big crowd of inquisitive local onlookers, surrounding the smashed and up turned car. Some persons forcibly broke open the glass shutters to take out the unconscious person driving, lying in the car. It looked he was already dead; he was lying inert with blood covered face and body. It seemed he did not use the safety belt. The police had to disperse the crowd who were looking at the stretched body lying on the ground. Police searched his pockets but nothing important was found. It was later revealed that his mobile phone was snatched or stolen from his pocket while he was having his ear-phones of the cell phone plugged to his ears. It seemed he always had ear phones connected to his mobile kept in the pocket while driving. They searched for the instrument in the car as well in the crash site but could not found. But his purse was intact in the pant back pocket. As the car was smashed very badly it seemed he was driving fast on that narrow road. There was a mystery as to why he was driving on that road leading to a village on north west side, the family or the police could not get any clue!.

When they saw on page 27, connection of the news seemed to a document he prepared, on the next date. He did not write like a story teller, with creative writing. It was in plain write up giving the factual details.

'I prepared a back dated 'Will' as if it was prepared by late Romakantho Choudari to gift to his second wife (concubine) Shrimothi Chandramoni Debi. I was taken to her secretly in the night to a large old mansion called 'Kedargowri' at the outskirts of the town, where she was staying with her mother. It seems the property was purchased by Romakanto on her request. She was very attractive like a film star even though she was in mourning dress. She took me inside the house, separately and asked me directly but tactfully to prepare a back dated Will as if it was prepared by her late husband gifting the property with the Mansion in her name. I first became surprised to see her taking this serious topic without any general talk. I almost became dumb when she was siting so close to me and ordering me in a nice but domineering way. I never had any experience that beautiful ladies can control men and dictate to obey even with soft voice. There was also an indirect threat. I had to accept to create that forged Will. I had no idea how she got information about my ability to copy signatures. It was my first attempt to write a Will without prompting of a lawyer or my senior document writer. I got the back old dated non judicial stamp paper in the name of Romakanto. Her mother's brother Durjoy took me discretely to the city in a car and returned in the night. Suddenly Shoilen and Lolit were startled to come across the name of Durjoy, with whom Lolit had a talk on the phone, earlier!. Both looked at each other as some interesting facts were getting unfolded about Kalicharon!. They continued reading his diary.

'I finished writing an original will on a back dated stamp paper, which I procured from Kolkata. I carefully copied Romakantho Choudhury's signature as he signed the sale deed document as a vendee. The property was a large old mansion surrounded by a tree plantations and fish tank, comprising of 4.3 Acres land with a compound wall around. Chandramoni Debi was staying in that mansion along with her mother. The cost mentioned in the sale deed was Seventy five lakhs. That must have been the white money, double that amount must have been given as black money as was the normal case in selling and buying a large properties.

I came to know that Chandramoni Debi sold that property in less than three months' time for about Two Crore Rupees. That first dangerous creation made me realize how much powerful my hand writing was, to change the ownership of a very rich property. I was happy to see the lady gave me a large amount for my service. Durjoy warned me that if I leaked about the Will, I would be eliminated like Romakantho!. I was shocked at his bold revelation about arranged killing of Chandramoni Debi's paramour and trying to get his property in an illicit way. He threatened with dire consequences if I ever try to contact Chandramoni Debi in future any time. He showed me a pistol pointing at me when he came to drop me near my house. He warned me about the secrecy of the Will deed made or the money I received. He advised me that I should not put in my bank account, but convert the cash to Gold coins for safety. It was a dangerous deed I made and might be treated as a partner in forged will making and also may be involved in the murder. But I was very happy at my ability in making a forged document successfully first time in my life'.

Both of them laughed at his crooked out look!. Lolit asked with a smile:

"Dadaa! . . . why did he write his own participation in that forged will preparation! . . . if per chance this book lands to police . . . . well he might be arrested on criminal charges of not only making a forged will but also concealing his knowledge about the murder!"

"Lolit! You remember he mentioned that he had no alternative and was forced into doing a forged Will . . . well he might have written to protect himself!. Let us now look for clues by which we may be beneficial without getting involved!"

"We were already got a good unexpected booty from this crooked Document writer! . . . I think we should forget to get involved in his affairs, especially with dangerous cruel characters like Durjoy and Chandramoni Debee!"

Shoilen laughed loudly . . . then he said in an amusing way . . . .

"Lolit! Remember the lady who got that property . . . just by crooked methods . . . it definitely should have gone to late Romakantho's family . . . . if we don't take some action the crime would be never come to light . . . . we should also get benefit from the family or from Chandramoni Debi by cleverly twisting her hand. She would part some profit out of fear . . . we have to be very careful while dealing with her! . . . with her dangerous back ground!"

"Dada ! . . . . whether we can twist her hand or she might twist us! . . . . the way he became a puppet under her hands!"

Sholen laughed at his partner's pun.

"Let us first see the copy of the forged Will we might get some back ground of her"

They took out the File which had copies. They could easily get a copy of the Will on a plain paper including the signature of Romakantho. It mentioned that he was writing this will for gifting one of his personal properties, which he purchased from his own earnings not an ancestral one, to his friend and close associate to Shrimothi Chandramoni, out of love and gratitude, and her great help as a friend in some key business matters. Her permanent address of Bhowanipore of Kolkata was mentioned in the Will.

Shoilen told with eager curiosity,

"Lolit let us visit this address in Bhowanipore area and make discrete enquiries about Chandramoni Debi".

They decided to go not in their normal way but in a disguised characters!. After thirty minutes Lolit came out dressed like a well groomed modern woman with a fashionable loose hair and nice makeup. He came out and locked the door from outside, and went towards left side of the corridor. After five minutes Shoilen came from the other front door located next to the door from which Lolit came. He had a white haired wig and with well-trimmed beard. Dressed like distinguished academician or high profile professional!. Even his close colleagues would not recognize as Shoilen!. He went to right side of the corridor. The building had two stair cases and two lifts located at either ends of the six storied block, as the building located between two roads, it had entrances on both roads. They normally enter or come out separately each from a different road. The same flat has two front doors side by side giving impression of two separate flats!. Shoilen got that new door after they decided to start their new venture. They met at a particular place, which also would change for their each outside travel.

Shoilen had contact with a Taxi company, they send the taxi whenever he requests. They send as per their requirement that is ordinary yellow taxi cabs or posh sedan Cars of high price range, with a uniformed chauffer. This time they asked posh car. Such vehicles do not carry normal yellow board taxi number. They went to Bhowanipur and got down near their destination. It was a small independent two storied old type of house, with a gate. Outside there was a name plate of the present resident, Ashok Rama Seshan, Charted accountant. He pressed the bell, and both were looking at the narrow but posh residential lane. Some had even watchman near the gate. It was a quiet area, not very far from the main road. One elderly woman came and opened the door, looked like a typical south Indian lady with completely greyed hair but looked neatly dressed and enquired with smile whom they want, in Bengali. Both greeted her respectfully with Nomashkar. Lolit asked her whether she knew Chandramoni Debi. The elderly lady laughed at their query and called someone loudly.

"Chandi! . . . ingevaa" ('Chandi come here' in Tamil.)

Both were surprised and eagerly awaited for Chandranmoni, to their utter surprise a small girl of eight came there running from inside and stopped suddenly staring at the strangers.

Both of them could not control their laughter . . . . Lolit asked again telling that he wanted to know about

Chandramoni Debi owner of the house. The old lady looked at them with surprise.

"my grand daughter's name is Chandramani . . . I thought you were asking about her! . . . just a minute I will call my daughter in law"

She went inside and came out with a younger lady who also looked typical south Indian with a sober looks and dressed in simple way. Seeing their high profile outlook smilingly she greeted them with Namaste and requested them to kindly come inside. She requested them to be seated in a sofa and she and her mother in law sat after they two sat. She said something in Tamil and the small girl went in and came with two glasses of water in a small tray. By that time Lolit again asked her they came to see the owner of that house, Chandramoni Debi who was her friend. The younger lady understood She replied with a courteous smile:

"Yes she was the owner earlier she sold the property to us . . . I do not know her present address my husband may know"

"Sorry madam! We did not know she sold her house . . . where can we meet your husband"

"His office is in the Chittaranjan Avenue, should I contact him"

"No madam we are anyhow going that way only we will meet your husband on the way and get her address . . . thank you . . . . your daughter is so sweet and nice!"

She laughed and told them that her name also was 'Chndramani' that's why her mother in law got confused!.

She took out a visiting card of her husband, where in his address was printed.

"please wait . . . pl have coffee in my house . . . . I will make quickly"

They both got up staying they will come some other day but they were in hurry. They rose and came out thanking profusely both the ladies. They got inside the car and left for Chitteranjan Avenue. In a twenty minutes-drive they reached Asok Ramseshan's office. Shoilen gave his card to the receptionist and asked her to contact mister Ashok. She just dialed him and told about the visitors and was about to read the card and found to be printed only in Bengali.

"I am Beniprosad of Notta Ronjita Bongo Kala Manch"

Shoilen said with a smiling look. She said something and within a minute a smart person of average height came from inside and extended his hand to welcome them:

"I am Ashok . . . did you go to my house . . . my wife said that you may come to meet me . . . . Please come in"

As they entered his cabin, Shoilen introduced himself:

"I am Beni Prosad of Natto Ronjita Bongo Kola Manch . . . . this is Ujwolita of our group.

Lolit also extended his hand Ashok felt surprised at the hard touch of that good looking lady's hand. He offered them seats in a sofa away from his office table and sat in a single sofa facing them.

"Mister Ashok we are just arrived from states . . . we wanted meet Chandramoni Debi . . . she is friend of us . . . . Ujwolita is her very close friend . . . . Do you know her present address?"

Ashok's face almost lighted up hearing her name "Oh. I knew her . . . as we were her tenants first and later when she decided to sell her Bhawanipore house she offered us . . . and I was thus had the privilege to buy that house . . . . She used to consult me for advice regarding her tax matters . . . . She is a great lady . . . more important . . . . of course you know her well . . . she is most beautiful lady I ever saw!" . . . suddenly he felt little embarrassed for praising another lady before one lady . . . he quickly added "Of course as beautiful as this young lady Ujwolita!"

Both laughed at his nice way of talk. Before they could even start to talk he rose from his seat and went to his table to bring his laptop . . . and within a minute both were staring at the photo of really charming lady, on the lap top screen; she had classy features!, with a sexy feminine look . . . which likely to attract any male. She had rich ivory colour skin large eyes nice fore head, thick dark hair . . . and attractive shapely lips and mainly her longish oval face with long eyes slightly prominent cheeks with a provocative smile.

"You know we were staying in her house as tenants when she left for Midnapore . . . sorry Medinipur . . . . When I was blessed with a daughter in that house I wanted to name her as Chandramani as her name fascinated me as her good looks. When I told her the good news and my request she was so happy and blessed her. She came to see the baby next day and brought a nice gift to her. She felt so happy to see her and was almost in tears with emotion to see the baby with her name in her house!."

Shoilen asked him "Ashok . . . do you know where she staying now we understand she left medinipur . . ."

"O yes she is now in Allahabad . . . . once in while she enquires about my daughter . . . She is married again . . . . she told us . . . we are not close about her personal life . . . it seems her first husband died in an accident and she could not stay any longer at Medinipur . . . . It is good she being quite young decided to marry I hope she has happily adjusted to her new life."

"We are so happy that she accepted her loss and taken partnership with another gentleman! . . . good bold decision!"

"As you also know her well about her . . . . I am sure you will agree . . . her presence will make a man happy . . . . she has that nice qualities . . . sorry please don't misunderstand me . . . . as a her friend I am telling in a lighter vein . . . . she lives in a beautiful modern mansion on the bank of Ganges . . . she even has her own artistically carved boat for pleasure boating in the river . . . we went last year at her invitation and stayed two days with her . . . poor woman still she has no children . . . . her present husband also a nice person bit older than her with very good business . . . . she would not leave my daughter even for few minutes when we stayed with her! . . . she acted as my daughter's God-mother! . . . showering all wonderful gifts . . . she adores my baby!"

"Do you know her uncle Durjoy also?"

Ashok suddenly changed his face clearly indicating uneasiness to talk about him! he said casually "I had seen him with her later; at Medinipur . . . . I don't know much about him. I understand he stays in Kolkata somewhere near Beadon street"

"Do you happen to know her address and phone number of Chandromoni . . . we are eager to visit. Her . . . please don't inform her before . . . we want to surprise her! . . . we are seeing her after so many years . . . she was very close to Ujwolita!"

Lolit was continuously staring her photo, while he was talking!

"Dear Ashok . . . can you please email this beautiful photo to me. I will give my email ID"

Lolit suddenly told with happy mood and he wrote something and handed him . . . Shoilen was fuming inside at the hasty action of Lolit but could not stop him. Ashok took that email address and kept with him.

He later gave them her address and smilingly informed them "By the way . . . her present name is not chandramani but . . . . Manonmoni Devi! . . . quite an interesting name!"

"Ashok . . . a good name for your future second daughter!"

Shoilen laughingly interrupted in his typical jocular way.

Ashok laughed and looked towards Lolit.

"well . . . yes it is really a good name . . . I will suggest that to my wife for our future third actually I first thought of Ujwolita!"

He replied with mirth. Both laughed for his good humor. They left his office bidding farewell.

"Lolit I can understand your appreciation of Chandramoni sorry Manonmoni! . . . . I was also was most impressed seeing her picture . . . well . . . . but why expose our identities by giving your email address"

Shoilen could not suppress his annoyance at Lolit's offering his Email address.

Lolith smiled and said:

"Dada! . . . Dont worry . . . the email address I gave was of my elderly colleague in my show room, I only created for him including the password. He hardly uses his email . . . he requested me to create one for him out of curiosity. I will open my lap top in the room when

we reach and transfer that mail, if sent by Ashok to my
address and delete from his emails"

"Lolit! how about our going to Allahabad . . . just to
see that Tribeni Sangam of course!"

Yes good idea . . . . Tribeni Sangam dip and darshon of
Manonmoni Debi! . . . ha ha !"

"No Lolit . . . i am serious. Secretary of Bengali
welfare association of Georgetown of Allahabad had called
me a week back for a show of our three act play . . . .
Charulotha on their anniversary celebrations . . . . in that
connection he requested me to come there before to chalk
out the program"

"Oh . . . original or stand by Charulota will act in that
play?!"

Lolit asked with a smile . . . .

"Of course both would go . . . but for prelim only
we both will go . . . I am thinking to book air tickets to
Allahabad . . . as you know we have to hit the iron when
it is hot . . . we will of course do some deep study on
our friend's Kalichoran's diary and other documents. We
will also see his other escapades . . . may be some good
materials for exploitation of our new ventures! . . . . he was
a valuable patron of our venture!"

They reached the house in the same way as they left
returning separately. Lolit found there were two missed
calls from Durjoy in their absence . . . he dialled him and
waited.

"Madam! I tried to contact you after you spoke to me
earlier . . ."

"Yes Moshay! Sorry for that. I had to go on some work
and forgot . . . . the mobile . . . your lady interested to visit
us . . . at what time should I book for her tomorrow?"

"How about today . . . I will send . . . . bring my wife"

"Just a n minute sir."

He closed he covered the mouth piece and spoke to Shoilen who just put on the TV local news . . . . Lolit whispered the conversation . . . he thought over for a minute and told what to say.

Our staff's services are booked today for a TV serial artists make up . . . kindly contact me tomorrow sir"

He heard other person's talk and replied with a giggling laugh "Thank you sir for your complement . . . I cannot meet you even if you come. I am going to park street metro station to go back . . . my duty is over . . . ."

"you want to meet me at park street . . . sorry sir . . . . I will meet you tomorrow"

"Of course you may . . . . if you are keen to talk to me . . . . if you come in another two hours . . . . So nice of you sir . . . . I can wait for you at . . . . Park street station or best why not you come to Flury's* in Park street! . . . meet me there at Bakery sales show room . . . which is close to my place you may meet me, I will wait for you for thirty minutes . . . . I have go to train as it is rush hour . . . am in dark blue dress with light blue sleeveless Kurthi . . . and Red colour bag . . . the counter manager knows my name . . . . nice of you sir . . . what dress you wear and how . . . . OK sir so nice of you. I will be delighted to meet you sir . . . ok sir I will wait . . . so nice of you sir"

Just then there was a local announcement with visual display . . . . in the TV news . . . the announcer was telling about a passenger of Kalka mail who was also was robbed in the train after consuming a sweet . . . . all other passengers got consciousness and left for Delhi, after train stopped for police investigation . . . . only

---

*   A popular cake shop of Kolkata

one passenger . . . as per the ticket it was mentioned his name as 'Gadhador Kar' but he seemed to have taken more sweets and could not come to senses for a long time . . . Police believe he might have been one of the gang of train robbers as some bags and valuables of other passengers were found on his berth and below. He seemed unknowingly might have consumed more of drugged sweets! . . . He had also four sweets in his pocket which they sent for analysis about the drug used. Doctors somehow got him to senses . . . . it seemed he was mentally shocked at the loss of his bag . . . . He was in delirium for a long time after getting out from coma or deep sleep his name is Gadhador Kar as per his ticket. He seemed got confused about his own name!, He mentioned only one person Durjoy and another two women's name 'Chandramoni Debi' and 'Debjani.' When he was told his bag was not found in the train he seemed to be very upset and behaved very violently and tried to escape and fell on the floor and was hurt. He again went into a coma or deep sleep.'

His photo was exhibited on the screen, saying anyone knowing him to contact the railway police station 'Dehri-on-Sone.' Railway Police or any other police station!. The police have not revealed further information about him.

Both heard that news with grave silence!. Without his long hair and beard he looked very differently!.

They decided to see Durjoy. Before that they went through the Diary about some more dealings connected with latter documents and were stunned at his new escapade in Kolkata. They studied the interesting but shocking material given by Kalicharon about a latest gory crime!.

*   *   *

CHAPTER 7

Inspector Deepankar Chatterjee rattles Durjoy!

Shoilen and Lolit decided to go through Kalicharon's recent escapade in his diary of recorded back ground version about his documents preparation. They again found a paper cutting of a murder in the middle of the Diary, which was seemed, was his latest descriptive details about a new document. There was a letter addressed to Lalbazar police Headquarters office of Kolkata, which also was connected to the documents.

The newspaper news was about a murder of a bank officer by name Nilesh Sanyal, whose body was found in Hoogly River near Panihati Ferry ghat, of Kolkata. He was killed in most brutal way with tied up legs to a boulder in the river. His swollen face eaten by fish, when his body floated and got struck up in a mesh grid near the river bank. He was missing since three days and his family reported to the police. Only little suspicious clue were three un-cashed new cheques with back dates, were found in his office table. They appealed for any information from public of his murder, by contacting or writing to the police headquarters confidentially.

They were surprised initially how and why Kalicharon decided to inform some secret information to the police regarding that bank officer's murder. He wrote in a neat Bengali script. Shoilen concluded that he must have been upset to see the murder and must be in the knowledge of some link to a property document, which he prepared.

They saw his diary in that connection. It read like this: 'I was summoned by Durjoy Basak to come from Medinipur to do an urgent job for him. After reaching Kolkata and met him in his private office located on fourth floor of a building in Beadon Street. When I entered the building called Jyotsna Bhawan, I felt it was wrong building I entered seeing ladies only in different types of dresses, in all the floors. But when I was about to return, he came out and called me. I was surprised how he could see me entering. Later I found he had a closed circuit video camera near the entrance and he has a small TV screen on his table showing whoever comes to that building. He informed that he called me to prepare a true copy of about 70 years or more, old original sale deed along with a later date gift deed of a property. He wanted me to copy in same style and exact way to look like the originals. It was a property document of an old two storied building in that neighborhood belonging to Jnanendra Guha. Durjoy did not reveal more details. He first got a colored Xerox copy of that original document, as well as counterfeit blank stamp papers of the same like originals. The non-Judicial stamp papers used in the originals were of British Government ruled period. I made the blank stamp papers look like faded old copies with my expertise. Durjoy arranged the exact replica of the old rubber stamps printed on the originals. I successfully forged the documents in the same style like the original including signatures of vender and vendee, signature of the sub registrar of 24 Parganas and witnesses signatures all alike. My fake documents were having almost as exact appearance as the originals. The original documents were smuggled out of a bank, and replaced with fake documents. The original was pledged to the bank by the present owner and got a loan. Durjoy was waiting for the owner to leave India. I was told the owner stays in America. I was informed that he was scheduled to return at end of this month. He may not come back to India within three years. The owner doesn't stay in that building but in Lake Gardens in south Kolkata. After the original owner's departure, I was to prepare a new sale deed to sell the property with original brought from the bank. A new person will impersonate the owner and sale would be complete in a deputy registrar's office.

Shoilen and Lolit were flabbergasted at the well thought out master-plan of selling another person's property by trickery to make a huge gain!.

"My god . . . . what dangerous world! . . . Durjoy hatched a plan to sell a valuable property without the knowledge of the owner with connivance of a bank officer!."

Suddenly he got a flash—the bank officer who helped Durjoy to smuggle the original and replacing the fake copy . . . . must have been murdered!. Now he understood the link of this murder!.

Then they read Kalicharan's letter. There was a sealed cover with a letter and another hand written copy. They carefully opened the envelope with postal stamps addressed the DIG Crimes (Hooghly) and found to be exact copy written in the same type and style of script like his personal copy. The letter was written as under:

Sir,

The murder of Nilesh Sanyal, Bank officer, of 'Help Bank' whose dead body was found in Hooghly, was committed by Durjoy Basak, of 42, Jyotsna Bhawan, Gaurav Sanyal lane off Dhani Ghosh Sarani (part Beadon steet), Kolkata. (His phone No is 012210012210.) He paid some amount to the bank officer to smuggle the registered original Documents of a property, a two storied building belonged to Jnanedra Guha of Lake Gardens. The owner pledged the original documents in the bank, and got a loan three weeks back. Durjoy got the originals smuggled from the bank records and replaced with fake originals in the file, through a secret deal made with Nilesh Sanyal for some huge cash payment. Durjoy later got him murdered, so that in future no link with him would connect him with the disappearance of the original documents from the bank. The river pleasure cruise was tempted and arranged to Nilesh Sanyal by Durjoy, whom he met him in a lunch in a restaurant in Sonar Bangla Hotel., on last Wednesday. He went there by car Durjoy who met him disguised like a Panjabi Sardar, (I do not know the reason.) The lunch was arranged by Nilesh Sanyal, the bank officer at 1PM. During lunch Durjoy invited him for a night boat party with entertainment, on river Hooghly. He gave another temptation saying a young Myanmar girl would be accompanying him in that luxury launch to entertain him. He conveyed that he was arranging a happy boat ride for his great help in getting original documents from the bank. The unsuspecting officer agreed to avail that boat ride, with enthusiasm. I do not know details of the boat trip and how he arranged to murder him in the boat and thrown him in the river.

The original property documents of Jnanendra Guha are now with Durjoy and fake document in the bank records. He intends to arrange to sell that property to another person, with original ownership documents.

I also wish to tell a previous crime committed by Durjoy, at Medinpur about a year back. He murdered Seth Romakantho Choudhari of Medinipur making look like an accident. A forged will was made for a large property with a mansion called 'Kedargowri' in Medinipur which was owned by Romakantho. The will was prepared for the property to be inherited to Shrimothi Chandramoni Debi, mistress of Ramakanto, She is Durjoy's sister's daughter. The fake will was made with back date, after the murder. The court accepted that Will, when produced by Chandramoni Debi. You can interrogate the two witnesses signed on that Will, to get the truth.

Sincerely,
'Anonymous'

Shoilen and Lolit were puzzled at Kalicharon's bold step in exposing Durjoy!, as he was also involved in both cases fully.

Suddenly Shoilen remembered they were to meet Durjoy in the afternoon. Lolit cleverly found the name of the caller as Durjoy, from Kalicharon's three mobile phones. He had impersonated with a woman's voice by telling Durjoy as Rupali from a beauty parlor in Park Street. Durjoy was enticed by Lolit and agreed to meet him at Flury's shop in Park Street.

Both reached that street by taxi and got down in a lane near that street. Lolit, made himself look like a modern lady with a fashionable outlook. He wore a Red Dress, carrying a large blue bag and dark glasses. Shoilen came out as a senior Muslim person, with white beard and knitted skull cap (Islamic Kufi cap). He also wore dark glasses and holding a walking stick. He followed Lolit a few feet behind, as he entered the Flury's bakery and went near the counter seeing the display. Shoilen remained at a distance looking at the cakes in a show case near the entrance. There were many customers and the sales staff, were busy. After few minutes Durjoy entered the shop alone and started looking seriously all around. He then saw Lolit dressed in red dress and carrying Blue bag!. Shoilen saw him and immediately could realize he must be Durjoy, he tapped the floor as if drawing attention of a sales woman. Lolit understood and slowly turned around and started to move towards entrance. Durjoy recognized and was puzzled seeing Lolit as a very beautiful lady but her dress was Red and bag was Blue!. He wondered, whether he correctly remembered her description, as he was looking for a woman with Blue dress with Red bag.

He went quickly close to Lolit and asked in a gentle way with courtesy:

"Madam are you Miss Rupali? . . . . from Sundar Bonita Beauty Parlor?"

Lolit saw the burly well-dressed man, looking at him intently with a broad smile. He was holding a bouquet of flowers. He could understand that he was impressed with his nice make-up. He studied him with interest, then gave a sweet smile and looked at him with puzzled stare.

"Sorry no! . . . Please excuse"

and went out fast, walking with style.

Disappointed Durjoy excused and turned towards the other lady customers.

Shoilen took a snap of Durjoy with his concealed camera. In few minutes Durjoy's phone rang. When he lifted he saw it was from Rupali, the lady who spoke in the morning.

"Sorry mister Durjoy . . . I was slightly delayed In my work and had to go station straight. Did you wait for me in Flurys?"

"Oh I am sorry . . . I came with my wife to meet you . . . . I am in Flurys by the way what was the dress you said you would be?"

"Blue dress and Red bag . . . why!?"

He laughed and said he got confused . . . and said he was much disappointed.

"Sorry! For missing you . . . as a matter of fact I was also was keen to meet you . . . but it is late already . . ."

"So nice of you . . . Miss Rupali . . . I will be happy to meet you tomorrow . . . when I should come?"

"How nice of you sir! . . . . Can we make it tomorrow afternoon . . . any time that suits you" Lolit gave a giggling sweet laugh "You are taking so much care for your wife to take her personally to a beauty parlor!. Ha Ha Ha! . . . I would be happy to meet you tomorrow" Durjoy hesitated "the real fact is I was attracted by your sweet voice I was keen to see you and spend some time with you . . . why not have a lunch together . . . if you don't mind"

Lolit giggled and coquettishly said:

"So bringing wife only to see me . . . how naughty you are! . . . what your wife would think of me . . . I have to behave in a guarded way . . . so you also in the restaurant!"

Durjoy became bold at her hint . . .

"Miss it will be my pleasure to meet you during lunch in a restaurant . . . . my wife may not be able to come"

"Oh how nice! . . . . It is easy for me to reach Zen or Mocambo . . . in park street . . . . sorry I just now remembered . . . I may have to go to Bally-Ganj tomorrow noon time! Being in public relations in-charge . . . . I have to do roaming a bit! In that case we might try 'Bluzz' or 'Park Plaza' restaurants in that locality"

"Dear Rupali! . . . You seemed to have good taste . . . Whichever place you choose I will accept. But How do I know where to meet you . . . . whether in Park street or Ballyganj?"

Lolit again laughed with a mischievous giggle. "Ok it is my pleasure to meet you also . . . sorry for disappointing you today . . . . I should not inconvenience you again sir . . . . can I give you a ring to your office or . . . . your place at 12 noon tomorrow afternoon . . ."

Lolit said bit coquettishly, with a slight whispering way.

"OK Rupali I will drive to your place to pick you . . . thank you dear!"

"Please don't do that please . . . Sir . . . I am not sure when I will be free . . . and where I will be . . . . But I will

inform you and meet you directly in the Restaurant . . . .
wait for my call please then you come to that place . . .
I will tell you what dress I would be wearing . . . to
recognize me . . . I will tell you the time I would be
reaching"

"Ok as you wish dear. I will wait for your call at 12
noon meet you . . . Thank you"

"So nice of you Durjoy . . . I will contact you at that
time please wait for my call and meet me I would wait . . .
bye and good night . . . have sweet dreams!"

Lolit said with mischievously.

"Bye Rupali dear!"

He kept the phone in his pocket and briskly left the
shop smiling. He called his driver and drove away.

* * *

Next day Durjoy was waiting in his room anxiously
for a call from Rupali at 12 noon. Suddenly his phone
rang at Twelve Five.

He picked it instantly with a big smile and
disappointed seeing a different number. He said with a
serious voice.

"Yes whom do you want?"

He again wondered . . . seeing a new number on his
particular mobile . . . which he does not generally reveal to
unknown persons.

"Can I speak with mister Dhananjoy Roye sorry! . . .
Durjoy Basak please"

Durjoy was startled at an unexpected caller using his
real name as well his secret name! . . . he was surprised at
the courteous call from some gentleman.

"Speaking"

"May I come in to meet you . . . I am just waiting outside your door"

Durjoy was visibly shocked at the sudden unexpected intrusion . . . also using his real name he was about to say no but before that one tall middle aged police officer in uniform, with a gun in a leather holder at his waist, barged-in in a quick way and closed the door. He had a strong booming voice and sharp big eyes and long nose and broad forehead with receding hair line. Durjoy was startled to see a police officer with a batten In hand. He looked smart and tough. He gave a light shake hand and lifted his cap. Durjoy was annoyed as well surprised to see a senior police officer entering without giving him a notice of his visit! He did not see that officer entering his building on the TV screen on his table!. He introduced himself as Deepankar Chaterjee. Durjoy felt slightly nervous somehow managed a smile.

"May I know sir on what purpose you came to see me?"

"Mister Dhanonjoy sorry Durjoy can we sit on the sofa and more relaxed than this office table seats"

Durjoy uneasily went to sofa at the other end and both sat facing.

"Mr Durjoy do you know a person called Kalicharon Kundu, he is in police custody, He was picked up from Delhi Kalka mail at Dehri on Sone Railway police station . . . arrested as a member of train-robbers' gang"

"You say Kalicharon Kundu? . . . none of my staff or person with that name known to me sir, must be some mistake"

"Strange he said he works for you and was traveling to Allahabad on your work. He informed that he stays in a one roomed flat in the neighborhood, which you arranged . . . he works as document writer for you"

"No sir I do not know any Document Writer of that name"

Suddenly his phone rang and saw it was Rupali.

"Inspector can you please excuse or postpone our talk . . . I have a business appointment they are waiting I promise you I will contact you"

"No Durjoy it is not possible . . . rather my visit was delayed . . . If you refuse I have no alternate other than taking you to police station in our police vehicle for interrogation. Those are my orders from higher-ups."

"Without arrest warrant you cannot take me . . . . Ok one minute"

he tried to talk in low tone on the phone:

"Madam I will contact you latter . . ."

He tried to tell something. Suddenly the Inspector took the phone "Mister Durjoy I cannot allow you send coded messages on phone . . . please try to cooperate with me"

He switched off the phone and kept aside. Stunned Durjoy, who was at his wits ends!, was looking with bursting anger trying to control himself. The Inspector talked with a little tough way.

"No arrest warrant required for taking you to police station . . . It will only embarrass you to be taken with policemen holding or hand cuffing in your own building before all . . . . Please cooperate with me in your own interest"

Durjoy stared at him uneasily.

"Mister Durjoy . . . is it not true that you came by car to a restaurant at Sonar Bangla for an arranged lunch with Mister Nilesh Sanyal . . . Bank officer of Help Bank on 10 th of last week?.

"I refuse to answer. I do not know who was Nilesh Sanyal! . . . . I wish to contact my lawyer"

"Ok another question You have the original property document of Jnanendara Guha, of Lake Gardens, owner of a two storied old building in this locality?"

Durjoy was suddenly enraged and shouted "Inspector you have no right to put baseless allegations!"

Inspector advised him to keep cool . . . as the building is surrounded by police and told in an authoritative way:

"Mister Durjoy I came only for preliminary enquiry but not an interrogation! . . . of a murder case don't try to act funny!"

Durjoy was fuming and understood he is in week position, he sweating profusely . . . fear started to haunt his thinking. He is still at wits end confused how that police officer new his real and false names . . . his contact with the bank officer!.

"Do you happen to know anything about the murder of Nilesh Sanyal bank officer, ... in Hooghly river few days back?"

Durjoy looked blank as if first time he was hearing about that "No sir!"

"Do you know of Seth Romakanto Choudary's death at Medinipur and about his Will made in favor of Chandramoni Debi?"

"SSir these are wild charges without any base!"

"Listen Durjoy . . . we have not charged you yet I asked whether you know"

"I reside in Kolkata . . . no idea of Medinipur murder"

"But I did not tell you Ramakanto was murdered! . . . was he!?"

Durjoy was shaken for uttering wrong word . . . .

"No sir I thought you were referring only murder deaths! . . . by mistake I uttered that word"

"I see . . ."

"I sincerely plead sir . . . I am unable to understand how my name is dragged in these unknown cases! . . . I beg sir please believe me"

"So tell me . . . have you not used Kalicharon Kundu alias Gobindo Laha alias Gadhador Kar?"

"I do not understand sir, When I don't have any personal contact with them why my name is linked . . . you have any proof sir other than what some document writer told . . .

Sir can I arrange a cool drink or tea, as you visited my office it was my privilege to honor you"

"I am not a fool to accept someone's vague talk and question your involvement . . . I have a very strong proof . . . but I am also human . . . I came alone to meet you and talk straight with well-planned murders . . . Involving master mind person like you . . . fool proof you tried . . . but I have got one original scripted letter from your Gadhador alias Kalicharon . . . alias Gobindo . . . . The original is only with me describing your criminal deeds."

Durjoy stared at him blinking without answering.

"I made a Xerox copy of that . . . here it is . . . see the letter addressed to the police Head Quarters"

He took out a Xerox copy of Kalicharon's letter.

Durjoy read the letter and was visibly shaken, he was shocked beyond belief that he couldn't imagine Kalicharon to create such a dangerous damage to him and he had given far too many clues which might tighten round his neck. The fake document in the bank locker itself can gobble him to a very serious problem. He was aghast at his own blunder to plan to eliminate him at Allahabad, instead in Kolkata itself. He unnecessarily took wrong precautions which unexpectedly brought him to police net, which never happened earlier. He asked with an exclamation:

"But there was no signature! . . . it is written as anonymous!"

"Yes . . . but I found it in his yellow color personal bag which was handed over to us along with him. I will show you a photo of that bag . . . see it . . . We found lot of finger prints on the bag . . . . photos of all and we found and also as this was new superior quality bag we found label of the shop inside pocket"

Deepankar found that information brought a little visible change of fear by the body language of Durjoy!. He understood his strength to deny or resist is allegations getting y diminished.

"Sir! I never saw or knew about this personal bag of somebody! . . . why informing about a private bag of someone whom I never knew?!"

"Mister Durjoy! . . . I brought this information to tell our police department looks minor details also We found a letter inside that bag which the Bihari police could not read the Bengali scripted letter. I was curiously going through his bag and found this un-posted letter, presumably written before journey and kept it aside may be to post after returning to Kolkata from Allahabad"

"Sir my name is Dhanonjoy not Durjoy! . . . seems some wrong mix-up or misunderstanding!"

"Dhanonjoy we know you are hoodwinking with a false names . . . but we have our own sources . . . of your suspicious activities . . . we also found out your both names . . . as we kept a tail to watch your movements! . . .

do not under-estimate Bengal police department! . . . would you deny this photo?"

Durjoy was shocked to see his photo in his hand!. He really felt the heat and angrily cursing Kalicharon in his betrayal and double crossing. He knew if the police investigate they could easily unearth some truths. He suddenly remembered the officer telling that he only had seen that letter and started investigation!. He said that on his own!. There must be some hint!. He decided tactfully tackle the officer and make high value offer to take the original letter from him. He saw this type tough officer will not agree for small amounts, he must be ready to shell down high price to save him from two serious criminal cases. Once he comes out from this nuisance created by Kalicharon, he thought many opportunities are there to make more fortune. He decided to lure the inspector. He decided to be liberal in his offer to soften the officer. He knew he cannot bluff any more but tempt him with bait, as they discovered his false name and real name.

"Sir, let us talk more practical way . . . . you can be highly benefitted . . . . you are a real intelligent officer . . . I am nowhere before you . . . why not help each other . . . . you handover that letter and in return . . . . you can earn a fortune . . . . which you will not make in your entire career"

"what! . . . . You are offering me bribe to handover the original . . . how dare . . . . !"

"Sir please don't misunderstand me . . . . it is not a bribe that is a bad word . . . . sir, I believe in quick action . . . I don't believe in delaying and having more meetings . . . . Please sir think in practical way . . . by taking up the case you would not get extra laurels . . . you might even get transferred while the case still being investigated and some other person might be benefitted, as many times it happens in government jobs . . . think sir . . . I promise to hand you at this very moment, in this place here itself . . . . a large amount as you desire and hand me the letter after receiving the reward"

Police officer, still keeping his stiff attitude, understood the reality, in his indirect threat and future action. He stared at him for a minute very seriously, not reflecting his reaction. Durjoy felt slightly nervous thinking whether his gamble would fail. But he decided to lure him with real bait.

"Sir can I bolt the door, so that no intruder comes in, you can hold your pistol and shoot me if I do any wrong move . . . I am human, I don't want persons of this building to stare at me if being taken out with police escort. I have a good reputation. I want to open my safe hidden behind that painting, for that I do not want any other to be in the room except we two . . . sir please"

Inspector became little relaxed at his pleading,

"Don't go near the door. I will bolt the door"

He said stiffly. He went and bolted the door.

"Ok . . . go ahead . . . but as I warned you if you try any mischief it will be your noose"

Durjoy reached a large colorful original painting of Jaimini Roy on the wall. He pressed a small knob on its side, the painting opened like a shelf shutter. There was a 'Godrej' safe built in the wall. He lifted a metal cover under which numbers keyboard was located. He pressed quickly some few knobs and a green light came. He simply held the handle and pulled open the heavy door. He smiled and showing huge stacking of currency notes as if it was a large bank locker.

He closed the door again and took a large calculator and quickly pressed some numbers and showed him. It represented 10 Lakhs. The inspector without emotion expressed not acceptable with horizontal nod. Durjoy changed figures to increase the amount, still he did not accept. The inspector took the calculator and pressed 5 followed by 6 zeros.

Durjoy stared at the figures, thought for some time without showing any emotion and finally accepted.

"Sir. I fill that amount in a brief case, all 1000 Rupees bundles of the agreed amount and hand it over to you then you can give me the original along with that Xerox copy?"

The officer took out the original manuscript letter written by Kalicharon and two copies, he made.

"Believe me I had taken only two prints, and no other officer or others knew about the existence of this letter"

He told in a low voice first time.

Durjoy quickly took out 50 bundles each with of one hundred 1000 Rupees notes, neatly packed them in a large brief case. He handed that bowing his head and telling:

"Thank you sir"

The officer tore one copy of Durjoy's letter and handed him the original letter and one copy, in his hand. He also said briefly, with a smile.

"The case is closed" and stood up.

"Mister Dhanonjoy! please do not accompany me as I leave the building even my men should not see you That is my request, Your Kalicharon would be discharged from the hospital after a week, if he gets back to senses, he was handled roughly by the Railway police, as they suspected him to be part of Train robbers gang"

"Ok sir I will pick him after he is discharged from the hospital. Thank you sir for this great help, I will not move out of this room till you give me a missed call on my mobile. You are great sir"

He laughed and said:

"Durjoy please don't offer me joy boat ride in Hooghly with Myanmar or Nepalese beauties!"

He laughed at the sarcastic taunting, but said smilingly:

"Deepankar Moshai! . . . Durjoy is very practical . . . he has beauties to give joys as well beasts . . . . to chase enemies . . . good bye sir"

Deepankar just smiled and walked majestically left the room with a heavy brief case, opening the door he moved out of the room and gently closed the door. After that he left the building in a fast gait, followed by another person in a constable uniform, who was standing outside the door. After few minutes Durjoy's phone rang and stopped.

He waited for that ring in an uncertain suspense!. He first destroyed the original and copy of letter. He was burning with hatred towards Kalicharon. He decided to take stringent action on him. But he was very happy that he could tactfully tame a very tough officer with a good reward, and escaped nuisance criminal cases. He felt Deepankar to be man with practical outlook. He was agitated with deep anger at the cut-throat tactics of crooked Kalcharon. He was surprised that he somehow secretly found his real name and spilled to police. He felt relieved of the stress from a dangerous situation he unexpectedly faced.

He rang Rupali, to have a relaxed lunch with her.

"Hi Durjoy dear . . . you disappointed me . . . why you cut off my call . . . and calling me madam!"

Lolit speaking as Rupali responded.

"Sorry Rupalee dear! . . . I was suddenly struck up with unexpected visit of my wife . . . . She just left . . . . had to discontinue my talk with you"

He said with a laugh. Lolit giggled:

"I can understand dear . . . wives ruin husbands' joys"

Durjoy laughed and suggested "Can I come now . . . which restaurant? . . . I will join you in less than twenty minutes"

"OK dear . . . meet me in Mocambo in Park Street . . . if it is not inconvenient . . . . I will reach that place in fifteen minutes will it be alright? . . . will wait for you . . . I am wearing Light Golden Yellow top with black polka dots with long transparent sleeves and Black skirt . . . . with stockings and shoes . . . . I hope you like western dress . . . . I am very hungry please come fast"

*   *   *

Lolit switched off the phone, and he and Shoilen roared with a hearty laughter. They were at that time sitting in Lolit's Maruti car, parked close to Jyotsna Bhavan's service stairs. They just returned from Durjoy's office room after cleverly fooling him. He was rattled with Shoilen's tough talk which made him desperately come to his feet to escape from the two criminal charges!. He fell to his cunning bluff!. His sudden meeting him came like an un-expected bolt from the Blue!. He was cleverly tricked to shell out 50 lakhs rupees!. Both were very happy at the big haul of a unexpectedly high payment!. They were surprised at their success in their very first trial run.

They parked the car close to the service stairs of that building on a side lane at the end. Both wore the uniforms of Kolkata police. While traveling by car, both covered police uniform dress with a long loose Panjabies (Kurtas) over the shirts concealing their police dress. After removing the outer false covering dress they went up by service stairs with uniforms like real police personnel. At first floor they reached the front stairs and reached fourth floor, where Durjoy's office located.

They made a recce previous night and found way to reach Durjoy's office without getting caught on video camera. They went as two customers in ordinary dresses both with beards and normal hair. They visited few entertainers' flats and left without engaging them. They roamed inside the building talking loosely as if they were slightly drunk. There was a closed sliding grill shutter with lock near the stairs of third floor. It was found the office is of Dhanonjoy Roye. Shoilen had a hunch that Durjoy also must be also in that office or Dhanonjoy might be using that false name to do illegal transactions. He discretely tempted a guard, with a small bunch of 500 notes and secretly asked one young lady wishes to meet Durjoy, in that Jyotsna Bhawan. He asked in a very low voice taking him aside. The guard looked around and whispered that Dhanonnoy and Durjoy are same. He advised him to inform her not to ask by Durjoy name but only to ask for Dhanjoy Saab after 11 in the morning to the duty guard. He quickly pocketed that money and went on duty.

Thus Shoilen found the secret of Durjoy!. They found entering by back stairs they would not be facing video camera. Shoilen dressed as Inspector and Lolit as constable. He stood near the door when Shoilen went inside. Lolit sent away the building guard to stand near third floor landing and instructed not to allow anyone to the floor. When Shoilen came out with a heavy brief case they briskly came down and reached the car with fast gait. They returned to their flat, covering the police uniform as they did earlier, while on drive.

*   *   *

They decided to do their next action, after keeping the booty safely in their place. They again started by their own car to Lal Bazar street and Radha Bazar street junction. Lolit parked his car in Radha Bazar street. Both came out walked separately. Shoilen was in is normal dress but Lolit came out in a different make up. He was having a small beard, slightly longish disheveled hair, heavy rimmed glasses, side hung red cloth bag with cloth straps over the left shoulder. He was wearing white Kurta Pyjama and cheap rubber sandals. He was carrying white sealed envelope of Kalicharon with his hand written address to Lal Bazar Police headquarters, also some few papers and a book-'Yatadura mane pare: Rajanaitika atmakathana' by Jyothi Basu.

Both reached a well-established but crude Tea shack on the road, close to most impressive Police Head Quarters building. That Tea stall was on the broad pavement on the road, popular with staff of the head-quarters as well visiting middle class public and workers. People sit on the wooden stools sipping tea and munching some small eats served there. At that time it was deserted except one or two customers. Both reached there separately sat at different places. Lolit sat there and ordered a tea and reading the book he was carrying; after ordering and sipping tea in a cup. He requested the tea serving young person to do a small errand for him. He discretely put a 100 rupee note in his pocket and requested him to hand over that letter to the clerk in charge to receive the Dak in Police Daftar. He gave a Lal-Salaam (Red-Salute) sign. Communist party workers greet the fellow comrades that way and get cooperation with fellow workers. He said in low voice: "Dhonyo Baad Comrade!". The serving young man smilingly took that letter and walked to the head-quarters and entered inside the building, to handover to the Dak receiving counter.

Lolit briskly walked away seeing him entering the head-quarters building. He reached his car and sat inside, and quickly removed the beard and hair wig and thick rimmed glasses. Shoilen remained in Tea stall; he was looking towards the main entrance of the Head Quarters building. After Ten minutes, that young man came along with a constable outside. They reached the Tea shack. The server was looking for Lolit. He said meekly, the comrade who gave that letter has gone. Shoilen who stood and about to go; intervened and asked what happened. Tea boy asked whether he had seen one Bhadralok (Gentleman) who was sitting here and gave a letter to be handed over in the office. Shoilen inquired: "Are you asking about bearded young man with red bag who took tea here?" "Yes" "Oh . . . he left towards Bentick street I think and entered a bus" The policeman told the boy not to worry and left the place and returned to headquarters building. Shoilen seriously left towards Radha Bazar Street and reached the parked car of Lolit. As he sat Lolit started the car. Shoilen smilingly said Kalichron's letter reached safely to the police headquarters! . . . . the Fireworks would start in few hours! Durjoy would curse the inspector Chatterjee and may hunt for him later!" Both laughed in high spirits with joy!.

They started to reach their destination after buying two air tickets to reach Allahabad that night. Both were looking forward to meet the graceful beauty Chandramoni Debi alias Manonmoni Debi. They were yet to plan to contact her in their own dramatic way!.

*   *   *

CHAPTER 8

Operation Code Name—'SUCHITRA'!

Durjoy was puzzled at the disappearance of Kalicharon, from the train. He sent two of his followers in the same train separately, they were to contact him at Allahabad station, as if sent Chandramoni Debi; to cleverly mislead and eliminating him in some deserted place and return with his belonging. They did know about the robbery in the train during their journey to Allahabad and stopping for a longer time at Dehri on Sone station and police taking away unconscious Kalicharon on a stretcher.

He did not give much importance to his followers report on the phone. He now got the information that he was detained on the way at Dehri on Sone station. He observed Kalicharon;s concealed happiness when informed that he was to meet Chandramoni. Durjoy laughed when he got report that he went to Howrah station, carrying an old big steel trunk box along with a new yellow colored travel bag. He thought the steel trunk must be with his life earnings. His secret follower reported that he deposited his steel trunk box in left luggage room of Howrah station.

He decided after eliminating him he would collect his life's savings from that steel box. He was wondering why he wrote that nasty letter to Police Headquarters, and kept in his bag. He thanked his stars for able to control the great damage. He was unable to control his fuming anger; he decided to hang him in his room, once he reaches from the police. It will look like a suicide. He decided to make him write his own letter stating that he decided commit suicide unable to live after the police torture for branding him as a train robber. He was planning his death to details. He was about to inform about Kalcharon to Chandramoni at Allahabad. She was not even aware about his travel to that city. He decided not to tell anything about him and the problems he faced due to him. He was in bad mood for not able to meet Rupali at Mogambo restaurant at Park Street. He wasted more than an hour waiting and trying to contact her. Her phone was switched off. He sent an SMS message. He was keen to meet her and tactfully planning to introduce to some rich businessmen who discreetly get through him, high profile ladies. She seemed smart and ambitious!. He knew such ladies bring fortune.

He did not reveal the serious situation; he faced with a police officer, and narrowly escaped dangerous consequences, to his close aids in that building.

They can get frightened and try to run away from him. He seriously was planning to change his present den and his name, as Kalicharon dangerously exposed some of his secret endeavors, which might have gone into police records!. He could never imagine that a crooked document writer would create such damage to his well-knit money spinning organization!. He was much disappointed at losing well planned taking over of a very high valued property near Shova Bazar, for which he made a very meticulous planning and almost was successful to get high returns in few days. Now he was sure it has slipped from his hands!. Kalicharon is still in police custody and still had potency to expose his present activities. He decided to take some quick action to shift his activities to a new place in a stealthy move.

*   *   *

At that very moment a high level meeting was going on at Kolkata's Lal-Bazar police headquarters building in one of the conference rooms. One of the senior most officers of the Kolkata crime department was discussing the anonymous person's letter giving lot of clues to catch the man behind the murder of the bank officer in Hooghly. They could understand that the person who wrote letter seemed authentic information; giving clearly person's name and motif for committing murder. It looked a person who was closely connected in that criminal offence some way had scripted that letter in hand writing. His writing was well in a clear way with neat pen work. It looked the writer might be a professional Document Writer. But they knew that his role might be secondary. They noted the name Durjoy Basak was not found in the recorded photos or list different category of criminals of Kolkata, in the computer.

The chief made four senior officers each with required staff and infrastructure to deal and investigate. Durjoy was to be brought immediately for interrogation. That he would be overlooked through a one way glass panel in the adjoining chamber by the chief, the psychologist and other officers to observe and suggest points for interrogation. Another group of officers will seize his office premises and thoroughly find for other evidences. They decided to get magistrate's order after initial interrogation.

The same team would investigate in Sonar Bangla hotel and The 'Help Bank' premises to inspect the documents in the bank records. The private luxury boats of Hooghly River would all be checked regarding their activities and ownerships.

One team would go to collect information from Medinipur regarding Romakantho's death and the Will details.

All groups will be organize and ready for action without delay. One of the lady officers was asked to talk to Durjoy on the mobile number provided in the letter.

That was the first action to be done in the conference and everyone would be able to hear his voice and answers. They were sure the person with name of Durjoy may not be aware of the anonymous letter reporting on him. As the address of him was part of Kolkata's famous red light areas, the lady officer was to tempt him with false story, to see his reaction, and cleverly trap him. Her phone was connected to amplifier so that all present in the hall would be able to hear.

She rang the number given in the letter, with a smile. In few seconds a gruff male voce responded.

"Whom do you want please?"

"I wish to speak with mister Durjoy please"

"Speaking"

"One of your friends told me to contact you"

She said with a little tender soft voice.

"Is it Rupali? . . . . of Sundar Bonita Beauty Parlor in park street?"

"How could you guess!?"

She asked with a jovial laugh.

"I had a luncheon appointment and she didn't turn up . . . I waited more than an hour sipping beer and looking for her"

"Very bad of her to keep a gentleman waiting in a restaurant . . . You didn't contact her"

"I tried many times but she switched off . . ."

"Oh! Sir Rupali actually requested me secretly; to inform you that her close member in her family became very serious and she had to rush. Poor girl was emotionally upset . . . yet she discretely told me to contact you!"

"Is it! . . . . oh how sad! . . . She was so happy when she talked! . . . . I am very sorry to hear . . . please tell her if you happen to meet I can help any financial need for unexpected expenses . . . ask her not to hesitate . . . as a friend if I will try . . . or could you tell me she is in which hospital now?"

"Dear Durjoy could you wait for some time to get that information. I will try all the sources . . . . As she suddenly left I didn't ask her that question . . . I am sorry . . . please wait . . . you seemed to be very intimate with you knew her since long?"

"That is our secret . . . any how since you are her friend if you wish I can take you also in my car to the hospital I mean if you are interested to go including any other of her friends . . . she is very close friend of me"

"Durjoy I feel you look real nice gentleman! . . . very sweet of you . . . why not . . . I can't say about others . . . I am keen to see her being a colleague but I stay far . . . can you arrange any transport to reach home to Behala . . . I mean afterwards"

"Don't worry madam what you said your name . . ."

"Suchitra"

"From hospital I will drop you at your house . . . . I hope your hubby wouldn't mind"

She laughed and said with little shy way "No mister Durjoy. Im single I stay with few other friends in a flat"

"Miss Suchitra . . . please don't worry. I will drop you to your flat . . . no problem . . . I have a driver . . . . I take it as pleasure to help you"

"Ok Sir! . . . . please wait for getting the address of the hospital or nursing home . . . very sweet of you by the by where you are now"

"My office is in Beadon street . . . . you don't have come to my office I will meet you in Park street"

"So nice sir . . . . just wait in your office I will give ring within 15 minutes"

When she switched off . . . all gave an encouraging support. Chief said in five minutes two vehicles with siren have to reach the address and surround and followed by local police station to send more support if required . . . . His car may be parked in a parking lot or near that building take over the car and keep the driver under your control . . . remove his mobile . . . . guard all entry and exit points. If there are any video cameras block them" . . . .

He looked at his own scribbling and said "Immediately contact Park street Police station and ask the in-charge officer to make fast but discreet enquiries regarding some lady by name Rupali of Sundar Bonita Beauty Parlor we have to contact her fast as we might be able to get details about Durjoy . . . . she seemed only casual acquaintance but we have to tail her or get the records of her conversation with Durjoy "Wish you all the best . . . the operation will be called 'Suchitra' the fictitious name suggested by our Inspector Miss Chitra . . . I appreciate her nice efforts".

In less than five minutes two powerful vehicles roared towards the exit and proceeded towards the north via Rabindra Sarani.

*   *   *

Durjoy was waiting for a call from Suchitra, smiling at the luck that another young fish is about to come near his net.

Suddenly there was a ring "Mister Durjoy sir! . . . . This is Suchitra . . . . please wait I am not able get her other number . . . sorry for the delay. I will call you again"

Durjoy replied "Ok miss Suchitra! . . . no hurry I will wait for your ring"

After ten minutes there was another ring:

"Durjoy Moshai . . . I got information that Rupaali's dear grand mom was admitted in a hospital in a serious condition . . . I am trying to find the name of the hospital . . . . did she contact you?"

"No Suchitra! . . . . very Kind of you I would like to know the name of the hospital and her grand mom's name"

He waited after another fifteen minutes. There was a ring on phone at the same time there was a Red alert light blinking from his staff!. He was surprised . . . before that he wanted to talk to her

He thought the same woman ringing . . . . he saw it was his guard near the entrance.

"what happened?"

"Sir a police vehicle stopped and . . . sir another one came behind They are entering the building!"

"What? . . . how many?"

"One officer leading four following others are surrounding the building"

He saw police in the Video . . . . and found two officers and some constables seriously entering the building. He immediately guessed that Suchitra and Rupali were police decoys to trap him!.

He quickly switched off the phone and came out and locked the room and quickly went to third floor in one of the flats and closed the door.

Within no time there was sound of heavy boots climbing the stairs. The officers saw the locked door, of his office; they were enquiring the building guard. He said he did not see when Saab has left the office.

"Is there any other entrance to his office . . . when he is likely to come?"

"There are no other entrances sir, I do not know when he likely to come"

The officer made a call on the wireless set and contacted his superior and conveyed the position. He barked "Check the surroundings and keep little away from building . . . if he finds you in the premises he may escape . . . . don't allow any one inside to go out for some time . . . keep a record if emergency"

"Rojer sir! I will do . . . . Sir there was a Video camera near the entrance . . . he might have seen our coming . . . we have blocked it"

He might be hiding if he found out! . . . go to the terrace as well keep a strict vigil . . . we don't know yet how he looks wait some message is coming to Chitra she is signaling I will come on line within few minutes"

"Roger sir"

He put off the phone and waited. In few minutes his chief came on line "Durjoy left his building in a car going towards Park street, He might have left before you reached there. He informed Chitra to meet him near Mocambo . . . . He gave some description of his car and his dress. He would wait near the place with an unlighted cigarette . . . We have alerted park street police station to surround him and catch. You keep away from the building and watch if he returns to his office. Keep no one near the building but keep a sharp eye on persons entering and don't allow anyone to leave without permission. If we catch him I will give you further instructions . . . wait close by to that building . . . end"

"Roger Sir"

Durjoy suddenly heard the heavy sound boots getting down from the fourth floor. He got information that both vehicles moved away from Jyotsna Bhavan parked near to a close by building. He smiled within; he had telephoned Suchitra saying he is driving away from his building and on way to Park Street. He told her to contact him personally near Mocambo. He gave false description about him and his car. He quickly made a plan to escape.

Durjoy alias Madhu alias Dhanjoy went to his office clad in a black Burqa like a lady. He went up by back stairs, from third floor where he was hiding. He went to his room silently bolted the door from inside; he opened the secret safe and collected all the currency notes, documents and valuables and put them in a large suitcase. He secretly carried to his flat in third floor in the same outer garb.

There was a suddenly sound of a siren after 30 minutes. It was an emergency service Ambulance. Three staff members quickly got down from the van came out with a stretcher and entered the building asking the way to a flat in third floor. Within five minutes the persons carefully brought a patient on stretcher fully covered and he looked unconscious was being carried; his white hair was only visible. They carried him into the ambulance and immediately put an oxygen mask on his face. Two ladies in Black Burqas followed the patient and entered inside the ambulance. Both ladies were crying and trying to control their sorrowful outburst. They brought with them a very large suit case.

The police officer tried to talk but ladies were not responding with tearful emotion. The senior person who was in charge was trying to check his heart beat with a stethoscope. He requested the Police that the patient's condition was serious he has to be taken to the hospital as he seemed to have severe heart attack every second delay would be dangerous. The police noted the patient's name a Mohammad Fatehkhan, came as guest to flat no 34. That flat's resident was Raheela Begam. He is being taken to Dum Dum Nursing home. As the vehicle left fast that place with loud siren.

Police were still clueless about Durjoy's whereabouts. Latter police found no person by name of Mohammad Fatehkhan was admitted in that nursing home; on that day even their ambulance did not move out. The number noted of the vehicle was also spurious!. His visit to Park street also was to mislead the police. The search for Durjoy intensified. The Police were baffled that no tenants staying in that building knew about Durjoy and no one even heard that name. They were of the opinion some person by name Dhananjoy Roye and another his partner Madhu

Nag had an office there opens during day time only, on some days and leave by 4 pm or earlier. They reach the fourth floor by lift. They were clue less as how they use an out of order lift. Raheela Begam of third floor also vanished with Durjoy!. Nothing was known about her even to the neighboring flats. Police new in that locality many lady tenants just leave permanently to unknown places, and never return.

*   *   *

The Forensic laboratory confirmed the documents now in the safe custody of the bank were not original and were cleverly done fake copies. They could easily found that papers were having watermarks of recently manufactured blank document papers.

Jnanendra was shocked when he heard that his original documents were replaced with fake documents. He did not know that a document writer had saved his high priced property which would have been sold by a fake owner!. They compared with his personal Xerox copies and could decipher number of differences which to the normal persons would not be able to find the changes. The officer who was murdered in Hooghly had sent those fake documents, for safe custody after the necessary legal verification.

The police found that there was no beauty parlor with the name of 'Sundor-Bonita' in Park street area!. They also found there were no further phone calls from Rupali's mobile to Durjoy!. Strangely Durjoy's mobile also found to be permanently switched off.

After some investigation they found the address of Dhanjoy Roye. He was found that he had a leg fracture, which was plastered and restricted to remain in the house since last fifteen days. He was a registered member as a share market broker. He had a separate phone. He was completely surprised to hear about the name of Durjoy and he was completely blank about him. He said he never came across that person. He confirmed that he only uses the lift exclusively in Jyotsna Bhavan and rest of the time he arranged to put a board as 'out of order' so that other residents and visitors do not use, as he made an agreement with the owner of the building. He looked genuine with no past history of any criminal record. He revealed that never heard about Chandramoni Debi!.

The investigation team went to Medinipur to look into the death of Ramakanto. The case it seemed was closed after thorough investigation, as Ramakantho's death was by an accident and the Will of Ramakantho was found to be genuine regarding gifting 'Kedargowri' mansion to Chandramoni Debi who was his mistress.

*   *   *

Unexpectedly a message received the from Head Quarters of Eastern Railway protection police force to Kolklata police department, regarding, Gadhador Kar, of train robbers' gang who was in their custody in Dehri on Sone railway hospital. He has two other names as Gobindo Laha and Kalicharon Kundu.

From the interrogation of Gadhador it was revealed, he was from a gang from 'Sona-Gachi' area. Their leader's name, seemed to be Durjoy and he revealed two names of ladies who might be their accomplices. A beautiful woman by name Chandramoni Debi who owns a mansion called 'Kedargowri', may be a top earning woman of the red light area. The second lady's named 'Debjani' queen of 'Jyotsna Bhawan'.

They got information that Durjoy and one of the ladies might have acted as bride groom and bride fooled all the passengers by clever acting and robbed by giving sweets laced with drug. Gadhador seemed involved in the murders of Ramakantho choudhary and Nilesh Sanyal. Nilesh Sanyal has an aviary with Mainamar parrots. Gadhador also might have dumped his wife in an ashram in Brindavan, after cutting her hair. It seemed he took dowry in his wedding. Gadhador was having a false beard and long hair, while traveling, he was found unconscious as he might have eaten drug-laced sweets. He was arrested and taken to hospital in unconscious state. He seemed upset about the loss a new yellow bag in the train. It seems there was lot of cash in that bag. He was abusing vulgarly at Durjoy for his loss. He went into a shock mentally affected it seemed due to the loss of his bag.

That report was forwarded to the officer dealing with Operation-Suchitra', along with a photo of Gadhador.

The police brought Gadhador (Kalicharon) from Dehri on Sone to Kolkata. He was found to be in living completely unaware what was going on around him, and existing like a vegetable!. He was only staring blankly and not responding to any questioning. He was admitted again in a hospital. They could also arrest one young lady named Debjani, (from the Railway police report). The residents laughed to hear about being called as the queen of

'Jyothsna Bhawan'. She was average looking young woman with cross eyed vision. She had no background with any criminal record. She was completely at loss about Durjoy or Gadhador. After seeing Gadhador in the hospital, she only recollected that one day she accidentally met him in the stair case; she revealed that he was searching for Durjoy. She jokingly told him that she was queen of Jyothsna Bhavan. She never met him again in that building. After interrogation and enquiring about her with her close relations and friends she seemed truthful and Completely innocent about the train robbery or Durjoy's activities.

Police were still analyzing all the clues connected and continuing their investigation on 'Operatio Suchitra'!.

*   *   *

Durjoy was most upset at the sudden collapse of his organization!. He got the some inside information about police investigation through one of his moles in the department. But when he got news that they may question Chandramoni Debi he decided to warn her to be vigilant and never reveal her present address to any known person, or change over to another influential partner. He decided to shift his activities to another place or another city, as he knew the Kolkata police may still hunt for him and keeping a sharp eye on him. He was stunned know of no trace of Deepankar Chatterjee, in Police department!. He had no doubt on him as he gave the original letter of Kalicharon. He felt the Railway police must have sent a report based on dirty cheater Kalicharon's squeaking!.

He decided to eliminate him now in police custody in a hospital.

He also felt the officer's real name might not be Deepankar, but could be a different one!.

He least expected him to be a stage actor !.

*   *   *

EPISODE 3

OUTLINE STORY

In this Episode, Shoilen and Lolit, accept a secret but dangerous drama to enact in real life, to help ailing Bonomali Das of Odisha, He was also an actor in Shoilen's group. Das was seriously ill and his death was imminent in few months. Earlier he was betrothed in his village to a girl of his sub caste, as per their old tradition, when they were children. Das informed them that if he dies, the girl would be treated as a widow and none from his caste would marry her. But if he marries another lady, the girl's parents can perform their daughter's wedding to another boy. To save the girl, Das tear-fully pleads them for help him, to rescue that unfortunate girl. Lolit agrees to enact disguising as a woman in a fake marriage, as Lolita, with Bonomali. Shoilen was to act as girl's father, Tejuddin Rehman. Their registered marriage was performed successfully. Bonomali's father Bishwonadh and Das's friend Damodar Sahu sign as witnesses. Das's father much annoyed and angry with his son for cancelling the betrothal and marrying woman he loved, but relented to witness the wedding. Bonomali's death occurs after two months in his village. His family tried all sources to inform his bride at Kolkata. Das did not give any details

179

of his bride at Kolkata. Shoilen and Lolit came to know that Das was from a rich family. They set their cunning eyes on the share of his property to the legally wedded wife Lolita. They felt that since they took extremely dangerous risky step of agreeing for the fake marriage, they deserve to get Bonomali Das's share of property in Lolita's name. They reached his village, Lolit in the make-up as Lolita and Shoilen as Tejuddin. They stay in Das's house and start demanding that as the daughter in law, Lolita should get Bonomali's share of the property. They found Das's family are god fearing simple people. Bishwonadh Das was well respected in his small town. They started to make the joint family's life miserable constantly brawling and loudly fighting. No body suspected any foul play, as Bonomali has taken Lolita as bride, through a Registered wedding. Lolita, threatens to take legal action on all the elders of the family with allegation of harassment. All the members were vexed-up with fear from loud mouthed Lolita and her father's daily ruckus. Bishwonadh got frightened to face legal case. He finally makes a truce with Lolita, decides to give his son's share of landed property in her name. Unexpectedly Shoilen and Lolit got information about Bonmali's friend Damodar Sahu, now settled in another town in Odisha, is about to visit Das's family. They knew Damodar to be very rich and miserly person with lot of ill-gotten money. They wanted to fool him by tempting him that he being a widower could remarry a young widow Lolita, who would come with lot of money. They wanted to extract another rich haul by trickery from him!. Will they succeed!?. Lolit, falls in love with Sunonda, a member of the Das family who becomes his only close friend!. She was Bonomali's cousin's wife. She was a beautiful damsel. Lolit tries utmost to keep his passion under control.

(Part of 'TRANSPARENT SHADOWS'—A Fiction. Author: M.V.S.Rao)

CHAPTER 1

Lolita agrees to Marry Bonomali Das

It was Sunday, Shoilen and Lolit were discussing in the morning time at Shoilen's two bed room flat in Manictola, of Kolkata. That large old type Commercial cum Apartment building had approaches on two parallel roads. That first floor flat also has two front doors side by side, giving impression as two separate flats. In that floor most of the flats were rented for small offices. Top floors were all Residential flats. The location had helped their activities as the occupants of neighboring flats were least inquisitive about the adjoining flats.

That day they were sorting out the various ornaments, laughing at the various interesting anecdotes they were recalling while doing their serious job of fooling various persons.

Suddenly when there was a ring in his mobile phone, Shoilen switched on and saw it was from one of their theatre colleague, Bonomali Das. He immediately spoke with genuine friendly way.

"Hello Daash moshaay (gentleman) how are you . . . no news from you since long time!"

The other person replied with equal familiarity and with a little hesitation requested him that he wanted to talk some urgent personal problem with him and Lolit. He requested him to visit his premises at the earliest as he is not unable to move much. He pleaded him to preferably to come that day itself. Shoilen assured that he would try to come with Lolit after an hour. Whenever Shoilen or Lolit get individual phone calls in the flat, they would never reveal about each other's whereabouts. Both of them were surprised at the sudden invitation with no clue of the purpose. They knew him since a very long time as an associate in the drama company, doing minor roles only. He was a mild natured and gentle person with sincere attitude. Normally he would have come to meet them in the theatre group to discuss any personal problem. He did not visit or participate in the theatre activity since about an year.

They never had any knowledge about his personal life. They both knew him to be a bachelor like them, working in a private firm.

Shoilen was perturbed by the strange request. His words reflected a nervous anxiety for some personal help. As both knew him since more than five years they decided to visit him that day. After getting his house address, they both came out to drive to his flat with keen curiosity. When they come out they would also generally leave separately with a gap of ten minutes; and meet at some other common point. Each of them would enter or leave by their doors.

Das's house was in lower middle class area in Khidirpur. It was a small independent old type of single story house. That locality was a congested area with narrow roads. As it was their first visit both were surprised to see him living in such surroundings. But in many Indian cities, some upper middle class or slightly higher class families get accustomed to live in such localities due to getting adjusted for long time in such surroundings and live happily.

They could easily locate the house. Before getting to his house, they informed him over the phone as they reached that neighborhood. When Shoilen pressed the doorbell button, he opened immediately, as he was waiting for them only.

Both were visibly shocked to see the change in their friend Bonomali Das's personality. He was looking lean as if he aged ten years older. His cheeks were shallow and face looked angular instead of the previous fleshy appearance. His eyes were still had the same glitter but sunken, giving of his young age, but he looked like a person not in good health.

He showed great enthusiasm to invite them with a happy friendly gesture. He took them both affectionately. He closed the door and made them sit in the front sitting room. It had sofas in that neatly kept small room. He went inside to bring cool drinking water.

The first thing that attracted both was a big framed photo of Das holding a well-dressed young woman joyfully. Both were astonished and surprised to see that, as they immediately recognized the woman with him. The lady in the photo was Lolit, dressed as a woman and acted in his first maiden role as Charulota, a woman character of a play.

On the last day of a prestigious play, the woman who was to act as the main important role, did not turn up to act; due to which the director and all the actors were in tension as there were no other lady was available for that role. To avoid the strong public resentment and disappointment of all the actors and supporting persons, Lolit accepted to come on the stage dressed as a woman to act that role. As he was associated with that play from the beginning and acted as prompter he knew the dialogues well. It was one of their prestigious plays played longer time than most. Lolit knew the main characters' dialogues well as he used to do prompting as well as reading that dialogues during rehearsals whenever heroine was absent. Till then he never acted in any major role earlier, but he used to minor roles occasionally. He was also was acting in main roles from school and college days. He was well versed in organizing stage props, enact during rehearsals of any role. Prompting from behind the stage made him an important asset and a helping hand to the group. Being a slim and medium height handsome person with soft voice he was transformed into a beautiful woman on the stage with suitable makeup. He acted that woman's role so convincingly and realistically, the audience were not even aware that a man acted!.

After the play was successfully staged, Lolit became the darling of all the persons associated with that play. Everyone praised him with utmost appreciation, and congratulated as well thanked him for coming to their rescue and did an excellent job. As it was a last day of the show the usual bash party followed the play. All the actors and the director requested Lolit to attend the party in that woman's makeup, just for celebrating the success. Most of the male actors and others took separate photos holding him closely for fun.

That was the same photo taken with Das holding Lolit in a woman's attire!. In the photo he was in his normal clothing without makeup but Lolit looked like a well-dressed charming young woman!. Both were laughing joyfully holding each other.

Lolit was a bit annoyed at seeing his photo with Das exhibiting it as a main attraction in that room!. As soon Das came, Lolit said with a disgusting attitude:

"Dash it is not in good taste to exhibit my photo as your girlfriend in your house . . . I never expected the photo to be used for your personal whims! Have you displayed to impress your friends to boast about your imaginary girlfriend!?"

Normally Lolit was a sober and mild mannered person. He lost his temper for the cheap display of his picture. He did not see the picture as something to boast. Even Shoilen was not that much amused at that big display of the picture.

Das immediately understood the situation and humbly sat on the floor near Lolit and seriously looked at him and said in a pleading way:

"Brother Lolit please forgive me for hurting you with that silly display of our drama night picture . . . but please believe me I did that intentionally only this week for a particular purpose and not to demean you . . . . please believe me, as a matter of fact I had to search for that photo for quite some time"

Both of them were astonished at his words as well his serious attitude in which there was no hint of fun or fooling. Shoilen could understand that Das was not acting but telling the truth. He made him sit next to him in the sofa.

"Dash! . . . please tell us what was the particular reason for hanging that picture so prominently!"

"brother I invited both you for some sincere help for my personal problem . . . this picture has some connection with that . . . I know no other person can help me except Lolit and you . . . in my present situation."

Both heard him with true surprise and stared at him without interrupting him.

"First let me tell you that I am not from Bengal but came from Odisha. At home I speak only Odiya which is my mother tongue"

Both were surprised to hear that, as he always spoke Bengali fluently and acted in many Bangla plays, but mostly minor supporting roles.

"Really it was amazing that till now never I could guess that you are not a Bengali"!

"I come from a village in Mayurbhanj District of Odisha now settled in a small town called Soro in Baleshwar district and I had mostly Bengali friends from childhood and during my studies, and as you know Odiya and Bangla have lot of similarities in the language as well living habits, much closer. After graduating from Kolkata I had a job here and continued to stay . . . . As I was interested in dramas I got few roles in your group and luckily I got acquainted with you."

"But you did not come to us for more than a year and no news from you . . . what happened?"

Shoilen asked him with a genuine surprise.

"Dadaa how to tell my story of misery . . . since a year I am not in good health. I suffered quite a lot and visited many specialists . . . . now I know the truth . . . .

I am very unfortunate to develop a very serious ailment . . . . I was diagnosed for Cancer in my liver . . . I am getting treatment regularly . . . please do not think

I requested you to come here to get monetary help from you for my treatment . . . . please listen"

As they both tried to say something he requested them to hear his story . . .

"I know I have no hope of survival as the decease had spread and only may be few months are left . . . I am planning to go to my home town and depart this world peacefully . . . . it is God's will and now I no longer having hope or fear"

Both became silent with genuine sympathy. Lolit tried to say to try another hospital or use of new treatment methods. Das only smiled with a grave look "I know where I stand and saw the top specialists . . . . but I am not fearing about me but unfortunately another person's life is about to be destroyed due to me"!

"what! . . . how another person's life is involved . . . . I have not understood.!"

Shoilen got up and reached him with a surprise . . . sitting closer to him.

"In our old village of Mayurbhanj district in some families they decide about marriage alliance of very young boys and girls; they finalize by holding a simple betrothal or engagement ceremony. Marriages would be performed when they reach adult age. My parents also performed an engagement to me with a girl of a known family of my village. I was Ten years old and the girl was less than Six! . . . I was postponing my marriage since few years. My main worry is that girl whom I was to marry will be doomed as she would be considered as widow as no other family would come forward take that young woman!. But I if I marry another woman, the girl's parents may object, but cannot stop it. The village Panchayat or our sub-caste seniors can cancel publicly annul engagement held in childhood. After that the girl may marry another man. So far I did not tell about my dangerous decease to my parents. My father and was about to come last week to finalize about my wedding. I am desperate how to stop my wedding . . . That is the reason I requested you to come here . . ."

Shoilen and Lolit both became sympathetic on hearing his story. Shoilen interrupted:

"Dash . . . You can count on us . . . . We will definitely help you . . . . but in what way we can interfere in your personal life . . . . Have you thought of any solution?"

"I am coming to that . . . What I am planning was only to help that poor girl . . . . I feel it was a burden on me more than my life . . . her life . . . I want to save her . . . .

I had seen Lolit in that drama even off stage also he looked like good looking female in his attire! . . . it suddenly struck me as an only alternative . . . to tell them that I have been in love with a Muslim woman who also agreed to be my wife . . . and I will show this photo to prove it . . . ."

both were stunned to hear his serious but dubious thought of strange imagination.

"Dash I don't mind your using my photo as your girlfriend . . . But why think of a Muslim woman you could lye some Hindu woman only . . . ?"

Lolit asked with a surprised look.

"This part of Kolkota lot of Muslim families stay . . . another main reason was if it is a Muslim family my father will not discuss with the girl's parents . . . he is against marrying from such families out-side our religion . . . . I would say that girl accepted to become a Hindu and her father reluctantly agreed to this marriage"

Both laughed at his convincing idea . . . .

"Dash I have no objection to use my drama photo as of your would be wife. I definitely will not object as you are doing for a noble cause"

"Daash! I somehow feel it would not look authentic and your people may not accept this marriage. As you said you would go to your village . . . all will see it as a fake marriage and the poor girl would have a pitiable future"

"I thought of that . . . . my plan is to make it look more authentic . . . . with folded hands I wish to request you to help me as actors to succeed in my convincing drama . . . . for that I sincerely was hoping . . . . you both would help me . . . Wish to show Lolit as my bride for that he will dressed as a woman and you come as a Pandit to perform simple marriage . . . after the registration . . . . here before my father and a close friend in Kolkota who stays in a distant place from here who would help as a witnesses before the registrar in a simple way and please do not kindly refuse me . . . I will get the marriage registered so that no one would disbelieve I am not going to take bride with me when I go to my home . . . so Lolit need not have to face our relatives in my village . . . I will somehow manage with other lies"

He almost got tears while requesting them with a very pitiable way. Both were stunned at the strange turn of events and his pathetic request.

"But you require a month's notice in the registrar's office for getting a registered marriage in that office"

"yes I knew . . . I have already . . . sorry I took this step without consulting you . . . I just took a chance that you would agree and I gave a written request in the registrar's office and there is a provision that registrar would come to house see we exchange garlands and solemnly register the marriage for which an extra amount is to be paid and arranged on a Sunday"

"Oh my God . . . Das how could you do this without consulting me . . . it is very risky . . . . If I refuse?"

Lolit said with a serious concern; not at all wishing to be part of this fake acting as a bride in real life.

"Shoilen Da and Lolit Da . . . im requesting you in a humble way . . . that too please do not refuse this will be conducted with absolute secrecy, even neighbors would not know. No other persons would be invited . . . main thing . . . kindly do this acting to help. I am not doing for myself but to save a girl . . . I wish to pay you one lakh each for the help in this acting . . . kindly do not refuse I beg you"

He got up from the seat and went to a table nearby and took out two bundles of currency notes all of thousand rupees notes and sat on the floor with crossed legs in front of them with tears and folded hands. Both were moved by his gesture and were shocked at his benevolent attitude. Shoilen lifted him gently and made him sit on the sofa keeping the cash on the table. Das was really in an emotional way with uncontrollable tears and trying to control his grief, unable to talk more.

Shoilen and Lolit saw each other in a serious way and sat silently for some time. Shoilen looked at Lolit in questioning way. Lolit said "Dada let us go out for few minutes outside and talk"

Both rose and Shoilen said:

"Dash . . . pl allow us few minutes to talk . . . plese don't be panicky we would try to help you"

They both went outside and seriously discussed among themselves in a low voice. Finally they came to him

"Dash are you sure the girl's future would be saved . . . if you go through this fake wedding?"

"It is hundred percent certain . . . the girl is really good looking and somebody from our family itself might marry her. I really want to save her"

"Dash . . . I am very nervous but I am reluctantly agreeing but see that it is for only that day and never talk about this at any time everything for one day only"

Lolit said:

"Dash . . . please don't make another drama involving me coming as a Pandit to do as per Hindu rites . . . please drop that. I will come as the father of the bride reluctantly accepting the marriage of my daughter to a boy of her liking . . . . I will come as an old Muslim gentleman . . . once the garlands are exchanged the marriage is registered it is supposed to be legal . . . . that would be sufficient . . . collect the marriage certificate at the earliest, and give it to Lolit for safety"

The next episode started that way, both again accepted to do fictitious roles in real life; Shoilen as an old Muslim gentleman and Lolit, in a young woman's role, as his daughter. Shoilen picked that amount silently.

They both were slightly in tension, as they have to act for friend, taking a risky adventure to help for a noble cause; but would have to face real life wedding drama publicly.

*   *   *

Everything was well planned to minor details. On Saturday Das's father Bishwanadh and his betrothed girl's father came to his house, as soon Das called them to be in Kolkata on a particular day. Both were dismayed at his urgently summoning them without having least idea about what was to take place. Both persons were shocked to see him at the Howrah station in an unhealthy weak condition. He just said that he was not well for about fifteen days and due to fever. He assured them he is alright now and will recover in few days. He did not utter anything about his planned wedding; he talked only talking general topics, while returning home. But he was feeling nervous and shaky to reveal about his decision to annul the earlier betrothal as it was breach of family honor; which the senior persons would not be able to digest. He was sweating and feeling depressed but tried his best to control his nervousness whether things would go smoothly as he planned alone with his drama friends. But he was in a desperate state, to go ahead, in a determined way!. Finally when they reached his residence, he got down from the taxi and gently knocked his door. Within a short time a young lady in a veil opened the door and went inside. Both the elderly persons saw her in a short glimpse but did not attach much importance. He took them to his small drawing room and as the driver brought the luggage inside; he paid and closed the door. As he expected both of them were staring at his large framed colored photo of him tightly caressing a woman and in a joyful mood!

Both were stunned to see him with a good looking well-dressed young woman in an intimate way!. It was unimaginable scene and both the senior persons were visibly shocked at his personal un-respectful photo being displayed in spite of their visit!. Das first looked at his engaged girl's father mumbled in a shy way. Bonomali was convinced that his plan hit in a better way than explaining with words. He felt sorry to see the reaction in both their faces of utter dismay!. They both were standing and staring at the photo unable to comment!. His father dauntingly asked him:

"Bonno! (his pet name in his home) . . . what sort of silly photo you kept in the house! Are you out of your mind?"

Bonomali just ignored his father and he meekly addressed his engaged girl's father . . .

"Sir! . . . I am very sorry . . . but since more than a year I became a close friend to that girl and . . . our relationship became very deep . . . at my age I cannot keep this as secret anymore and we both decided to become husband and wife . . . . I know about the engagement vow my family took when I was too young . . . but in life at my age I don't want to cheat your daughter . . . please excuse me . . . I love this girl and my decision is final . . . I am not a small boy to be reprimanded please excuse me I cannot help . . ."

That gentleman was too embarrassed as well bursting with anger. Held his fore head and weakly could only sit on a sofa, looking at the floor. He was speechless and shocked at this unexpected turn of events!.

Bishwanadh was in a fit of rage at his eldest son's shameless attitude and revealing unexpectedly as a characterless person!. He knew from childhood as a well behaved and good natured child and also a sincere and sober young man, always respected elders and good hearted person. He was aghast at his irresponsible decision to marry another woman after knowing that he was engaged to a girl since long time!.

Before retirement he was a teacher in a high school and he used to treat his pupils friendly way and rarely did he shout at any of them for their indiscipline. But he was shivering with rage at his own eldest son's taking life as a children's game. He shouted at him first time in an uncontrollable loud voice;

"Bonno! . . . Don't talk absurd way . . . you are part of our family . . . you cannot behave so irresponsible way!"

"Boppaa! . . . (father or dad in Odiya) this is my life . . . It is final decision. I called you for this purpose only . . . please listen . . . please don't shout loudly . . . My friend Lolita is in the bed room . . . kindly understand my position, She converted to be a Hindu to marry me defying her family, who follow Islam . . . . That formality is over yesterday in Arya-Samaj and her new name is Lolita . . . She made a big sacrifice to marry me and has no other place now . . . . she is staying with me as we are getting married!"

Bonomali told in a low voice, without looking towards him. His father was flabbergasted at his son's words . . . He was shocked to hear that his bride was a Muslim girl; he remained stunned unable to digest the information.

He lowered his voice in a feeble way controlling his anger . . . he could see the affair gone too deep!.

"What? . . . . She is a Muslim! . . . you are staying together already . . . Oh God Jogannaadho! . . . . I never knew I will see this day!"

He sat too astounded to utter any more . . . he also sat on a sofa; his face became red with pent-up rage. At that moment Lolit dressed in a woman's makeup was hearing all along from behind the curtain, being a small house, he could understand the tense atmosphere even though he could not follow Odiya!. He came to the room timidly yet making his presence as a well groomed young woman; her arrival was revealed through sound of the silver anklets with little trinkets and the bangles in both hand giving a nice light sound with his movement!. A tray with two plates Rosagullaas and other sweets were in his hand, bringing with a happy and shy way. He covered his face and head with sari pallu as a normal custom in front of elder males. He kept the tray on the center table went and touched their feet humbly bending the head exhibiting utmost reverence.

Both put blessing hands reluctantly, not even looking at the woman. Lolit tried to give both elderly persons one each, plates of sweets, but both did not accept. They did not touch and sat there in a depressed mood. Bonomali introduced both, one as his father and other his friend. Das's father told Lolita,

"Please take away these sweets . . . we are not hungry now"

Lolilta once more touched Das's father's feet with high respect and told in a shy way:

"Sir please excuse me for daring to come to meet you in your son's house . . . I may not be able to speak or understand Odiya but I will make it a point to learn and live in your family . . . I never met any person as nice as your son! . . . . I could understand you are all very cultured and respectful family . . . . I thought mother-in-law and others also would come to bless us . . . . I wished see other elders also . . . I insisted Bonomali to call . . . . I thought they will all be happy when we both will get married tomorrow"

Both were startled at her telling that the wedding would take place next day. They were stunned at her announcement, and looked at him with glaringly. He bowed his head and said in a low voice:

"Yes our registered marriage would take place tomorrow in this house. The registrar would come. We have to exchange garlands in front of him and sign before him . . . sorry I could not write or inform you on phone earlier. She was expecting mother would come and happily waiting . . . she is a nice educated girl"

He requested Lolit to go inside as he wished to talk some urgent matters with his father. As Lolit went inside, his father-in-law rose and said in an angry tone to Bonomali,

"I take it as an insult to me . . . I do not wish to stay any longer here, I will go to Howrah station and go back . . . . I cannot remain witnessing your one side decision and forgetting us and treating us as if we are beggars at your mercy!. I do not know why you called me all the way to hurt me face to face! . . . . Please tell me how to get a taxi I will go immediately"

His father also in an angry tone said that he would also go back with him.

"Please Bishwanadh! . . . my relationship is broken with your family . . . . But I don't want to break your relationship with your son . . . please stay with your son, that is my request . . . no more arguments please and I will just now go back . . . we are unlucky to lose Bonomali. But the situation now cannot be altered that girl left her family for him . . . I cannot ask him to throw her out for my daughter . . . she is as good as my daughter . . . I accept our fate"

Bishwanadh also was too much upset at his son's unimaginable behavior and his un-thoughtful action ruining the family's name for his personal passion . . . he was unable decide what he has to do . . . since last one year he hardly ever came home always telling that he was not getting leave . . . twice he said he would be arriving and last minute he would bring some excuse for not able to get leave. He looked very weak and sickly which caused much worry to him when he saw after a long period . . . but his falling in love with a Muslim girl and least caring about the girl he was betrothed was a very annoying unfaithful act . . . . He never expected that his son would ever do such undignified act to another family who were waiting for him for years . . . . He decided to go to his village and avoid seeing his son's registered wedding.

"Bonno I have also decided to go to village to day"

Bonomali sat near his father's feet with tears and requested in a pleading way to stay for the wedding. Seeing his son's pathetic appeal he felt touched and changed his mind to remain in Kolkata for that day only. He lifted him and sat in a pensive mood.

At that time, Banomali's friend Damodar Sahu, came to the house. He greeted both father and son and congratulated Bonomali for getting married next day. Damodar Sahu is his friend, who was also from, Baleswar district of Odisha. He was working in Kolkata since more than 30 years, after his marriage also his family used to stay in his village and he was continuing in his job in the city. He and Bonomali were friends and occasionally meet each other both spoke Baleswari dialect of Odiya, which was another binding factor. Bonomali earlier requested him, to come on Sunday to sign as a witness for his registered marriage. He was happy yet he could not understand why he was getting married at Kolkata, and not his home town which is about 6 hours' journey only from Kolkata. He asked about his welfare and enquired details of the wedding registration timing.

Bonomali took him inside to talk to him aside, to talk about next day's program and also to request him to accompany his earlier betrothed girl's father to escort him to the Howrah station. When they entered to his only other room in that house; Damodar was stunned to see an extremely beautiful well-dressed woman boldly sitting on his bed unmindful about her sari Pallu on her thighs and wearing a sleeveless blouse!.Lolit was sitting in relaxed way unmindful about his lady attire and talking in low tone on his mobile in a happy mood. Bonomali introduced his bride Lolita, to Damodar, when they went inside. She hurriedly lifted her slipped sari which exposed her provocative body. Lolit rose and covered his head and touched his friend's feet. He was amused at the fat round person with big pot belly and shining bald head. He was reeking with disgusting smell of sweat, which he was wiping with his small Gamuncha (Small hand woven towel). He was staring crudely at him with an open mouth shining with dark stained teeth, and Tammaku Paan. Bonomali introduced Damodar, to Lolit, as his friend from Odisha and accepted to sign as a witness to their marriage. He informed that he was resident of Kolkata, working in the city for more than 30 years and now as a head chief in a big restaurant. That he was also a big land lord in his village with lots of properties. He said smilingly that he may look humble but he is a very well to do man and a very helpful person. Damodar just smiled and said he was simple salaried person not as rich as Bonomali described. He said he is still working in the city to survive. He said that he felt happy to come and sign as a witness. He assured her that he would assist them for any help in future also. Damodar was shocked to see the bride shaking hand with him, when introduced!. She enquired him in a happy way weather his wife would also attend the wedding. Damodar slightly felt uneasy and told in a sad tone that his wife died a year back. Damodar was astonished to see that beautiful bride came very close to him and putting her hand on his shoulder in a consoling way to say she was sorry to hear his tragedy, in a very affectionate way even though he never met her earlier. He was also surprised to see Das did not feel anything unusual at his bride's strange mannerisms!.

Lolit was aghast at Damodar asking Bonobir unashamedly money for taxi expenses to arrive next day to sign as witness. Das took out ten 1000 rupee notes and gave him and requested him to kindly accompany his father's friend to the station that day before going to his home. He also quietly hinted him not to discuss about the wedding next day and only talk general topics, and also requested not to pry his relationship with the family, while going to Howrah station. He made a sign of secrecy informing not to ask any more details about the wedding before the elders, assured mildly he would tell latter in a whispering way.

Bishwanadh was in no mood to discuss or talk any other family topic with his son in the presence of the bride, who was also, was staying in the house. He said seriously that night he would sleep in Damodar's house and come with him next day at the time of wedding. He decided that way to express his displeasure at his son's insistence to be present at the registration of wedding function.

*   *   *

Next day the scheduled marriage registration was held in a simple way as planned, before an officer representing the Registrar of Assurances office. Lolit dressed as bride exchanged the garlands with Bonomali Das in a joyful way, smiling happily. Both solemnly accepted to abide lifelong as husband and wife, as was told by the officer. They both signed in the register. Bonomali's father Bishwanadh and Damodar Sahu signed as witnesses to the wedding. Lolita was looking very pretty dressed in a rich bridal attire and makeup, but looked shy and conventional. Damodar was most impressed at her charm and sophisticated makeup of the bride!. He felt she looked like a beautiful film-star!

Surprisingly there were hardly any invitees to that function held in Bonomali's house. Bishwanadh Das, Damodar Sahu and Shoilen cleverly disguised as Tejuddeen Rehman a senior Pathan, with beard with shaved-mustache, wearing a dark Sherwani and Pyjama and a Mussulman cap. He looked serious throughout during the ceremony. He only talked only with Lolit only most time. She was in a tense mood, even while showing happiness. She seemed worried lest her father create any bad scene, to express his displeasure. Lolit told so discreetly to Das but made sure that Bishwanad heard the words.

Both Shoilen and Lolit made the scene emotionally touching, after the ceremony, with their histrionics as if father and daughter unable to control their separation!. The bride was weeping profusely while bidding farewell to her father; He also burst with tears of extreme sadness and uncontrollable emotion. He left Bonomali's house with a sad posture. He did not talk much, but was showing his displeasure about his daughter marrying against his will. He requested Das in a tearful way to look after his daughter well in future, and also requesting him to allow her to stay in his house, for few days, before leaving for the groom's ancestral home in Odisha. He briefly requested Bonomali's father also the same, gently said as if he was doing a formality, reminded him to kindly accept her ignorance of their family traditions of Odisha, and requested to kindly guide her. Bonomali bowed and touched the feet of father of the bride, in a most humble and respectful way before him. When he went into his bed room, he touched Lolit's feet also to convey his heartfelt gratitude. Lolit lifted him, and told in a serious way:

"Dash please don't be so emotional, we are friends doing a drama act only for a good cause, I may be younger to you and please don't embarrass me, we are members of the same fraternity, to impress others by our acting, I am happy everything went well so far . . . . thank god whatever planned by Shoilen Da looked very realistic".

The function was over within a short time and the officer left after completion, stating that the marriage certificate would be handed over next day in the office. There was hardly any gaiety or laughter, normally associated with weddings. Only Lolit as Lolita, made the occasion, a bit interesting acting joyful way, as a newly wedded bride: brimming with joy, after Sholen left, to bring some realism. When Bishwanadh left with Damodar, after the lunch, Lolit also removed his make-up and changed to his normal dress. Shoilen also came back in his normal dress beaming with happy feeling. He was also tense acting in presence of Bonamali's father and Das's friend. He was amused at the clumsy behavior of Damodar and at his greedy display of grabbing and eating too many sweets and snacks kept on the table for the occasion. He could control his laughter with difficulty seeing him presenting a packet of Kerchiefs as a wedding gift to the groom, after the wedding function. As he had to act with dignified sorrowfulness he avoided passing any amused remarks, at Damodar's antics. He however had a private talk with him to get to know his address and his living style. He came to know that Damodar was a very well to do person. He saw his clumsy greediness with selfish outlook He decided to fool him in future to extract good sum of money!.

The three had some discussion about the future management and safety measures to avoid any leak about the fake registered wedding function, fooling some known persons and committing a fraud using an established public office, making an illegal marriage between two adult males.

Thus Bonomali Das married Lolita, a male disguised as a woman, in a legal way!. Such peculiar happenings may occur in a big city like Kolkata!. Also Lolit didn't know this mock wedding would bring changes in his as well others' lives!.

*　　*　　*

Chapter 2

Lolita decides to visit Bonamali's home at Soro

Three days after the registered marriage function at Bonamali Das's house, Shoilen and Lolit were busy with new drama rehearsals in one of a theatre's rooms. Lolit was holding a copy of the drama script and following while two characters of a play, being enacted by male and female artists. Director, Shoilen and other actors were sitting around watching the slow process of a new drama enacting. When the heroine has forgotten her lines in that scene and was not making good attempt to act in a realistic way. Lolit was prompting her dialogue and constantly helping her, with little acting taking the role of the director and advising her. He corrected her sentence in a mock up way, telling how the woman must express the complete dialogue. The female actor laughed out loud thanking Lolit's nice expression and came to him to pat him in friendly gesture. She seriously told the director that she wished to see how Lolit would do that scene. Director as well Shoilen and others welcomed him to do that little act. Lolit sportively went and acted that scene in a most realistic way modulating his voice to express in a dramatic style!. It was a humorous scene wherein a loud mouthed wife taunts her henpecked husband, and irritates him with continuous nagging, as he listens and helplessly pleads. Lolit did that effectively showing provocative body movements and loud outburst, while acting that small scene!. His acting attracted everyone in that group; they all applauded with clapping and cheers. He did similar acting to fool the fellow passengers in one of their train robbery episode. Shoilen trained that type of scene to Lolit before, in their flat. The role was similar but dialogues were different. Lolit shyly acknowledged the response. He and Shoilen smiled at each other remembering their memories. Lolit had developed a great talent to act like a woman and guiding excellently!.

The female actor went to him and patted with warm appreciation. She expressed that Lolit did that role so well that he must guide her like a Guru.

He told her laughingly, he is ready to give her some personal coaching at her place in acting. All laughed at his joking stance. Other women on the stage also came round him and hugged him and patted him encouragingly; volunteering to take lessons from him. One lady informed in a lighter vein that her husband would stop her to participate acting on stage when she starts learning this type of talk with husband!. All were laughing and enjoying that break.

At that jovial moment, his mobile ringing sound disturbed his attention. He just took out and looked at the phone. It was from Bonamali Das, whom Lolit agreed for the fake marriage. He excused the director and went outside the room to talk.

When he responded the call, Bonamali informed him that the registration certificate of the marriage has been received and requested him to collect. He also informed that he would pay the balance of on lakh as promised. He thanked him profusely again for his great help. Lolit told him he would come with Shoilen as soon their rehearsal session was over.

Latter as they were about to leave to meet him, another call came to Shoilen from Das. He talked to Shoilen with little tension, saying that Damodar Sahu arriving in his house to have a dinner with them. He was unable to dissuade him as he was asking to commit a day for a party with Lolita or arrive in his home town to attend the family wedding reception.

Shoilen understood his grave problem decided help him. He requested him to arrange the dinner in a classy restaurant for privacy as well to avoid meeting known friends when he comes as Lolita to accompany him. Bonamali laughed and mentioned that he also decided to arrange in a star hotel restaurant for his privacy. He confirmed that only Damodar would come.

He explained to Lolit that Damodar was pestering Das to host a dinner with his bride. He requested him to go alone dressed as Lolita to finally get rid of this problem. He laughingly told him not to act in the restaurant as a bashful newlywed bride. He hinted to collect all details about Damodar as well as Bonamali's family discreetly. Lolit told Shoilen, that Damodar is a miserly person with idiotic outlook. He was informed by Das that Damodar would stoop to any depth to make others spend. He got information that he had made lot of money working in a good hotel mainly recruiting young men and boys from Odisha arranging jobs and squeezing big amounts from them besides good shares from the suppliers of reataurant, other money lending resources. Shoilen and Lolit decided to exploit Damodar cunningly, as he knew such persons could be easily trapped.

Lolit went alone in his car to Das's house and there he changed his makeup to look like a very fashionable modern lady in a provocative way. He went much earlier to be ready before Damodar arrived. The three went to a classy restaurant in Alipore. The ambiance was very nice furniture and surroundings. They preferred an exclusive partitioned enclosure to avoid any unexpected friends seeing them.

When the waiter enquired whether they would have drinks before dinner is served, Bonamali Das told Lolit to excuse him but to go ahead and order whatever drinks they wished to. Lolit took that opportunity "Damodar Moshay can I recommend you some nice cocktails they are like appetizers . . . . I am sure you will enjoy before the dinner is served . . . unfortunately I don't drink but give you company with a soft drink . . . please don't feel shy . . . I got information about drinks from my friend who is doing hotel management"

He felt too happy "Madam I am too eager to take cocktails please order as you desire, I don't know much about them . . . hope they are not strong?"

"No mister Damodar! they are like good appetizers with little alcohol . . . I am sure you would enjoy . . . . Would you try 'Arizona Twister' or 'Bolshoi Punch' . . . . I heard they are very popular".

Damodar was completely blank about cocktails, but he was eager not to miss chances when offered free!. He was not aware that Lolit mischievously ordered cocktails which were strong, to enjoy seeing his reaction in slightly drunken tipsy condition!.

"Madam! . . . . You are so well informed . . . I will first start with the Twister and later I would try the other one as well! . . . he he he he!"

When Lolita ordered, the waiter was confused and called the bartender. When Lolita casually ordered cocktails requirements to the surprised senor staff member. He wrote them and placed before the bar in charge. Both made those cocktails after referring to book, as he never mixed those cocktails earlier. Actually Shoilen cunningly suggested those names knowing the strong contents to give a good kick. Damodar was over whelmed to have dinner and drinks in a posh restaurant, in the company of a beautiful sophisticated lady. Lolit excused Das and went to the bar, to inform how many of the two cocktails to be served and also informed the bar man to make for him a small vodka with coke, with more ice cubes.

When Lolit went boldly walking towards the bar, Damodar was astonished at the stylish way the new bride going and talking with the barman. When she went from the table he congratulated Das, and told in Odiya with utter surprise:

"*Bonomali! . . . . muu sotto kohuchi . . . . Teme bhollo bohu payicho! . . . sundoro ebom chalaak mohila . . . . ette adhuniko jubati ko mu kebbe dekhinai! . . . . motte bodo aanando hevuchi!*"

(Bonomali I am telling the truth, you got a very good bride! . . . she is goodlooking as well very smart woman! . . . . I never saw such modern woman. I feel very happy to see!")

Bonomali just smiled at his friend's comment, laughingly he told him

"*Bhayinaa! Tume pai Lolita ko gutteye bhollo bohu dekhibaaku kohibhi? Tume kayiku single rohibo . . . .*

tume bessi byaso hai nai . . . kuhontu mu nischoyo tanku pochharibi!"

(Brother! Should I ask Lolita to see a good bride for you? Why should you still stay single . . . . you are not much aged . . . tell me should I ask her?")

"Nai Bonomali . . . . se bishoyo somoyo asle kohibhi ibbe nai . . . pore dekhibhi . . . motte dekhile sundoro pilla baghjibo!"

(No Bonomali! When the time comes I will tell not now . . . . will see later . . . Goodlooking girl will run away seeing me")

He said laughing loudly. Just then Lolit came and saw both friends in a laughing mood.

"Why both of you are laughing heartily please share with me your discussion!"

Bonomali told her laughingly:

"when I asked him to marry a woman now that he is still in good age . . . . he was telling good looking women would run away seeing him You tell him to accept"

Lolit went close to him and held his hand told with a humorous way:

"You are so good looking and healthy any woman would agree happily . . . . If had seen you before meeting Bonomali I would have become your girl-friend . . . . you are strong and handsome!"

Bonomali also laughed out loudly and said "Thank god Lalita saw me first or She would have become your girlfriend and refuse me"

Damodar shyly laughed and felt very happy at their talks. When the drinks arrived he took a sip while Loilta said "cheers"

He was overjoyed with first time seeing a charming newly wedded woman recommending and ordering drinks!. Lolit as Lolita slightly behaved in a coquettish way with Damodar intentionally to find about his personal properties and family life. Bonomali showed least concern as Lolita became close confederate to Damodar not caring the required etiquette, expected from a bride in front of the groom. He was in reality enjoying it as a fun, seeing his friend Lolit Sen acting nicely in a woman's role, fooling his friend!. Damodar was pleasantly surprised at the boldness of newly married Lolita in least caring for her husband's presence while talking with him as an intimate friend.

As he quickly gulped half the glass he found the drink to be too punchy and with an exotic taste. He was fascinated to see the glass top edge was quoted with salt to give an interesting taste for every sip!

Lolit discreetly hinted to Bonomali to advice his friend not to gulp but take slowly!. Bonomali under stood Lolit's hint.

"Damodar Bhai! . . . A cocktail could be enjoyed more if taken in small sips . . . than gulping . . . ha ha ha!"

He said with a good humour.

After another half hour the drink mixture of different alcohols, made Damodar tipsy and started to blabber about his success in becoming a rich man. He started boasting about his ability to fool many in his job and activities. Lolit intentionally asked Damodar in a casual way many queries about his life's achievements. He sat close to him and poking him with fun joyfully taking the role of a hostess to look after the guest. He was continuously talking to him in a most intimate way!; touching him and holding his hands and talking many times in a whispering way as if long known friend. He was too much attracted to her beauty and her perfume.

The cocktails made him behave like a fool forgetting the surroundings! He started to moving still closely towards Lolit and talking in a romantic mood. Bonamali was watching with fun!; he also encouraged him to tell details about his success.

He ordered one more twister followed by the Bolshoi Punch and narrating his secret method of making money from various sources and how much he made all irrelevant talks telling his secrets as the drink controlled his head!.

He foolishly narrated how he would make money from young job seekers from Odisha who would offer whatever he asked by taking loans and arranging money to him. He laughingly told those silly boys prepared to massage his legs to get jobs!. Bonamali quickly made him to change the topic.

Lolit encouraged him to reveal more by not caring when the sari was slipping and exposing her feminine beauty. Lolit looked at him as if she was attracted by his manly attraction. Damodar, developed a bulky body, due to regular gulping of rich and fatty foods of Hotel kitchens!.

Lolit mischievously many times was discreetly holding his hand below the table and touching his hand intentionally to bring a happy feeling to Damodar. He became a bit bold and responded with discreet passion. He willfully boasted about his good property and his benevolent nature. As she ordered fourth drink for him he decided to show his good nature by secretly giving a gift to her.

On that day he had put on two thick gold rings and a thick Khada on his right hand, when he came to the party. Lolita showed little inquisitiveness and praised his gold kadha and rings as if they looked very artistic. Damodar discreetly asked whether she would accept if offered as a as a gift. Lolita replied whisperingly that she would take it as a lucky charm and keep as a lifelong memory. He took out first the ring and handed her as a wedding gift with a great show, while Das went to the rest room. Damodar felt very happy to see he could passionately please Lolita with that ring. She happily expressed her pleasure by almost hugging him and holding his hand with happy smile. He was so overwhelmed and happily took out his gold Kadha (Armlet) and put to her hand. She was overjoyed with happiness and once more hugged him tenderly before Bonomali reached. But he saw the mischief of Lolit and enjoying from distance.

Lolit disecretly praised Damodar's broad mindedness and hinted to contact him in future to meet in a park or cinema. He was overwhelmed at her secret hints. He felt that the lady was more impressed with his strong body than her weak looking husband!.

Lolit thus made a fool of him to part two gold items and information of his ill-gotten wealth and properties.

After the dinner they dropped him in his house lest he might lose his way or fall somewhere. Damodar never took drinks earlier and with the strong cocktails he became uncontrollably talkative!. He also gifted his two gold ornaments. Kadha and ring, which normally would not dream even to do such benevolence!. When they reached Damodar's house Lolit went alone with him to his house and helped to open the door lock. While shaking hand telling good night he took out his second ring also and kept in Lolit's hand. He quickly came out lest he might do some more boorish outbursts.

He was happy that he could make Damodar part with three gold items foolishly. Lolit went to Das's place and removed the makeup and changed to his gent's dress. He gossiped with him for some time. Das handed him the certificate and the balance money he promised. Lolit quietly listened information about his family details, property and his address and family businesses, while talking as a friend. Bonamali gravely informed his plan to shift to his village, winding up his house at Khiderpur. He decided to tell his parents that his bride decided to stay with her father some days and come later. Then they parted as friends

*   *   *

Shoilen and Lolit laughed seeing the marriage certificate issued by the authorities. (They got an affidavit for date of birth certificate of Miss Fairooja alias Lolita, from a notary, as it was required for marriage registration, contacting him outside the registration office; Shoilen and Lolit went, as Tejuddeen Rehman and Loit in black burqa as Fairooja alias Lolita). Shoilen advised not to destroy the certificate for some time to watch the situation.

Bonamali Das gave them his final farewell call before leaving the city for good. He requested them not to call on his mobile. He said he would delete all his phone calls from his mobile. He profusely thanked them for the great risky help.

After two and half months they saw his photo in the newspaper in the obituary columns, which his family inserted to inform about his death to his known persons in the city. They also felt sad at his demise, and both remembered his noble deed to save his betrothed girl, from life long suffering.

After a month Lolit telephoned Das's mobile from a public phone booth. He requested to call her friend Fairooza wife of Bonamali. They understood that some lady was asking for Lolita by her Muslim name. Bonamali's father, Bishwanadh, answered the phone and lamented about his son's death. He pleaded her, that he was unable to contact Fairooja or her father, after Bonomali's sudden death, as he was ignorant about her family's address or contact number. He requested to inform him their Kolkata address and contact number.

Lolit quietly conveyed regrets and expressed to try to contact her, and disconnected. He just wanted to know the reaction from Bishwanadh Das. He was genuinely looked eager to contact Bonomali's wife, expressed real sorrow towards her, for losing her husband at a very age. He said he was eager to take her to his house.

*   *   *

They first decided to visit the Das's town as strangers to gather more information about his background and the family properties. They restrained for few months to get their bearings correctly to get first-hand information directly about the family. They initially thought only to help him to solve his personal dilemma in a humanitarian way. They helped him with a risky illegal venture which was known only to them and Bonamali Das, about the fake marriage and fake bride. Lolit feared if there was any doubt or Bonamali's family reported about the missing daughter in law, the police might enquiry and investigate. He feared if by oversight if they left some minor clues which might lead to their involvement. He took from Das the enlarged photo as well original photo copy, lest their back ground might reveal.

Till Das's death, he used to fear, that he might prattle his dangerous plan unknowingly in semi-conscious condition in his sickness. It would be treated as committing a serious crime if reported to police. He would have been in serious trouble if the marriage secret was found!. After a month after Bonomali Das's death Lolit felt relieved from his mental fear. He and Shoilen had some plans to fool Damodar Sahu, to cunningly make some money. Shoilen was happy that he has now enough dirt on Damodar to blackmail. Both decided to tackle him later. They made discreet enquiries about his place of work and his activities. They collected enough information to black mail him or lure him to part a good amount. In few months they came to know he also left the city permanently, before they could take some action. They decided to black mail him later by going to his village and posing as police investigators from Kolkata. They decided and planned to threaten him exposing his exploitations with youngsters from Odisha running the jobs racket.

Shoilen and Lolit had a basic information from Bonomali about his family and their properties. Later they got confirmed news through Das's close persons, that he was from a well to do rich family, with lot of landed property; they seriously started pondering the possibility to exploit their late friend Das's family as their target. They thought they were entitled to get a much better deal from the risky venture after Das's death. They felt they deserve a better profit for taking a dangerous risk involving their future career and life. They went in disguise to Das's town Soro almost ten months after his demise and discretely collected on site information about his family and their social position. They found they lived a sprawling large two storied building where they stay as joint family. Das's father Biswanath Das was present eldest member. They found him to be simpleton retired as a senior school teacher. That small town being close to Bengal, majority can understand and speak Bengali language which is close to Odiya. Das's family also all the elders knew Bengali. Biswanth was considered to be gentle and un-ambitious type person with reputation of fair in his dealings. He was much respected in town. Bonamali had three younger brothers and two sisters.

They first got the full details of their property mainly rich agricultural lands and the house. Their lands were located at out skirts of the town. They also came to know the property was divided among the brothers, by Bishwonadh's father. Bishwonadh Das's one elder brother died. They had a look at the property when it was ripe with crop. They realized that the land would be easier to sell before the new crop is sown.

After another three months they arrived in Soro, in the late morning. Shoilen, as Tejuddeen Rehman, disguised as a rough Muslim elderly person and Lolit as a converted Hindu Bengali woman, who removed the burqa as soon they entered inside the compound of the Das's house. They came to town with a clear plan to implement, their well-rehearsed drama in real life!; to claim the share of property of the daughter in law of the family.

They decided to be tackle gently initially to achieve their objective. They decided to use first Mercy pleading, then demand with rude approach and make them disgusted with them. If that method also doesn't work they decided to threaten them by bring pressure from legal angle; to get the rightful share of property as legally wedded wife of late Bonamali Das. They decided to act aggressive to scare them to come to reason, by instilling fear in them.

When the entered the house, in the front room, Biswonath Das was reading a newspaper sitting on an easy chair sipping tea. His wife sat on a chair close to him talking with a young boy.

Suddenly the doorbell gave shrill ring. Both of them were stunned to see a young woman standing near the door profusely weeping. Her head was covered. She was wearing ordinary sari with no ornaments. An elderly tall stocky Muslim gentleman was behind her. He had greying beard without mustache, skullcap on the head and wearing Sherwani and with Luknovi type Churidar pyjamas. He was wearing black glasses; he looked serious and stiff.

Thus Lolita entered into the family house of late Bonamali Das, whom she married at Kolkata. Biswanath immediately recognized Lolita and her father, as he was present during marriage registration event. He invited both of them to come inside with a happy attitude. He introduced them to his wife who was looking at the most unexpected guests with surprise.

A framed photo of Bonamali Das was on the front wall with a garland. Lolita went straight to that photo and vent up her emotions of loud outburst. She was hitting her head on the wall with un-controllable grief and shedding tears profusely. The young boy in the room, rushed inside the house to inform others about the strangers. In no time all the members of the family rushed to the front room. Bonamali's mother was holding Lolita and trying to pacify her grief.

Suddenly the Tejuddeen Ahmed addressed Biswanth with angry tone in rough booming voice. "Your son has ruined my daughter's life. He left Kolkata without informing his wife whom he converted to Hindu and married her. He sent her to my house and left Kolkata without informing to her or to me! . . . He cleared his house resigned his job and left the city. He never responded to her phone calls. He gave only one call from here to tell that he would come and bring her to his house and that he fell ill . . . he requested to wait a month, for auspicious time!

. . . . after that, there were no calls from him. When we got the news of his death she fainted and fell down the steps. She was two months pregnant . . . she lost the baby and went into a coma for some days. She was unable to bear the double loss of husband as well as baby . . . She became depressed and in my age I have to witness her sorrowful life! . . . tell sir . . . . why you also never cared for your daughter in law!?"

He was unable to talk more due to emotion. He was breathing rapidly and shaking with anger.

Lolita went to him and pleaded to control. She took her water bottle and gave him a tablet from her bag. He sat on a chair and closed his eyes to take rest. She told Biswanath das in a sad voice in a feeble way that her father was a heart patient with high blood pressure. He requested him to gently pacify him. Biswanath was moved by Lolita's father's outburst. He felt real pity on both of them.

He sat near him and tried to narrate how much he tried to contact them "unfortunately my son developed Lever cancer and when he came almost serious he returned to our house. Local doctors also confirmed and we took him to Baleswar for treatment but with no luck, He lost his voice fifteen days before and staring blankly. He was not able to reveal your phone or address. He suffered a lot before death we were stunned at his untimely demise . . . . I am very sorry to hear about my daughter in law's condition and her losing our grandson. We are equally sorry for her and accept her to be with us . . . please take rest today we will talk tomorrow"

Ladies all surrounded Lolita hugging and sharing her grief. They took them inside and gave her a room for them to stay.

For two days they both acted with restraint and then to put up real action plan. They started the next day with a mild way with sober acting to bring them closer. Tejuddeen first raised in mild way pleading that they must be considerate to their daughter-in-law by giving her husband's share of the property as she was legally entitled.

Biswanath as well his brothers went inside and talked over. They came out and said that that was reasonable and in future he would divide his property to his children and Bonomali's share would go to his wife only.

Tejuddeen spoke bluntly rejecting future division. He said that she may not like to stay here as she never lived before as you seemed intentionally avoided her to contact after Bonamali's death.

"Because you also never wanted her . . . and really never accepted her to be your daughter in law as she was a Muslim by birth. I will know she would never be accepted in future also . . . I fear to leave my daughter alone here as she might be insulted and work as house-maid with no respect . . . My innocent daughter would treated as an out caste . . . . I cannot believe your sweet talk now . . . you may force her to run away from here. Sorry Mister Biswanadh I do not agree for that proposal."

Biswanadh pleaded sincerely that his family is not such crude character heartless persons to insult their eldest son's wife or drive away he said we would give respect to her as the eldest daughter in law of the house.

He further added.

"I sincerely promise you Tejuddeen saab we respect you and we will never ill-treat her because of her former religion, I personally have no objection even if he married a girl of different faith . . . We respect both of you and consider you as my close relatives . . . please do not imagine that we are anti-Muslim and insult her . . . I take oath on God Jagannadh to treat her as part of the family."

"Ha Ha . . . . Dont imagine us to be illiterate dumb heads! . . . . I do not believe you and all your family members . . . . Your son ran away with least concern to his loved wife . . . quietly ran away from Kolkata even a day before his departure he never revealed about his illness or going away permanently from Kolkata keeping secret to himself! . . . . A person who was in love with my daughter for more than a year . . . . just deserted her after enjoying her! . . . in spite of her pregnancy, which he also knew . . . . ah! do you expect us to believe your family that you would treat her as an equal and respect her as a senior daughter-in-law! . . . Biswanadh ji . . . . let us separate in good terms and give her share which as your eldest son's wife . . . . she legally entitled . . . that is my earnest request"

Biswanadh was silent for some time and requested him time to resolve with his family's consent. He felt it is difficult to convince him and was in deep distress as he could understand that what was done by his son is inexcusable . . . he felt his son might not have been knowing the seriousness of his illness at the time of the marriage but became panicky and unable to think what was right, when faced with stark reality.

He was genuinely sympathetic to his daughter-in-law, but thought with little peaceful atmosphere and exposure to the good natured family might bring change in the thinking of her. He thought she could defy her father in marrying Bonomali, and if she feels staying in family would be better for her, she might convince her father and remain as part of the family.

He decided to postpone the discussion by keeping the Lolita and her father, in good humor and diverting them with nice general talks and treating them with nice hospitality.

Shoilen and Lolit could understand the thinking of the old man and his family. Both of them thought over to act fast to bring them to accept their demand. They decided to be on the offensive with aggressive attitude and crude behavior. They knew Biswanadh's family would be shocked and get fed-up and accept to their terms. Shoilen as Tejuddeen decided to shift to a hotel to stay and Lolit as Lolita to remain in the house. Their plan was, to frighten them as well make them to hate their daughter in law. They decided secretly plan and review the strategy in the privacy of Shoilen's room in the hotel. Their sole aim was to forcibly squeeze good chunk of money as the share of Bonomali and quit for good.

Next day, the family was busy and ladies commenced to do puja blowing a conch shell, after bathing and wearing fresh Saries.

In an adjoining room, Shoilen, acting as a pious Muslim put on loudly a recorded Moulvi's prayer in

Arabic, spread a small mat and putting a scull-cap began to do various Namaj rituals mumbling within. Lolita did not do prayer acting but sat nearby covering her head, and requested everyone in that room to be quiet!. All were attracted by the loud recorded prayer rendering, went to the hall where he was praying; all were stunned at the scene!. Biswanadh putting on a finger near the nose silently warned his family to be quiet. He sat in the room calmly but respectfully remained watching Tejuddeen. Others elders left that room fuming within, unable to digest, that scene.

When Shoilen was offered the breakfast in the drawing room, he refused to take alone; Biswanadh sat there and took with him, even though he was to go to the temple and take after that. To please him, Biswanadh praised Tejuddeen for his devotion to offer prayers so sincerely. He respectfully told him that there was a mosque close by where he might offer his prayers amid people of his faith. Tejuddeen was furious at his suggestion, he shouted at him in an angry tone "You want me to get out of this house!. Is that the way to treat your Sambhandee! . . . . I know you all hate me and my daughter . . . . you cannot even tolerate my devotional prayer in your house how badly you disrespect me on the second day itself of my stay in your house!"

"Sir please do not misunderstand me . . . . We have no objection to your offering prayer in our house . . . As a teacher I always treated equally all students irrespective of their religion or language . . . If teachers and professors have biased views about persons of other regions or faiths . . . then they don't deserve to be in the noble teaching profession . . . In real life also I follow same principles . . . kindly excuse me for my suggestion. I told only for your own convenience but not to discourage you . . . please continue to pray whenever required by you . . . treat this house as yours sir"

Shoilen felt ashamed of his own acting of exhibiting bad manners before Bonomali's father, who seemed to be a thorough gentleman; but he did not show it, as he was a matured actor and just as on stage he must live in the role of angry Tejuddeen's character.

"Mister Bishwanadh I was also present when my daughter and your son got married at Kolkata . . . I could feel how unhappy you were at that time . . . and did not bring your wife or other close relatives . . . . but you are talking as an idealist!"

Bishwanadh felt upset at his remarks. But coolly he told in a mild voice "Sir! Unfortunately you were not knowing the back ground . . . I was unhappy for his marriage for some other reason . . . He was to marry another girl to whom we arranged betrothed in his childhood . . . I agree it was wrong on my part to decide his marriage when he was a boy . . . we have some deep family traditions of my caste and community, which now I feel it was incorrect . . . we discontinued that old traditions now . . . also unfortunately my son urgently called me without telling about the wedding . . . due to that reason my wife or other relations did not come . . . . Now we all fully accepted his choice of his bride . . . unfortunately he left this world at his young age . . . but we honor his decision we accepted your daughter as our true Bahu . . . sir please do not misapprehensions about us in this regard, we will treat her as our daughter"

Suddenly there was a shouting from adjoining inside room. Lolita's loud out bursts were audible!. There she was, it seemed, objecting to one of the ladies who did not offer Puja Sindhur kunkum and other offerings to her as she being a widow. Lolita was upset at neglecting her and raised a ruckus. All the ladies were shocked at her loud outburst before her mother in law in a most indecent language. Lolit also started to act his role to misbehave with the family!.

Bishwanadh went there hurriedly to inquire the cause. All the ladies covered their heads with respect, but Lolita least cared for him and continued her onslaught increasing her voice, shouting in fast spoken Bengali.

He reached near her and pacified her with kind voice and told her "Bodo Bohu! (Elder daughter in law) please forgive them who neglected out of ignorance . . . If you feel sad my son's soul would be unhappy . . . everything would be done as per your wish as you are still new some ladies are not that intelligent but followed old customs . . . I promise you will not be disrespected. In future you gradually control our house affairs . . . I treat you as my daughter"

Lolita left that room with angry face and went to her room bolted the door and sobbing loudly. Bishwanadh went to the door and pacified in a humble way as he was upset at her sobbing. He silently called his wife to request her to come out. She also requested her to come out and forget this minor incident.

After much persuasion she came out and defiantly went and stood near a window with down cast head, still sobbing.

The lady who did not offer Sindhur earlier to her, came near her, with a genuine respect to apologize; she bent and touched her feet with respect and asked her to forgive her. Lolit saw her attractive face and beautiful feminine body; he was immediately drawn to her delicate charm!. For a moment forgot his role and stared at her with passion!!. She was very fair young woman with big nice eyes bouncy cheeks and youthful attraction; she looked innocent and was upset for her fault. He felt sorry at shouting at such charming damsel. Lolit could not take away his eyes from her and affectionately took her close to him with affection. That lady put her head resting on Lolit's shoulder and requested her to forgive her. He could not resist that inward temptation to be close with her. She was Sunonda, wife of Bonomali's cousin. He benevolently put arm around her and took her close to his body expressed more emotion by taking closer tightly and hysterically shedding tears with feeling. Luckily Shoilen did not see Lolit's unexpected close encounter with a young beautiful woman!.

Bishwanadh called his wife to another room and quietly explained to her as she was not originally Hindu woman but was converted later before the wedding she would not be knowing our old customs about widows. Muslims respect their widows in the same way as married ladies and they do not follow different rules. Poor young woman never lived with us earlier, doesn't know Hindu customs and the bad way we treat our widows. She felt we were insulting her, I cannot see her to live like a widow in our house . . . please consider her also as married woman, tell other ladies also my decision. Let us follow exception to our elder Bohu, I sincerely feel no god will punish us for treating a widow in par with a married woman. Madam please try to understand me and let us keep our Bohu in a good mood as a married woman only. May be in future she might accept our age old customs but for now let us forget the old traditions."

His wife was also a broad minded lady and sincerely felt that her husband's decision cannot be wrong and she always accepted his radical views without any reservations. She also understood why Lolita felt grieved. She went and put little Sinduur on the top of her forehead in spite of protestation from Lolita. Other ladies were stunned at her act but no one showed any negative thoughts, in that joint-family they all respected elderly head couple.

*   *   *

A plate with breakfast was arranged for Tejuddeen in the drawing room. Bishwanadh humbly requested him to kindly accept their hospitality even the food may not be as good as in Kolkata. The Break-fast consisted of Singaras, some puffed rice with curd and rosagullas. Shoilen ate them with distasteful face as if he was consuming cheap quality food. He hardly took little part and washed his hands.

After the breakfast he again reminded Bishwanadh about the family's decision regarding handing over Bonomali's share, to his wife. Bishwanadh said with smiling face:

"Sir! . . . please forget that for some days, I am yet to discuss with my family, we are very fortunate to get a well-educated nice girl . . . your daughter. We beg you to let her live with us some days and make our house atmosphere more cultured . . . please sir"

"You and your family are real crooked . . . you seemed to be experts to eliminate us . . . keeping us in good humor with your soft exterior! . . . I am not impressed at your false acting to be pious with ulterior motives!"

Shoilen shouted with loud outburst least caring for the senior person's feelings.

He immediately rushed out with angry treading went outside to the road, without giving opportunity for him to reply even. Biswanadh also rushed out to pacify him but by the time he reached near the gate Tejuddeen was much ahead without looking back. Bishwanadh resisted going after him lest he would make scene on the road.

Shoilen, as Tejuddeen, first went and reserved a room in a hotel, as he decided to stay away from Bishwanadh's house. After having some breakfast in that hotel, he went to the local court to get to know a good Bengali lawyer if available. Luckily he could locate one person, by name Pijush Mukherji, to plead for Lolita. He made an appointment with that youngish looking Vakil who was having his consulting chamber, close to the local court, in his residence. He requested for an appointment to meet with his daughter in the afternoon. He finished lunch also after going in Riksha around the town to kill time.

When he returned late, everyone in the family finished the lunch. Only Bishwanadh was waiting for him to take food with him. As soon he entered the old man received him with a happy smile and asked him whether he had gone to see any friend or the town. He also requested him to come to the dining room for lunch, as it was late. Shoilen told in a curt way that he had already finished lunch after Namaj in a mosque he would like to rest. He went to his room without caring for him.

There after closing the door, he and Lolit secretly talked in a low voice, about their program. Lolit smilingly said that he made another fighting scene in his absence with another lady and threw some vessels and broke some cups etc., He said laughingly that the family were scared of him and avoiding even coming close to him. He said he did not spare Bonamali's father also after coming to front room and not finding him.

"I asked him about you he was stammering for reply in a tensed way and said he did not know where you went . . . I daunted him loudly for allowing you to go away alone in this strange town. And I continued to shouting going in inside"

Both silently laughed for their good starting to make Bonomali's family life miserable.

Shoilen had met a good advocate specializing in criminal cases at Kolkata, before coming to Soro. He discussed the legal aspect to fight justice for a known young widow deserted by the husband's family, in Odisha. He paid his fees and got the main points all well written quoting the concerned Indian Penal Code sections, to fight the case, to get her husband's share of properties.

Both went in the afternoon, hiring a Cycle-Riksha after coming some distance from the house, Lolit came out wearing a black burqa not to attract locals of the small town. When they went inside the house, he removed the Burqa dressed like a widow in a simple way. Yet he put on the makeup to attract the young lawyer. Many were staring at them being a small town. They thought some guests of local Muslim community came to their town. Even after covering the head, Lolit was looking like a very good looking woman with his makep!.

*   *   *

CHAPTER 3

*Lolita decides to seek legal aid to
get her share of property!*

When Lolit and Shoilen reached Lawyer Pijush's house, there was a small room near the entrance verandah where an old clerk was sitting reading some Odiya magazine. He quickly put the magazine in the desk. That room was made part of the wide verandah with wooden benches. The Lawyer's old clerk sitting on a Dari on the floor, he had an old type of a small floor desk in front of room. He looked at them above his reading glasses, which were at the lower part of his nose. He greeted Shoilen respectfully, and rose and took them to layer's room, and went back to his room. Pijush Mukherji's consulting room was the front room of the house. When Shoilen and Lolit went to him as Tejuddeen Rehman and Lolita, he was alone sitting behind a huge old table, reading a book. There were old book shelves behind him with bound law books.

He had a table top computer on a side table. He had a landline phone and a writing pad on the table. It was neatly kept office to give confidence. When they both entered Pijush found a young very good looking woman in white Sari, with no ornaments. Her eyes were red with continuous weeping. She was still in tears and rested her head on her father with emotion. Pijush greeted Tejuddeen Rehman and Lolita respectfully, and made them sit in the visitors' chairs facing him. He was attracted at Lolita's beauty; he felt sympathetic seeing her misery. Tejuddeen told him in low voice that he requires complete privacy to discuss some confidential matters, he said that he would like no one disturbs them or over hears them talking, as some of his clients might suddenly come. He spoke in Bengali. Pijush understood his request.

He told his clerk to keep any clients in his room only till his job finishes with the new clients. He went in, and came after five minutes and escorted them inside his home.

One elderly woman standing near a dining table welcomed them with greeting. He introduced to his mother to his and clients. Lolita still silently weeping went and touched the elder woman's feet with respect. She lifted her tenderly and advised her to face the problems boldly, seeing her in deep despair.

Pijush told his mother said not to tell anybody about his clients and request them to wait outside if any one comes to meet him. He took them to his younger sister's study room and closed the door. He made them sit in two chairs and he sat in another chair facing.

"Mister Pijush do you know Mister Bishwonadh Das, ex teacher retired as a head master of this town?"

"yes very much . . . I studied under him in the school . . . a very nice noble person"

"Are you his lawyer also?"

"No I am a junior in this profession . . . but I never saw him in the court premises. I don't think he had any legal problems, more over I am taking up criminal cases only as such I never met him on law matters . . . why you are asking about him?"

"We are from Kolkata, she is my daughter Fairooja now her present name is Lolita, she is daughter-in-law of Bishwanadh Das, wife of his late son Bonomali Das"

Pijush was visibly surprised hearing about their relationship with his old teacher.

"I never knew his son was married! I attended the last day rites, and offered my condolences; Bonomali was much senior to me and did his college studies in Kolkata. But it was real surprise to hear this news . . . I am so sorry for you madam . . . when was the marriage took place? . . . I do not think anyone knew about the wedding, as this is small town such functions would have been known"

"It is unfortunate sad story . . . . my daughter and Bonomali Das knew each other since a year before the wedding, she defied my advice and converted as Hindu to marry him. It was a registered marriage, took place at Kolkata a year back. Bishwonath Das came to the wedding and also signed as a witness . . . Unfortunately Bonomali came to know he had Cancer and my daughter became a widow within two months after the wedding. It was tragic affair for her in her young age"

"I am so sorry to hear that . . . now what is the legal problem?"

"See I am a middle class man with simple means . . . I wanted my daughter should get the rightful Bonomali's share of the property, so that she can live independently and respectfully at Kolkata . . . as her life is ruined"

"I see . . . so you want to file a case to get her husband's property? . . . sir it is a civil case I generally don't take up such cases . . . added to that he might engage a senior lawyer . . . and the case would go for years . . . I am honestly asking . . . are you prepared for such problems?"

"Mister Pijush I want to fight this on criminal grounds . . . I want to file a case under harassment and mental torcher . . . which is being faced by my daughter in her in-laws' house . . . they do not want her being a born Muslim and they never were happy with their son's choice . . . She is facing hell . . . they don't even feed her in the house with other ladies and give her food on back verandah as if she is their maid-servant! . . . both of us are living like beggars . . . at their mercy . . . we pleaded since months to give her share . . . they did not even informed about her husband's death before . . . even she could not see her husband in his last days even . . . They just wish to disown her and throw her out . . ."

He was suddenly became emotional and uttered crude words denouncing with vengeance.

As he was gasping for breath due to sudden over stress the daughter pacified him and requested Pijush to get a glass of water, rubbing her father's back gently and advising him to be calm for some time. Pijush went in and came fast with a glass of water. He told him to take some rest on the bed till he was alright.

"Yes Baba please take some rest . . . I will talk with our good lawyer"

Pijush was pleased at her words.

As Shoilen silently went to take some rest. Lolit as Lolita sat much closer to him and resumed their proposal to in a weak whispering way. He forgot to close the door when he went to fetch water. When she moved close to him to talk, he quickly rose closed the door. She smiled and asked whether he is married. He shyly replied "No madam I am a bachelor . . . I am the only son and took up my late father's profession . . . as we have land and properties I did not choose to practice in bigger towns . . . we are settled here since many years. My sister is studying in a college now not in the house"

"Pijush Moshai . . . as we are desperate our main plan now is we wish to engage you as my lawyer . . . first with your assistance I wish to file a F.I.R (First Information Report) case in the local police station . . . against my father in law, mother in law, and some other close relatives . . . . You see we consulted a senior criminal lawyer at Kolkata . . . he said we have to make my appeal on IPC 498-A . . . . which deals harassment of daughter in law by husband his parents and relatives."

She took out 10,000 Rupees as advance to help them and to meet connected expenses for court and police station and others . . . . She gave copy of Kolkata Advocate's complete guidance draft.

Being a small town lawyer, he was pleasantly surprised to see a big amount as the advance fees. He never got such a chunk of money in his the cases he dealt. Suddenly he felt a pang of pity on his nice old teacher, whom he liked him during school studies . . . he really felt whether he should fight against such a nice gentleman.

She said in a respectful way not to hurt his feelings,

"Pijush Moshai! . . . I was told by our Kolkata advocate about this IPC Number Four Hundred Ninety Eight A, passed by Government of India, to aid, helplessly harassed married women by husband or in laws and other relatives. He told me an FIR in the police station, would be even sufficient to file a criminal case against the in-laws and others in case woman is being harassed I am sorry I need not tell you as you are in the profession . . . you must be knowing fully about this penal code . . . My Advocate asked me to refer Google search to get information . . . in the Internet . . . regarding I.P.C section 498A. That's how I got some clear knowledge on this and . . . I do not want to go to court . . . but they are trying to ignore me and trying to drive me away ruthlessly . . . even though I was married to Bonamali Das . . . here is the copy of my marriage registration . . . as the wedding was done in Registration of Assurances office at Kolkata. I want my rightful share of the property as the daughter in law"

She gave him a copy of the marriage certificate. The young lawyer had a quick glance at the certificate. She gave also the draft given by her Kolkata advocate. He quickly went through the draft and understood the serious allegations, and complaint mainly quoting Section 498A of IPC. He could understand the implications if a case is filed against his respected noble teacher Bishwanadh Das. He then looked serious and nervous to fight a case against him but tried to suppress his feelings. He was it seemed undecided whether to take up the case.

Seeing his indecisive face Lolita could understand his dilemma being young and a disciple of Bishwanadh! . . . . and fight a case on her behalf with a good old teacher might be bothering. She gently held his hand:

"are you undecided to take up or not? In that case we may have to go to some other lawyer. But sincerely I request you not to miss this case and lose that money which may go to some another lawyer . . . because you can file a suit copying in Toto of that draft . . . it would be bit helpful to you".

He smiled and said "let me study and decide if you don't mind"

Suddenly her father got up and intervened.

"Sorry Pijush ji . . . They are confidential matters . . . we got from a popular advocate . . . your job is very much simplified . . . after FIR complaint is written in police as per the draft it will be referred to the court and court is bound to issue non-bail-able arrest warrant against Sala!. Bhishwanadh and his rogue family. We will have to influence the police officer to bring the offenders to the police station and later they would be arrested and sent to jail . . . . Those dirty persons deserve to be punished for harassing my daughter".

The young advocate was visibly shaken. He knew the same procedure would be followed and poor great man and family who is respected in this small town would face a shameful humiliation. Whole town would be sympathetic to him as he is well respected citizen. He may be noble but his family might be crude and hated the innocent daughter-in-law.

As Tejuddeen getting restless with that inexperienced lawyer, Lolita understood the situation suddenly as if a new idea came as flash!. She requested Pijush to leave the room for few minutes to privately talk with her father action to be considered and if he agrees she would discuss.

Pijush also felt a relief for the break as he was still in a dilemma!.

He understood if he takes up the case he may become popular and more cases likely to knock his door, but in the small town he would be seen as villain and public may hate him for putting a great person Bhishwanadh and his family in the jail. That matter weighed more in his thoughts; he also has a genuine respect to his good teacher.

Father daughter (Shoilen and Lolit) discussed something for almost ten minutes then called Pijush.

Tejuddeen sat on the cot looking undecided, but his daughter looked she made up some her mind for some action. She requested him to kindly close the door and listen. She sat still close to him and said in sorrowful at the same time with some determination.

"Pijush! Basically I respect Bishwonadh, he seemed kind hearted but rest of his family members were very rude with me and treating me with hatred! . . . I found it would very difficult for me to live in such environment . . . my life would be doomed . . . why should I suffer . . . because me and their son fell in love and married?! . . . . do not know why my fate is tied to such family who all hate my very presence, forgetting I have lost my future by loving nice Bonomali, I still do not regret marrying him he was really a good hearted person. But I never expected his family look upon me as some bad omen for his death, which really upset me . . . I want to live independently still as his wife only. I want some justice to live decently in future. I am against taking hasty legal action to trouble them . . . I still feel some compromise solution could be there and I wish to try that also, I found my father-in-law is more matured and may consider my appeal . . . . But If we fail . . . legal redress may be the only solution. I found if we go to some other lawyer they would encourage me only to fight legal battle . . . but I could see your reaction and respect to your old teacher . . . I feel you have still reservation to drag him to face the humiliation of police . . . courts . . . jail atmosphere. You could act as a goodwill messenger and first try to bring some reality what might happen and way to avoid. I request you to keep my name out of this as if I you are doing this on your own consciousness"

They had a long closed door discussions of their plan of action. Pijush not only agreed but appreciated the positive approach considered by Lolita with maturity. Tejuddeen did not participate but listening with a disgusted pessimism. Pijush wrote down systematically and assured her to do his part sincerely. He accepted the advance amount. The action was to be initiated after four days.

Tejuddeen told Bishwonadh, when they reached his house, from lawyer's house, that he would be shifting to a hotel; but his daughter would continue to stay with them. He pleaded sincerely not to shift, but of no avail.

From that day the offence started in real crude way. Lolita made the family shudder with fright the way she used to brawl for any reason, finding fault with someone or other. She did not spare even elders. She would never cover the head unless some out-siders come to house. Even with them she used answer curtly and used to ill-treat the family in front of them. She would ridicule whatever food or snacks prepared by the family. She used to beat young boys or girls, for minor incidents. She would throw any article in hand if she was in foul mood. Tejuddeen would visit some odd times but never used to take any food or tea. He would daily rake up the issue of handing over their son's share of property to his daughter. He would loudly shout in the front room with male members while Lolita would start crying loudly as if she was having a great pain or facing a new calamity!. Calmness or joy had gone from their house, since Lolita's arrival in their house!. All the

ladies used to leave the room to some other room to avoid her.

One night, Bishwonadh's wife, unable to face the daily chaos caused by her daughter-in-law, she burst into tears before her husband in the bedroom. He was also was getting upset and did not know how to tackle her uncouth behavior, in spite of her education, but he thought this was due to her father's upbringing. He could not imagine a city-bred young woman could be so nasty like an illiterate slum-dweller brawling women!. He found she doesn't even observe basic modesty or manners of a house lady. He felt nervous and unable to see any solution to tackle her daily onslaught on all at any time; if she remains in the house permanently it would be real hell!. He felt she must have trapped her son and must have black mailed to marry her. He was upset to see his very gentle and kind hearted wife also bursting into tears. He really felt deeply distressed and depressed.

Just at that time his phone rang. He gently lifted and said his name. Other side it was his old school student Pijush Mukherji, now practicing as a lawyer, taking over his late father's practice. He was very anxious to talk to him in spite of a very odd time!. He seemed to be in distress and wanted to meet him next day morning in privacy. His request surprised him as he was not that intimate, being much senior in age, to hear his personal problems. He always used to greet him with respect like all other ex-students, if by chance come across him in the town. When he invited him to come to his house, he requested for some other place. He himself suggested a place and time. He accepted and was surprised at his strange choice. Many people in that town come to him for advice as such he felt he must be having some personal problem. Strangely he requested him not to reveal his name to anyone in the house also. He did not tell about him when his wife asked about the phone call. He just avoided to tell her but became thoughtful.

As usual in the early morning, he went for morning walk to his usual place, a public park. As he started to walk briskly, suddenly, Pijush came in front of him and respectfully touched his feet. Both went to an isolated corner, sat on a park bench.

Pijush directly came to the point, after few general topics, after seeing no other person was in the vicinity.

"Sir!. I am in a deep dilemma, as I am unexpectedly accepted to take up to file a criminal case two days back for a young woman, latter I was shocked to know that my client was your daughter-in-law, Lolita Devi, wife of Bonomali babu"

Bishwonadh also was stunned at his revelation. He stared at him in an unbelievable shock. He just stammered:

"What my daughter in law approached you to file a case against me?"

"Yes sir, it looks she consulted a senior advocate at Kolkata and on his advice she is going to lodge a F.I.R. in police station based on Indian Penal code No. 498-A and few others . . . It is a dangerous clause and mandatory for the police to take up and the court also have to issue non-bail-able arrest warrant against you, your wife, and all your brothers and their wives . . . you may get bail after two days after depositing heavy amount and two sureties for each individual you have to report every month to police station as long as the case hearing goes on. Sir, even if I refuse to accept other lawyers may agree . . . that's why I wanted to contact you secretly and warn you . . . sorry sir . . . but it is a dangerous clause to help wives and daughter in laws against harassment of husband or in laws".

Bishwonadh was stunned beyond perception he became suddenly weak and felt a dizzy with a feeling of extreme fear!

He remained speechless for some seconds unable to digest at the dangerous situation he and his family going to face!.

"Oh God Jogannadho! . . . what sin I made to see such miseries! . . . son Pijush! I am extremely thankful to you for your early warning . . . but can we come out of this peril?"

"Yes sir! . . . even if you engage a good lawyer to defend you, you may come out free . . . but it may take months or few years . . . but initial damage of getting arrested cannot be avoided . . . This particular IPC has done havoc in many innocent families all over India . . . even high dignitaries or top officers were arrested if their wives or daughter in laws lodge cases on this dangerous legal clause!. I am not exaggerating but telling you the reality . . . you may inquire some senior lawyer also not informing your present situation as you are about to face . . . you cannot do anything except come to compromise before with her in a tactful way . . . . as if you decided to help her and lead her own life . . . Sir she and her father want your son's share of your property . . . since she is a legal heir please put a condition to give it writing that in future she should not claim any more as if detaching relationship for ever . . . . Sir . . . they will demand that if they file a case . . . You might consult an experienced lawyer or advocate . . . unfortunately you cannot apply for pre arrest bail in this case with no ground or reason . . . Sir, I advise you not to delay but please act courageously . . . . I am sorry sir. I disturbed you late in the night and this morning . . . but I was feeling restless as I have highest respect to you and your noble guidance"

"No Pijush I am extremely lucky to have such nice student like you. I am very thankful to you . . . you did a great help to me by pre-warning"

"Sir my sincere advise to you is discuss with your brothers without involving women . . . they may not understand and get scary, Please explain secretly about the IPC 498-A . . . . kindly do not quote my name as it will not help you in any way . . . but she might go to another lawyer . . . if she gets suspicious . . . please try to understand me . . . I am telling in your interest . . . discuss compromise with her only . . . her father looks unreasonable and greedy . . . but she might agree than go to court . . . which may or may not bring desired results at an early date . . . these cases drag for two to three years . . . . inconvenient to her also"

"Pijush! I am really impressed at your very mature advice young man!. It was indeed great help to our family which I will always remember . . . you showed me really very practical way to come out of this danger! . . . god bless you . . . you will have a great future!"

They both rose to go out separately . . . . suddenly the old man had a doubt-

"Dear Pijush . . . I will be able to demark the agricultural land . . . but is it necessary to give a share of the common house also? . . . it will pose many problems!"

"Sir . . . don't raise that problem unless she asks . . . As you are going to offer your son's share of landed property . . . with no knowledge about her proposed case . . . explain the practical problem of partitioning of the house . . . . only if she asks . . . . please take early action . . . I will delay another four days to help you . . . . all the best sir"

Bishwonadh felt much relieved . . . All the family were vexed with his daughter in law added to that he felt it would be disastrous to all of them if Lolita decides to take the dangerous step to go to the court!. He shuddered at her cruel method to punish them . . . and send them behind bars in a jail! He became panicky and sat for something with a heavy heart. He never faced in his life such a calamity . . . He could see his serious pupil Pijush also was shaken and could not see him straight in face feeling for his grievous affliction. He decided to follow Pijush's advice. As she has a right to her husband's property he felt it is his moral duty to hand over.

Bishwondh, had a little doubt whether the junior lawyer was real or exaggerating about I.P.C. 498-A, which was the main Clause Lolita got complaint draft made by a senior advocate, at Kolkata. He sent one of his nephews to make discreet enquires to Baleshwar city court to meet some senior lawyers. He got confirmation tallying what Pijush explained, the danger of that clause. Bishwonadh then made up his mind. He also imagined that many might believe the complaint by Lolita might be true, as he never revealed about the marriage of his son in Kolkata. Lolita's and her father's wild behavior also made him to hasten his final decision. Bishwonadh feared that crude Tejuddeen Rehman might even start make a scene in the town by his loud and crude booming voice also, shouting that injustice being done to his daughter!.

He decided to make truce with his daughter-in-law, as recommended by Pijush, He understood it would be better to hand over her share of the property. In the evening he separately told his wife to send Lolita to the terrace alone, as he wished to talk to her and to chide her to improve her attitude. He did not show any sign of annoyance or anger, when she came to meet him.

He spoke with her calmly with dignity. He explained he sincerely wanted her to stay with them, as en educated elder daughter-in-law, to bring culture and enlightenment to the family and also felt it would bring peace to her as a change from hectic Kolkata life. He said that he could understand that she was not happy to live in the present surroundings, which he realized it did not work in his expected way. He said he decided to make her live anywhere way she likes. He said that he never wanted to make her unhappy by forcefully keeping in their house, as such he decided to handover her share of property as desired by her. He clearly explained how much land he owns of which the rightful share of Bonomali would be handed to her. He told he would get the partition deed would be made in her name truly and said that it is up to her to keep that land or sell it. He promised to call his lawyer to draft the gift deed, in her name, and get it registered. He also offered to help her to sell out that land to a party, and get cash payment to her directly. Lolit was overwhelmed at the sudden turn of events in their favor!. As Lolita she mildly thanked him and said that she would consult her father and tell him the two alternatives. Bishwonadh said in clear terms with a firm note, that he does not wish to talk with her father in this matter and said only she should decide and participate as his daughter-in-law, also assured he would not try to deceive her. Lolita stared at him and understood his determination. She respectfully touched his feet with reverence; she informed him sincerely, that she understood him and would not allow her father to interfere any more in her family affair. She only requested for an early action. She listened to him in a satisfied good mood. He said with a smile to inform her father tactfully, so that he would not feel upset, and peacefully agree. Lolita smiled and said she knew how to tackle him, and assured him that she would see that he does not come to argue any more.

With slight hesitation he mildly told her that his lawyer recommended a written assurance signed before witnesses that she would not claim any more in future and would not demand or visit, to avoid future revoking. He said that since he (Bishwonadh) is old, he recommended that action.

Surprisingly Lolita laughed and said, she would sign that without any reservations, once her property share is received by her. She assured him she would never be so heartless to come to claim more with greed. She thanked him for his kindness to understand her sincere justified request and decided to handover her share. She also requested that she would prefer sale transaction was also done by him as she would be able to manage on her own. Bishwonadh was surprised when she discretely told him not to inform any others including her father, the value of the transaction, but hand-over the amount in cash only and not by bank draft. She said she would believe him and clearly emphasized her full confidence with him. She left him in a happy mood.

Bishwonadh heaved a sigh of relief and continued to sit in a chair remained pondering his next action.

Lolita reached quietly and was going to her room, seeing her mother-in-law, she respectfully smiled at her and unexpectedly told her, that she would like to accompany her when she goes to the temple later. The old lady was pleasantly surprised to see some change in Lolita, her head was still covered and observed there was a gleam of joy in her eyes!. She went up to the terrace to meet her husband. He told his wife with a serious note that he decided to hand over Lolita their son's share of property and for that purpose he called her to speak in privacy. He did not tell the dangerous legal problem, Lolita was contemplating, against their family. His wife responded with relief, it is a good decision, and said that she was praying god daily that peace to return to the house. She fully appreciated her husband's good decision.

Later, sitting in the drawing room he saw through window and found Lolita was sitting in the garden swing with Sunonda and happily chit chatting with her. Both were in happy mood and behaving like real sisters, Sunonda was telling some interesting topic and Lolita was holding her hand and responding with joy, laughing merrily!. They were slowly swinging in a happy way!. He heaved a sigh of relief at the change in her. Lolita over-heard Bishwanadh telling his nephew to request his lawyer to come and meet him next day.

That caused unexpected joy to Lolit, as Lolita he plucked a Rose flower and tenderly tried to insert it in Sunonda's hair. She happily was about to say something in good humor, but seeing their father-in-law, Sunonda covered her head, and found Lolita also did the same and held her hand and led her to the house.

Next day Lolita respectfully informed Bishwanadh's wife that she wished to go to the hotel to meet her father and asked her permission to have lunch with him there and requested not to wait for her. The good lady smilingly accepted and told her to return early after lunch. Other ladies were surprised at her unexpected change of modest behavior!. Earlier she never cared to ask her mother in law whenever or where ever she went out. That day she seemed was in good mood and did not misbehave or raise her voice against any one!.

Shoilen and Lolit were extremely happy at the sudden turn of events in their favor; they joyfully realized that their young lawyer Pijush, did his job well as prompted by Lolit. Shoilen laughingly said, that their gamble to pursue for these unexpected large returns really worked. He was happy that the result was much faster than they expected!.

Lolita rang up their lawyer and told that she decided to wait for another week, for her to lodge a Criminal case F.I.R. in the police station, as something positive might turn before that. The lawyer also was really happy at her decision. He only was disappointed that she did not come personally to talk with him. He was also attracted at her smartness and charm, and was waiting eagerly for her visit!.

He tried in vain to discuss the Plaint draft which he prepared for her to approve and also he was waiting to include the list of names and their relationship with Bishwondh Das. It was just an excuse to spend some time with her. Lolit pretended that if it was very urgent she would send her father. The young lawyer hurriedly told him not to send her father, as he would not understand, he said he would wait for her, and hung up.

Lolit laughingly said:

"Dada! both Bishwanadh and Pijush are scared to talk to you, you have earned such reputation"

"It is elementary my dear Watson! World loves heroines and hate villains . . . but I must congratulate you for your matured and convincing acting . . . You made us very rich now!"

"Dada I am not a heroine in this venture! . . . . I am doing the role of a vamp as directed by my villainous father! . . . . the laurels of success should go to Tejuddin Rehman only!"

He retorted laughingly!. Both were in a mirthful mood.

They celebrated that day with cool beer and nice lunch, as their venture about to end most profitably, bringing rich unexpected dividends!.

Lolit returned in the late afternoon. Before his departure, Shoilen cautioned him to be very careful and reminded him to get both time shaving, and keeping dress and makeup in good realistic form. He said he would avoid come to meet him as he cannot change attitude towards Bishwonadh so early, it might bring hurdles also to them. He cautioned that these last few days also very crucial lest they are not caught by any wrong step or cause suspicion. He said till they depart Soro, they should be fully on guard about their real identity. He hoped the transaction would be completed as early as possible. They decided to accept the option by selling the land immediately and get cash, as suggested by Bishwondh. Both felt a sigh of relief as selling of that land would be tough for them in a small town. Getting only cash was in the safe and best option. They decided to depart for Kolkata immediately bidding farewell to Soro, forever!.

Bishwanadh kept his promise, by calling the lawyer and did the necessary formalities to divide the land and to give Bonomali's share to his wife; he arranged the sale of that land to a land-lord of the adjoining property, without the hassle to make another sale deed in the name of Lolita as vendor. The sale deed completed and cash was paid some in white and some in black, the entire money was paid to Lolita. The transaction was completed within a week.

*   *   *

In an unexpected turn of events, Bishwonadh informed Lolita that Bonomali's friend Damodar Sahu was coming to his house, from his village Rupsa. He was expected to reach after a week. Lolit and Shoilen decided earlier to leave for Kolkata same day after the full money was received. But after hearing the news of visit of Damodar, both were tempted to trap him in some mischief as well squeeze an additional gain. They pondered the various possibilities and came to a conclusion to a new twist to catch him in the net with an attractive bait!. They decided to extend their stay for another week, in that period.

Shoilen decided to go to Kolkata to deposit the cash in their bank locker and come back, while Lolit as Lolita would continue to enact a new drama with Damodar Sahu!.

Bishwonadh's family were expecting that Lolita would leave Soro forever, as expected. They were restless to see that she was not making any attempt to leave them!. She continued to lead normal life in their house!. But she was in good mood behaved well with all. Yet It caused little tension to all of them, as they wanted her to be out of their house as well town, remembering her dirty behavior since she stepped in their house.

*   *   *

Except Bishwanadh, his wife and Sunonda, almost everyone in the family hated Lolita for undignified and uncouth behavior. Even, after she became subdued and tried to have normal relations with all, most of them still most avoided to talk with her. Lolita decided to give all of them some gifts before going to Kolkata, to remove their ill-feeling towards him. Lolit felt sorry for all of them, as he was only acting for success of their crooked plan! Sunonda was the only lady became close friend of Lolita. Being younger than Shoilen, for Lolit it became real problem to control his feelings since he was taken to be a woman by all the ladies and some used to come very close in the daily life. While they were informal move freely among themselves, Lolit was always on guard about his makeup and dresses, and used to move with modest way. His rough behavior as Lolita made others to be at a distance, which helped him!. He was always used to be neatly dressed and very formal. Once he was bit reckless and in a mood to smoke a cigarette to relieve his stress; unexpectedly one small girl came to the terrace at that time while he was secretly smoking!. That girl was staring with surprise, while he was looking another direction and was caught unaware. He was very wild and thrashed her for disturbing him, he severely warned her not to reveal to anyone, threatening to break her leg!. That girl timidly went down crying. Lolit knew that must have been reported by that girl. He determined to act roughly to deny if asked. But no one dared to discuss with him, and were more fearful of her!.

Bishwanadh's wife introduced to Lolita to other ladies of the big joint family, on the first day of Lolit's arrival. He touched the elders' feet with reverence. It seemed she became a darling to them. Other ladies also embraced her affectionately. Some ladies were surprised at her hard strong body like a man. (they thought Muslim young ladies have a muscular strong bodies!) Each did not reveal to others. She embraced the younger brothers of her husband also affectionately when they came to her with respect and to offer good wishes. The Bonomali's family was a simple people and they never were rude to her. They had all some reservation about her as she was from a different faith, whose customs and traditions are quite different from their conservative outlook with small town back ground. Among the ladies Lolita met Sunanda, wife of Bonomali's elder cousin brother Mayadhar. They had no children, even though they were married four years back. But his closeness to Sunonda came on the second day, when he created a noisy scene for the Sindhur issue. Sunonda felt very upset that due to her mistake Lolita felt ill-treated. She went to her to offer apology with tears and expressed at her affection and sympathy by resting her head on Lolita's shoulder and begged for excuse. When she hugged him tightly with real emotion of sorrow, Lolit was lustfully aroused with passion first time in his new role. He never felt such sexual attraction with other ladies whom he hugged earlier or his escapades in the train dramas!. He also willfully expressed his emotion with sorrowful weeping; putting his head on her shoulder and hugging more tightly with emotional acting!.

Lolit was awe struck at her beauty and attractive figure. She was a young lady of about twenty five, shorter than him with slim body and real feminine charm. He could not take of his eyes from her well-shaped body!. In spite strong effort his attention was drawn to her attractive presence!. Her every movement distracted him to control his lust!. Her face with large eyes, her slim figure with shapely body curves looked as if chiseled to perfection by a master sculptor!. He got real thrill out of this new experience. With great difficulty he could separate from her embrace and met others. He really enjoyed her close body touch and wished for more time of that joyful time.

When they whole heartedly decided for the new venture, Shoilen had strongly advised Lolit that they should observe one strict principle that they should never develop any personal or sexual relationships with women even if close contacts were unavoidable, with persons with which could bring troubles as well might expose their secret intentions. Lolit remembered his friend's advice decided to be utmost careful.

Sunanda also felt a mesmerized effect with the body touch of Lolita!. She felt a real sisterly attraction at her affectionate solace by putting her head on her shoulders with uncontrollable emotion. She felt a real sympathy towards her. She decided to be closer with her to help her to forget her grief. She was the only woman developed cordial relationship.

He also was unable to control or restraint his desire to talk and stay close to her. He was unable avoid lustfully looking at her when she was in close proximity. Sunanda liked Lolita's modern style of dresses and make-up. She was fascinated by her costly saris which Lolit used wear.

That day, after the happy news of about to get a nice chunk of cash, he was in joyful mood. He wanted to share his joy with Sunonda by generous desire to please her with some good gifts separately to her only. Lolit discretely told her when others were not in vicinity that he wished to give her some gifts which he brought from Kolkota. Sunanda whispered that she would come to her room and take them without others knowledge. She followed Lolit to his bed room and quietly bolted the door. He presented her a nice Necklace with ear-studs, nice silk Sari, and a good ladies hand bag with some perfume with facial beauty products. That Necklace was part of the loot he robed from a woman in the train. He kept that secretly, for future use without the knowledge of Shoillen.

Sunonda was visibly overwhelmed with joy, for all the costly gifts, which she never even dreamt to own. She embraced Lolita with joyful affection and whispered that how lucky she was to have such a nice elder sister. She expressed her deep sympathy for becoming a widow at a young age. Lolit enjoyed once more her embrace passionately and he also held her tightly but tried control his lust with utmost restraint!. He felt very satisfied for able make her very happy with his gifts. He developed a deep lustful desire to entice Sunonda to have still better and more intimate relationship before going back to Kolkata, and vanish.

Unexpectedly that became a reality even without his trial.

*   *   *

CHAPTER 4

Damodar Sahu falls in love with Loilita!

Damodar Sahu was returning to his small home town Rupsa, near Baleswar in Odisha; Bidding farewell to Kolkata city where he lived for more than thirty years. He, was traveling in a truck, to go by road to Rupsa town of Baleswar District of Odisha. He sat in the front by the side of a known driver. He was carrying all his belongings, consisting of some old furniture, buckets and pans, house hold items and Steel trunk boxes with his clothes other old linen etc. Mainly he carefully kept his cash currency notes of his savings in big amounts, carefully concealed under old clothes and linen. Majority of articles he was bringing were collected items discarded by original owners as junk; he always lived with such items only!. He used to stay in the city in a frugal way, saving all his earnings carefully. He never believed in throwing or discarding any of his out dated articles!. He was traveling in a truck to carry his old collected belongings to live in his permanent house. He came to Kolkata when he was barely fourteen years.

Damodar lost his father when he was ten. He could not complete even his primary schooling. Unable to live in poverty, his mother sent him to Kolkata, for any small job. From that village many Odiya speaking persons used to go to earn their living.

One distant relative, who lived many years in that city, helped to get a job for Damodar, as a domestic help in a well to do family in Ballyganj. He had a hard life due to many problems he faced right from his young days. Gradually he became a cook working in rich families.

He made a vow to work hard and earn as much as possible to live a better future life. With determination and courage he strived hard to improve his sources of income. The feeling of insecurity made him to live in frugal way and learnt the way to save his meager income and depend on others for his daily living. He learnt from life the art of acting in his daily dealings with cunningly false show of humility and sincerity. He changed his jobs to get better income. He never showed any change in his daily life and always pretended to be a poor to get as much sympathy and help from generally liberal rich Bengali families.

When he was in early Twenties, through one of his employer's influence, he got a cook's assistant job in a good restaurant. With hard work and sincerity he gradually rose to higher jobs in the hotel kitchens, as he learnt the culinary art of making good dishes. He used to get more money in those new jobs beside his earning extra income by dishonesty and clever deceit. He developed the cunning ways to pilfer money and whatever he could lay hand, wherever he worked!. He developed a personal circle of sellers of vegetables, grocery, meat and fish. He would get his cut from all hotel purchases!. With his experience he could land to higher chief's position gradually in years in bigger hotels. With hard work and sincerity he gradually rose to higher jobs in the hotel-industry. By his clever maneuvers he gradually able to save much money. He started giving loans to known persons at high interest or which brought more returns. He used to recruit young men from Odisha, in various minor hotel jobs, such as kitchen helpers, cleaners, watchmen, waiters and others. As most youngsters were from humble village background they used to work very hard and sincerely. As employment opportunities were less in Odisha many educated youngsters migrate to various cities mainly to work in hotels, restaurants and private establishments. They never used to join unions or politics for fear of losing their jobs, as they used send money to family also, from their earnings. Hotel management thus used to prefer Damodar's recommended candidates, for reliability. For Him that became a big money earning racket. He would charge hefty amounts from the candidates to arrange jobs. He would ruthlessly squeeze large amounts from the desperate candidates even for small jobs. He became greedier and was avoiding going to his village fearing loss from other activities than his monthly pay.

He would give temporary shelter and left over hotel kitchen food to young recruits from Odisha charging for them also. He could purchase lands in his village and built a better house and property.

He had a very strong attachment with his mother and always used to send her money even when he was earning a small wages. His mother was happy to see her son able to become owner of a house and lands. He used to come home at least twice in a year. He married, in his late twenties, only daughter of a widow landowner and increased his holdings. He never brought his family to the big city except for occasional visits. He had only one daughter. His mother and wife used to live with his daughter in the village. After his marriage his mother in law had serious illness, depended on him. He used to collect money from her and never attempted to give her proper medical aid, even deceiving his wife. Due to lack of required medical checkups and aid treatment she died in few months. He cleverly maneuvered to get her property in his name before her death. With his cunning dishonest methods he could amass reasonably good savings!.

Tragedy first struck him with death of his wife due to improper medication in the village. He was unable to decide whether he should bring his aged mother and young daughter to Kolkata or shift to his village and start life again there.

He put his daughter in the local school. He started visiting his family more frequently. Another few years passed before he could take a decision. He finally had to bid goodbye to Kolkata when his mother became seriously ill. She hardly lived few months, after his return. He never wanted to live with his daughter in that city due to his odd timings of the hotel job.

His daughter Neelobeni alias Neelu had reached her Fifteenth year. She looked much older than her age because of her height and healthy body!. Her grandmother and her father pampered her from her childhood, over feeding her.

With good healthy developed body appearance, she also developed a domineering attitude. She became an uncontrollable child. Her father used to shower all the affection and love to his only daughter. He used to bring many good gifts and dresses whenever he used to come.

From early life she developed an attitude that others had to accept her demands reasonable or not!. She used to believe that she was always right!. She would show her violent anger if any children argued with her or disagreed with her. In the school also all her class mates including boys used to get frightened due to her loud outbursts and violent attitude!.

Even her teachers used avoid punishing her for fear of facing her anger. She has once bitten a teacher who tried to punish her for beating another child. With growing age her anger and aggressive nature increased and she became an undisputed leader of the children of her group both boys and girls!. Her father was not aware her childhood pranks and naughty nature.

Even though she was young girl no one dared to argue or fight with her. She used to hit even her teachers with stones aiming with catapult from hidden places!. She was leading undisciplined life like a tomboy.

By her rough methods and naughty behavior she became a ring leader of some mischievous boys of the village. Nobody could dare to question her misdeeds. The absence of her father most of the time in the village, grandmother's over affection made her a spoilt child.

Her grandmother never reprimanded her if others reported of her misdeeds. In her view others were all envious of her granddaughter. Not only in the school, her rowdy errands, started in the town also. Petty shop keepers, venders and fruit garden guards have also faced her wrath when they tried to argue with her or challenge her.

Her band of followers would make their life miserable.

In spite of her young age she became notorious in their neighborhood. She would challenge any person, who tried to scold her or argue with her. She would use foul language with loud voice, inappropriate for a girl of young age!. After school hours she and her followers used to meet regularly in the out skirts, to plan their misdeeds and mischief. They all started enjoying the roguish way of childhood adventures!. All had cycles and used to roam freely. Neelu's sena (group) were being seen with fear by many a person in the village.

When a Circus company put-up tents in a town close to her village she visited to see that show with her friends. She was immensely thrilled and attracted to that interesting circus stars' performances. She liked the daring feats by the show artists, the trapeze artists one wheel cycling, horse shows, acrobat feats at high level, breath taking show jumps from roof tops and similar other attractions of the circus show.

She became very fascinated and used go three or four times in every week. She came to know that two Odiya speaking girls worked in the Circus Company. She made acquaintance with them with sweets and other presents.

Even though they were much elder to her, they overestimated her age by her looks. She used to meet them in their accommodation in small tent. She was thrilled to see their life of adventure and applauses from the audience. After closing of the shows the Circus company was winding up to go to another town. Both the ladies accepted her invitation to visit her home which was only half hour journey from the town. She treated them with sweets and homely food. Secretly she disclosed her ambition to join the circus company and wanted to know how it can be achieved. The ladies wanted to discourage her considering the hard life they had face daily with meager salaries and bonded type of work schedules.

She offered them two thousand rupees from her secret private savings for their help and agreed to give more after she gets a chance. Seeing her over eagerness they also tried to hook her. They took her to their boss for arranging for a job in the circus.

She gave that man also another three thousand for help. That person was impressed by the girl for her bold looks with tall well-built body. He felt she has an appealing personality to act in the circus. He also informed that she can be offered a job with the approval of her father if she is less than eighteen. She bluffed that her age will be eighteen by next year. He gave a printed form where in if the father signs, along with two witnesses signatures, she would be offered a job in their company. He promised to be in contact with her regularly, and gave her his cell phone number. He informed her she would have to deposit few thousands, if she joins the troupe. She was over whelmed by the assurance of a job in the circus to lead an adventurous life. She was sure her father would agree her wish as he never refused any of her demands.

In few months after her circus trials, her father arrived in the village to stay permanently. She and her friends used to mock some feats of show jumping and cycle driving!.

Due to death of his mother Damodar started to run the house by himself. As he was a cook all along, his new life has not caused any problem to him. He was satisfied with his comfortable living with his daughter.

He used to look after the house-hold needs and send his daughter to school. In the night he used to narrate his city life experiences in his long association with Kolkata. He started missing his habitual restaurant chief's job of ordering his staff and the luxury of daily having rich sumptuous meals!.

He used to tell her he would try to start a small restaurant in the town. He had very few known persons in his village because of his living away most of the time. He gradually started his new life to look after the lands, house rents and getting adjusted to the new environment. He did not know his daughter's notorious reputation. No body reported her misdeeds to her father, fearing the wrath from his daughter's nuisance gang. Because of his ever humble and unassuming weak appearance he was complete contrast to his daughter!. His philosophy was aggressive attitude does not help a poor person, whereas humility and humbleness give success. He was dishonest and deceitful to the core, with a mask of virtue!.

Only when she innocently requested him her desire to join the circus, he laughed at her as if it was a childish prank and smilingly advised her after completion of education he would allow her whatever type of nice job she wanted. He told her that she cannot live without her and after her marriage also he would live with her only. He was amused that her daughter was ignorant of dangers in touring show jobs. But she misunderstood that her father was not against joining the Circus.

After some months stay at his village, Damodar made a short trip to Soro, a town in Baleswar district, to see the family of his late friend, Bonomali Das. Both were close friends at Kolkata. He wrote ten days earlier to Bishwanadh Das, informing his date of visit to Soro.

At Bonomali's request Damodar signed as a witness to his registered marriage at Kolkata, with a good looking woman named Lolita.

He went with his daughter to visit his friend's family to offer condolences and to know about their welfare. He did not know that visit would change his entire life.

His friend Bonamali died a year back just two months after his wedding. He had seen his friend's wife

Lolita during the registered marriage time and later after a week he had a dinner with Bonamali and his bride. He remembered the close friendly way she talked during the dinner in a restaurant. She talked freely with him and made a very good impression on him. He was surprised to learn that it was a love marriage and she was from a Muslim family, and accepted to become a Hindu to marry Bonamali. He came to know that she changed her name to Lolita after conversion. He visited his friend's family few times earlier with Bonamali Das, which made him close acquaintance to them. He was received cordially by all of the family members.

As he was discussing with Bonamali's father, brothers, and other family members, Lolita clad in a white Sari and dressed like a widow suddenly came to the room like a hurricane fell on his feet weeping hysterically. He was about to ask about her to the family. He was touched by her grief and the pitiable appearance. Even his friend's family members were also seemed shocked to see her making such a scene!. Damodar tried his best to console her with emotion. After some persuasion she rose and handed him a small closed cover and told in Bengali with tearful voice that her husband gave that letter before his death to be handed personally to him. As she did not know the address she could not send it earlier. After telling the few words she left the room touching his feet with some sort of secret message which he only could feel. He was touched by her present condition, after seeing a year back, when she was in colorful dresses with a very sophisticated appearance and jolly behavior!.

Latter when he was alone he carefully opened the cover to see what his friend conveyed as his last message. To his utter shock it was not a letter from his friend, but a secret message in few words without signature from Lolita!. She simply wrote that her life has become a hell in her in-laws' house and everybody ill-treats her after his friend's death. She wanted to meet him privately alone at the weekly market place to talk to him as it would be difficult in the house!.

He was distressed at his late friend's young wife's pitiable condition. He decided to meet her discretely at the place and time she indicated. He went out alone telling that he has to meet a friend and also do some shopping. When he was searching her in the weekly market at the location she mentioned, suddenly he found she came very near him fully covered and requested in a low voice!. He found she was in a colored sari, and not in her white dress as he saw her earlier!. She told him to follow her discreetly after few minutes. Seeing her going with fast gait, he carefully followed her at a distance to avoid suspicion from others. As it was noisy busy market nobody noticed them. He gradually followed her to an isolated wooded place.

There she came very close to him and started narrating her pitiable story, with tearful emotion. She said that her in-laws, her husband's other family members wanted to throw her out after her husband's death. They humiliated her in all possible ways. Finally in desperation she took refuge of the police, with the help of her father, and reported about her dangerous living condition. The police and the Panchayat (Village heads) finally came to her rescue and directed the family that they would be arrested if any harm comes to her and forced the family to hand over her husband's share of the property in her name. In spite of that she said that she was living with them facing mental torture every minute. He advised her that she should have left that house and go to her parents place. She said her father would not take her back as she married against his wish to a Hindu person. He came with her to help her to get her husband's share of the property, as she was alone and in distress!. She told him that she still undecided where to settle, as her father was also a rude and uncouth person who would snatch her money and ill-treat her. She informed as her own mother died and her father living with a second wife, who is very haughty woman. While talking to him standing close, her covered sari gradually slipped and she was whispering getting closer to him.

Damodar has seen Lolita with her uncovered face, he remembered the dinner with Bonamali and her in a good restaurant, few days after the marriage. On that day she was sitting very close to him and many times touching him. He was also was mesmerized by her charm as well closeness during the dinner and envied at his friend for getting such a smart beautiful wife. He found the same charm and sexual appeal even in her sorrowful outlook. He kept staring at her lustrous ivory colored face with rosy cheeks and provocative looks!. Lolit could easily understand his lusty look, expression of stunned passion!. She suddenly as if carried away by an emotion, hugged him with emotional sadness. She was trembling with a feeling of solitude unable to face the depressed tragic lone life. She looked at him like lost child looking for help. She rested her head on his shoulder as if conveying a message to save her!. She could not control her flood of tears of deep distress!. But quickly separated and expressed her uncontrollable emotion and requested him to kindly excuse her bad behavior which was unintentional and impulsive!. After seeing him she expressed she felt first time felt happy after she became a widow. She enquired with sweet but guarded voice, expressing sympathy about his lone life as a widower in his still young life; he may not be having any person except his daughter in his house. She reluctantly but with a strong message she conveyed her request, that if he has no objection, she was prepared to stay in his house as a maid, instead of living in her present hell or her Father's house at Kolkata. She expressed the plight of unhelpful situation in society for women like her. She expressed her suspicion that he might not see her alive in his next visit, as was sure her family may take to any extreme action to get rid of her, and snatch the property back!.

That hint of her desire to come to his house acted as a flash idea on Damodar's mind. Her unexpected physical contact had aroused the deep male urge within. Since the death of his wife he never spoke to a woman in an isolated place. Her sudden holding her and standing very close to him touching his body attracted him in an uncontrollable way!. He resisted the urge to enjoy women's company when he was leading single life in Kolkata, fearing they would likely to squeeze his hard earned money!. Some new desire came into his mind. He was deeply distressed at her pitiable life. He suddenly took her hand and whispered with a shaking voice whether she would accept to marry him, as he was a widower. She stared at him with unbelievable astonishment and which quickly turned into coy joyfulness. She could not control her happy emotion at this sudden suggestion. She bent and touched his feet with shy gesture and told him she would be happy to stay near his feet. Damodar immediately came to a conclusion to marry her and live with her.

He first asked, as if it is a minor matter, about losing her share of property if she marries. His secret desire was she should come to him with her share of her late husband's property!. She smiled at him and whispered that she had already sold her property and converted to cash and put up fifteen lakhs rupees in bank and another ten lakhs given as black money is with her. For the first time after seeing no other were present in the vicinity, he put his hand around her and took her close to him and whispered in her ears if she has no objection he will raise matter with his late friend's father, Bishwonadh Babu, and tell his desire. She lowered her head said with tears and emotional voice that he came like a god and rescued her from the torture of living in their house. She urged him that the marriage has to be fast as she had to protect her money and gold ornaments to bring with her secretly. He was overjoyed at this new opportunity, and readily agreed in a serious note that he would come in week alone and marry in a temple and take her immediately to this village. He expressed that he was lucky to get such good hearted beautiful woman to come to his life.

They separated after secretly planning the actions to be taken for a quite marriage and departure. Before parting he warned to keep her head fully covered live carefully. He gave his cell phone number and address. She whispered that she doesn't want to wear the old ornaments came from earlier marriage, and hinted she would be happy if he bought some new ornaments as it would be look auspicious in bride's attire. While returning she gave a very happy look with a sweet smile. His desire had trebled with her attractive body movement. He was happier at the thought of getting a bride with twenty five Lakhs money and ornaments!. He thought he would buy her new ornaments for her after the wedding.

He was bit surprised her sudden transformation into a woman of boldness and talked with definite plan action!. He thought as she was fed up with her present life she does not want to lose the opportunity!. She took this bold step like a determined woman. Another thing he observed was she seemed to be habitual pan eater that too with perfumed tobacco zarda; as she took a pan from her small silver container kept in the folds of her sari and started chewing with a happy feeling. The moment he proposed to her he felt her eyes had a flash expression of slight mischief seeing him with a lusty side glances with an attractive modesty!. Her hand held his arm briefly but lustfully before her departure!. He felt a shiver of passion with that bold touch!.

A slight suspicion crept in his mind, about her character, but quickly he put that aside. He felt a real urge to take this woman as his wife. She had lived very few days of married life and has no children. He felt a strong desire to be with her and wanted to marry her at the earliest!. These facts also weighed strongly in her favor. After marriage of his daughter he would not be alone in the house.

He went in a to his late friend's house after some time, doing some marketing. Damodar decided not to inform his daughter also, till the marriage is over and come home with bride. He felt his daughter too require a woman help in the house and would accept her as a mother. It did not occur to ponder on this issue and take advice from relatives and close friends. His main important reason of hurry was that she should come to him with her large cash and gold before the in-laws snatch her lawful share!. He knew if he looked for a second marriage in his town, he could not expect a beautiful woman like Lolita with so much cash with no close relations. He met her father-in-law, Bishwonath Das separately aside and seriously yet with a sheepish smile, announced that if he agrees he has decided to marry his late son's widow and take her with him. He bluffed that was his son's last request to him!. The old man was surprised in an unbelievable way with a surprised look. He kept staring at him with stunned expression, he was actually very happy inward at that unexpected good news!. He felt had Damodar came fifteen days earlier, they would not have faced her dominating violent behavior or would not have handed over his son's property. She made all of his family members' lives, a night mare and made them fear even to see her shadow!. Even after promising to leave permanently, she continued staying with them with least signs of her going away to Kolkata. He did not show his real feelings. He put up a required seriousness in his face, as if undecided to agree or not, at the proposal. Finally with long face and keeping a same serious attitude told him with a sigh and speaking in a low voice "Though I am unable to lose my son's wife who is like a daughter to me . . . but considering her age I should not come in the way her happiness. It is better she settled with a nice person like you instead of staying as a widow. In this locality many have eyes on her to marry her. As my son's friend and a widower you really deserve such virtuous good woman as a wife. I am agreeable for this proposal. I will convince my other members myself so that they will also agree to her wedding. When do you wish the marriage to take place? . . . . Does she also know about your wish?".

"Sorry sir I happened to see her separately for few minutes alone and informed my proposal to her and also informed that was the message from her late husband. She was also astonished at my direct approach but from her reaction, I feel she is not against this as it was her late husband's desire. And my wish is I want to marry her within next week. I wish to do this function in a simplest way in a temple."

"Okay son as you wish I will make arrangements for next week but do not discuss with your known persons of this village till it was over, that is my sincere advice, as it may bring bad name to our family"

"I will be leaving today with my daughter and will come next Saturday for the wedding and will leave the same evening, I would not inform or bring any relatives or known persons to the wedding as I wish to help her and honor my friend's request"

He expressed his desire for an early action. The old man promised that he would see it would be done as desired. With a shy expression he handed some amount to meet the wedding expenses in spite of strong refusal to take money by the elder person.

After bidding good bye to the family, father and daughter left for the bus stand to catch a bus. It is normal tradition that no one in the family normally accompany them to see them off, when friends come to offer condolences. Unexpectedly Lolita came to the Bus stand secretly to see them off, again as an young widow!. She brought some sweets and new clothes to Neelu. He sent his daughter to bring water; and discreetly whispered not to give any hint about the wedding in front of Neelu. He also conveyed that everything going as planned. He informed that she should be prepared for the wedding next Saturday and leave on the same day evening. He also conveyed that he would inform his daughter later. She touched his feet with happy feeling of respect and tears came with joyful emotion. She demurely informed him "Sir I venture to request you to pay my father in-law some good amount to make arrangements for the marriage so that they may not feel the burden and sincerely help us. Ask them to make as simple as possible without any guests. Please convey them not to arrange any photographers. I feel it would be a waste to spend more money for this wedding"

Damodar appreciated at his would be wife's care for money and fore sight. He found from his daughter's looks and response, that she was cold and disrespectful towards Lolita!. He could guess that she did not like her to come to meet them. She avoided talking with her, except a few words of thanks.

*   *   *

When Damodar left the house, Bishwanadh called his family to inform the news. After he found that his daughter-in-law was also not in the house locking her door and went away. He closed the front door, and with bursting happy laughter he informed the good news to his family about the proposed marriage!. All the members were almost shouted with uncontrollable joy!, as if it was a happiest news!. Everyone seemed were greatly relieved from the news as it would bring peace and happiness family. They were all worried to see she was not attempting to go back and continued staying. The old man cautioned that they should not reveal this proposal any person in the neighborhood, lest Damodar may get information about her from them. Only the ladies regretted that they unnecessarily told about Lolita to his daughter.

But the old man said with conviction that Damodar looked very determined to his decision. He seemed to be in a hurry to marry by next Saturday. He informed them that they all would help him, to see that marriage takes place secretly and fast.

When Damodar left to meet Lolita secretly in the afternoon, Neelabeni was in the house with ladies. She told them it was really very sad for that good looking nice woman Lolita Deedi (sister) became a widow at a young age. All of them looked at her with an unexpected distaste!. She was completely surprised to see they all expressed dislike equally!. Even though they knew Lolita locked her room and went out of the house, yet they talked with low whispering tones!. One after the other told her that she was not at all a good woman. She is a devil in the woman's body!. They are living with fear, elders as well as youngsters because of her loud brawls every day with all the members. She even becomes wild and hits them if they try to reason with her. They lamented that Bonomali unfortunately fallen in love and got married due to pressure from her father. It was still a mystery how he died within a month after reaching here, barely less than two months after his registered marriage at Kolkata without informing them before. They lamented, that she never came to their house till an year after his death, but came now only with a sinister motive to claim her share of property. Her father looked as a real ruffian with foul language and crude behavior. She would shout without any provocation and argue that she had every right to stay with us them as the daughter-in-law. Daily she would fight for share of property, money gold and other valuables. Finally they decided to handover their son's share of land. They were hoping that she would go back and never show her face. All of them were fed up at her bad behavior with least respect to even elders. They got a written agreement from her stating she would not visit them again for any more property claims. They wanted to get rid of her after handing over her share being Bonamali's wife. But they were unable guess her further motives in staying further. They informed that she came to know of Damodar's visit to their house; it looked she was waiting for his arrival. They told all this information to convey about her to her father, as they saw Lolita's drama before him.

One small girl of ten who was sitting close to her finally spoke with angry complaining way "Neelabeni Deedee I saw Bonomali uncle's wife was sitting alone and smoking a cigarette in the evening on the terrace . . . aunty slapped me for seeing her smoking"

Neelabeni was surprised at their meek approach! She even asked them in surprised tone as to why they kept quite all these days instead of thrashing her and driving her away. As she herself a violent tempered girl, could not understood why the family tolerated such misbehavior!. She expressed her feelings in an angry tone!. She even volunteered to give a harsh rebuke to her when she comes now, for her misbehavior and even slap her hard if she dared to argue with her. She said being a Bengali woman she must be feeling we Odiyas are inferior; we must show our Utkalo Beerota!.(Valiancy of Odisha people). They all laughed at her outburst and told her leaving aside beating it requires courage even to talk loudly with her. She is a cunning and dangerous woman. Neelabeni was convinced that Lolita is a bad woman.

*   *   *

Damodar started to day-dreaming about how happy he would be from the next week, after his marriage with Lolita and how nice their house would be with her charming presence!. His thoughts were interrupted when his daughter woke him up from the slumber and started telling facts she gathered about her from the family. She narrated their fears and how badly she behaves with all of them. Laughingly she even remarked the family members are like silly goats, and fear her to be a tiger!.

Damodar felt a little fear from her revelation about Lolita; yet he did not believe that as truth. She made a deep impression on him by her narration of how she was being ill-treated with hatred and mental torture. To substantiate his reason he created his own version of her marriage. He told his daughter not to believe what was told by the family members. His friend late Bonamali informed him that even though she is very good woman with kind nature his parents and other family members were against their marriage. Whenever they came to village they used to ill-treat her. I understand they made her life miserable since her husband's death. She was denounced by her own parents as such she is now in a helpless stage with no help. She being a woman must be feeling very insecure. They were all treating her badly to get rid of her. That news he gathered from his friends in that village. He advised her not to hate Lolita just hearing the family's outburst. He met her at Kolkata in his friend's house and she behaved very well. He said that she and Bonamali were living very happily at Kolkata, unfortunately his sudden death turned her life to misery.

Neelobeni got into a confused mood after hearing her father's version about Lolita. Somehow the version of all the lady members including elders as well young spoke with hatred towards her; it was spontaneous and did not looked like prepared hate dialogue. Especially a simple family woman of Odisha would not dare to smoke, unless she was of a hot tempered girl like her. She was convinced that Bonamali Das's family spoke the truth.

*　　*　　*

CHAPTER 5

Lolit entices Sunonda!

As the Bus in which Damodar Sahu and his daughter travelling left, Lolit in the dress of Lolita smilingly took out the pan from his silver box and hired a cycle-Riksha to the hotel Manorama. He discarded his burqa that day, but covered his head. On the way, dialed a number from the cell phone. When the other side asked about the progress he laughed with a stage type giggle and told:

"The fish is attracted by the bait . . . . the real catch is expected on Saturday".

The other side male voice laughed in a big way "What do you mean real catch?"

"Dada I am on the way coming to you I will tell about the joker Damodar Sahu, my late husband's close friend".

After reaching the Hotel he took stairs. He was greeted by the sole receptionist who knew that the lady is going to her father in room number 6. Lolit went to the first floor room and knocked the door. A booming male voice asked "Who is there?"

The masquerading lady laughingly replied in a low voice:

"Mister Charulota"

The person inside quickly put his false beard and opened with a big laugh seeing his friend. He put hand affectionately and brought him inside with a good friendly greeting. He bolted the door after Lolita alias Lolit Sen entered the room.

He took off his woman's wig from his head and sat on the bed in a relaxed way smoking a cigarette. He was looking funny with male face and female attaire!.

Shoilen also sat on the chair with a cigarette.

"So! What is the latest scene?!"

"Dadaa you were right about Damodar Sahu he fell to my story, as you predicted he had a nasty lusty look on me . . . and asked me to marry him!"

He narrated the full story about his interesting affair with Damodar. Shoilen said with a big grin:

"So we have found unexpectedly one more bakra (goat) . . . let us postpone our journey for another week . . . . looks this trip is very profitable one. Our late friend Das had amusingly about as a very Kanjoos with good wealth mostly earned by crooked methods! You also found his illegal methods of earning a lot telling in drunken state! We are now certain of this silly fellow's greed to gobble our money also by getting married to rich Lolita! . . . Ha Ha Ha . . . .

I am sure I can black mail him to extract some more. Please give his address to make a visit before wedding takes place. After my success we will decide our next move. If he declines the wedding we will forget about him"

Lolit smiled and suggested him another point to black mail. They seriously discussed and planed their next moves.

*   *   *

After an hour Lolit as Lolita reached her in-laws house. She was surprised at the changed atmosphere!. Every one greeted her with smiles and offered Tea and sweets!. Her father-In-Law and senior members sat near her and gradually brought the topic and asked her whether Damodar proposed to marry her. She shyly burst into tears with emotion and gradually narrated:

"Yes . . . it seems my husband came to know he had few only months left due to serious illness, it seems he had a un-curable medical problem. He kept me also in dark after it was diagnosed. This it seems he kept secretly and resigned his job and returned to this town. Before leaving he made sure that I will stay in my father's house till he writes when to reach . . . My husband took pity and wrote to his friend all details and requested him to marry me as he has no hope to live, since he also lost his wife. He gave me that sealed cover to handover to him. After hearing all that unknown facts I was in a fix what to do. I reluctantly accepted to marry Damodar Mohashoy provided you all accept the wedding. I wouldn't be happy at Kolkata with my step mother. I have decided to settle in Odisha with Damodar babu . . . Sir . . . Do you approve my decision . . . I am upset because my father may not approve. I will tell him not now but one day before . . . . the wedding?"

"Suppose if he comes tomorrow and asks you leave for Kolkata?"

She said in low voice:

"Sir! To really tell you I am avoiding to go to Kolkata and live with my step mother . . . I am yet undecided . . . suddenly this marriage proposal came now I decided to remain in Odisha and with Damodar babu . . . . You are so good I cannot forget your affection to me.

Since you also feel it is better for me to marry him, I respect your blessings. I requested my father not to come to my house . . . if I tell him now he may not agree for the wedding so I will tell him just one day before and send him to Kolkata"

The family were stunned at her words first but felt relieved at her decision to marry Damodar and go away from them. Bishwonadh decided to help her to get married and so that she would leave Soro for good.

"My daughter we also feel you made a wise decision . . . and also my poor boy unfortunately hidden his illness to us also till he reached here. Doctors here had also confirmed his dangerous illness. We all had to face that tragedy we could never believe the God would take away our eldest son . . . . that is our very unfortunate bad luck . . . We had to face that calamity as it was the destiny . . . I feel personally that your decision is really good to you as you are still young and Damodar also not very old . . . . but please don't tell to others and keep that as a secret . . . that is our request . . . as people would think badly about our family . . . as you are young you would have a happy life with him."

"Do you know Damodar personally?. I hope he is a good person . . . He was also My husband's very close friend"

"Oh He is a gem of a man with money, lands and good properties. He is a simple man good at heart . . .

he would make your life comfortable . . . . By the way Damodar requested to make arrangements for the marriage to take place in a temple. I agreed to do all the needful"

"Sir, I thank all of you for this help . . . I agree to marry him on your kind assurance, please pardon me if I had offended you at any time, I could not imagine our love relationship would end so short period. I was out of my mind and angry with my life as well every one even my friends due to pent up rage! Please make it as simple function as possible as it is a second marriage to both of us . . . . Also please do not call friends and relatives to this function . . . that is my sincere request . . . as I would not feel that happy under the present circumstances . . . . Sir I would feel happy if you and mother-in-law, or any other of your brother and wife can do the konya-Daan as I understand that is Hindu custom in wedding!?"

"OK child I respect your sentiments we will be very happy to do that we will organize the function as you desire".

All of them felt sympathy and forgave her past attitude, as she would be going into another family. All the ladies hugged her with emotion and wept for her. Sunonda felt happier to hear about Lolita's proposed marriage with Damodar Sahu, whom she saw. She felt he was not good match for Lolita, who was very sophisticated charming lady, with good taste. He looked crude and fat, looked complete contrast to her nice fashionable personality!. But she found him to be humble and simple in nature. She felt being a widow she might have accepted him for some good male company for security and live as a housewife. She came to know that he was a well to do man living in Rupsa. She felt happy that she would be living in the same district, to occasionally see her.

Lolita's wedding news was a happy event to the entire family. But Sunonda became emotional with joy as well feeling of sadness as she would go away from her. She became much more intimate to her after the gifts. She came to her room and hugged for a long time with tears. Addressing Lolita as Badi deedi (elder sister as she was older to her),She expressed her desire to sleep with her that night to happily chitchat long time. Lolit was seriously perturbed at this unexpected turn of events as he did not want to displease her and hurt her feelings. In fact he was bubbling with joy for that unexpected luck. He first thought of informing the new development to Shoilen. He knew he would never allow such things to take place. He would have come to stay with him or would have taken him to his hotel. Lolit could not control his passionate urge to spend a night with her; he suddenly remembered that he had some sweets mixed with drug. He decided not to discuss his private opportunities with Shoilen. His secret plan was to use the sweets mixed with drug to make her unconscious and take advantage to enjoy her in the night!.

Luckily the guest bed room which was given to her was away from other bed rooms connected with only dining room Most of the other bed rooms were in first floor. It had also an attached bath room.

He avoided cigarettes and zarda pan instead only put in his mouth mint sweets which he always kept with him. In evening he once more shaved and applied lady's makeup.

After dinner she took permission from her husband and went to Lolit's bed room to sleep. Her husband was very pleased when his wife showed him secretly the expensive gifts given by Lolita.

Lolita and Sunonda talked happily for a long time both telling their nice days before marriage, in which Lolit did little talking and encouraged her to talk most of the time. He took lot of precaution to sit at a distance lest he lost his control. She smilingly expressed her desire in a low voice to apply the same makeup to her face also. She was giggling with joy seeing her face in the mirror after he applied with loving care. He lovingly whispered she was looking like a real film star with her fine beauty and makeup. He could not resist the uncontrollable urge to kiss her face. She also kissed him with a nice smile and addressing her as a nice sister. Lolit took the sweet and forced in her mouth with an affectionate gesture. Sunanda was overjoyed as she had weakness for sweets. She accepted happily when he thrust another sweet also in her mouth.

"Sunonda! shall we lie on the bed and talk or you want to go to your husband with this make up?!" Lolit asked humorously.

She giggled with shy modesty said:

"Lolita Didi . . . today I took permission from him to sleep to with you. Tomorrow you put that makeup before I go to him"

Lolit took out a new Night gown and gave her saying:

"Sunonda wear this night dress also as my gift along with makeup when you go to your bed room next day, your husband will love your nice glowing face and your night dress."

Sunanda shyly smiled at her remark. It was provocative thin semi-transparent chiffon nightly. She never saw such attractive woman's night dress earlier. She accepted it with real joy and said:

"Thank you Deedee I desire to wear it tonight, I cannot wait till tomorrow I love this dress!"

She immediately started to undress with least hesitation to take out her sari stood with her inner dress only! Lolit was dazzled to see her provocative beautiful body with minimum wear!. Joyfully he made her wear that new dress with utmost restraint controlling his burning desire. While helping to put on the new dress, he could not resist touching her voluptuous curves and her shapely legs; She went to the mirror and almost danced with pleasure!.

She came to the bed and rested talking with joy; Lolit also came to the bed and sat next to her.

"why you are not wearing night dress?"

"Sunnuu! . . . . I will again start wearing after the marriage only. She understood Lolita's words and pulled her body towards her and said:

"I am very lucky to have good affectionate sister like you . . . . I wish you all the happiness after the marriage . . . Lolita!! my real desire is to spend next few nights also with you only till wedding day as your company brings me joy, you are an intelligent good woman . . . I like you very much and will miss you after you go away!"

Lolit also felt very happy of this new prospect but had a lurking fear inside.

After talking some more minutes she started feeling sleepy. She happily went to a sound sleep in no time. Lolit took precaution to check the door bolt once more and closed the windows. He set his alarm, and lustfully took her very close towards him. He never had experience to sleep with such a voluptuous beauty. Sunonda did not know what happened to her in the night!. His only regret was he would have a much better time had she also participated joyfully.

Next day early hour he got up and took the bath and shaved and quickly put up the makeup. She sat in a chair to avoid any temptation. He was still happily remembering the joyful experience of the night!. As she was still sleeping he continued to ogle at her exposed body. While he was trying to cover her with a sheet, she woke up. She was in no mood to get up as was still feeling drowsy. Lolit smled and said "how did you sleep in the night? . . . you were singing nicely in sleep . . . To night you must sing . . . you have a sweet musical voice!

"Oh maa! I must get up as all the ladies must have got up already . . . I really had a sound sleep"

"Sunondaa! did you get any nice dreams?"

She shyly avoided her question and got up from the bed and was about to move in the night dress. She was scared seeing her own dress and quickly changed to her sari and folded the dress and kept under the pillow. Sunanda whispered her to get it washed as she would give her another new one that night. Quickly she rushed out of the room, hiding that night dress inside her dress.

Sunonda became over affectionate with Lolita after joyful way they spent three more nights. She became very dearest to her for her friendly manners and benevolent attitude. She used to hear her with keen interest whatever topics she used to narrate. Each night she used to get a happy surprise with the unexpected costly gift which she used to receive. A pair Gold bangles, a gold plated ladies wrist watch and a cute alarm clock with FM Radio she got in the three successive nights!.

Sunonda came from a middle class family discontinued her studies during high school studies due to arranged marriage her parents fixed. Her husband got a job with a meager salary. She never got herself or seen any one giving such expensive gifts in her life!. She used to secretly show to her husband only, all her gifts; she knew the other members in the family would not tolerate with envy. She never hesitated or refused any gift from Lolita as she was sure in her life she would never get such opportunity. She would eagerly wait for the sweets also from her. She became almost like a real younger sister to her, and gossip with her either holding her hand or lying on her lap or hearing her stories about Kolkata life. She became so fascinated with her love and respected her with high reverence. She started worrying as her wedding day was approaching closer. Every morning while bathing alone, she used have an exemplary feeling of joy remembering the gift and the nice time she spent with her. She used to feel a strange experience of different womanly happy feeling. When she remembered only two more nights were left as the wedding was to take place on Saturday. In the family also all the members became very affectionate to her seemed to forgot the earlier days of discord.

That night as soon she entered the bed room and bolted the door, Lolita came there silently behind her and embraced her very tightly and kissed her with utmost love. She also expressed how keenly she awaiting her arrival. Sunonda was startled at her sudden hug and felt as if it was like a hot manly gesture!. She smiled happily and turned towards her and she also hugged passionately. Lolita took her towards the mirror and asked her to close her eyes with her hands. When she opened her eyes, she found a costly pair of gold ear rings glittering with colored gems in her hands!. She was over whelmed joy seeing the lovely new gift. She hugged her tightly with affection. She just told for fun that her husband was getting envious because she only receiving all the gifts.

"Sunonda! I have forgot about him . . . . kindly excuse me . . . tomorrow I will give you gift for use by both of you . . . . I never had any younger sisters except my twin brother, I was looking at you as my God given younger sister. I never felt so happy in my life for the affectionate way you spent your time with me last five days".

Sunonda almost wept with happiness.

Lolita Lolita's wiped her tears and gently applied her good make-up as was her usual desire. She looked happily at her glowing face and shining lips in the mirror. She looked at her new glittering ear rings with pride. She took off her sari and wore the night dress came to her as she was staring her with delight. That night also Lolit spent happily after she slept unconsciously.

*   *   *

Friday morning Sunanda readily agreed to Lolita's request, that she and her husband should help her do some shopping. They went to Baleswar city, hiring a taxi. They first went to a very large cloth showroom and selected costly silk saris and dresses to all the members of her in-law's house. She made purchases for every one including children with Sunonda and her husband's help, never minding the expenses. She purchased many other gifts to all, from other show rooms. Lastly she took them to a Mobile phone shop. She requested Sunonda to sit in a sofa of the show room and gave the list of names of all family members and the list of gifts before the names. She requested her to check to see that she has not missed any one. She told her that she and Mayadhar will select a mobile phone for him. Sunonda started to check the list seriously.

She requested Mayadhar to select two good mobile phones. She got them registered one in Sunonda's name and other in her husband Mayadhar's name. She requested him not to reveal to Sunonda about the mobile phone purchased to her.

They both were overjoyed expressed at her big hearted generosity, when they completed the purchases and returning home. She requested them not to reveal about the purchases she made that day to anyone, as she wanted to surprise them.

In the evening Lolita requested all to sit around in their living room. She modestly requested to accept her humble gifts for getting married with their blessings next day.

She first gave a Gold wrist watch and clothes to her father in law, and deeply bowed him with reverence. She presented a gold chain ornament and a costly silk sari to her mother in-law, and bowed to her. She embraced her blessed her heartily, with beaming happiness. She gave dresses to all the family members along with good gifts. She gave two big boxes local sweets purchased that day. To Mayadhar she gave mobile phone and clothes. Every one of the family showered heaps of praises and expressed sincere thanks to her. All elders wished her happy married life to smiling Lolita.

*　　*　　*

CHAPTER 6

Shoilen robbed by Neelo-Sena!

Four days earlier, Lolit sitting in his room telephoned to Damodar's mobile number from his cell phone he got in local town. First two days he spoke for long time with Damodar, with love talking, and informing that he should have fixed marriage still earlier, as she was feeling eager to live with him. He said that he was getting restless waiting for that auspicious day to marry him.

Damodar also was also used to happily respond to his sweet talk.

Two days after leaving Soro town, Damodar recived a panic call from Lolita. She was weeping with fear as she spoke with him. She informed that her father unexpectedly arrived from Kolkata to take her. She informed about the proposed marriage with him to take place on Saturday.

"Sir, he was furious with me for agreeing to marry you. I cried and pleaded him to agree for the marriage. He was adamant but finally demanded to hand over the Ten Lakhs cash I had. I bluffed that I gave that amount to you for safety custody."

"That was a very good deed you did!"

"Sir, he is a dangerous man, with nasty manners . . . . I saw him kicking persons mercilessly if any disobeyed his orders, got your address from somebody of this family. He threatened me that he would take that cash from him otherwise he would not allow our marriage . . . He made me write a letter to you to handover those Ten lakhs to him"

She continued with hiccups of weeping on the phone.

"Oh God! . . . what to do now! . . . . shall I hide somewhere or go some other place."

"Sir please don't do such things he would get angry and wait for your return or come here and will not allow the wedding. Or latter he would try to take not only ten lakhs cash but also will demand more than half of the Twenty Lakhs Of my bank account . . . . If we refuse he may attack us which can be dangerous to you as well to me and your daughter . . . If he becomes angry he may do any dangerous act! . . . I am worried of your safety . . . please don't offend him!"

Damodar became nervous on hearing her. He was unable to imagine such big loss and but he was very timid person.

"Dear Lolita dont worry I will deal with him and bargain to reduce that amount to five lakhs or six lakhs. Our wedding will take place on Saturday as planned."

Damodar was not knowing that his daughter was secretly listening his conversation with Lolita. She was angry that her father decided to marry that she devil and bring her to the house. She decided to oppose her father to desist from that marriage venture.

Next day Shoilen reached Damodar's house disguised as Tejudden Rehman. Neelabeni saw a tall rough Pathan, looking like a ruffian, came to meet her father. (In Odisha they generally use the word Pathan to Muslim men)

Neelobeni was at the entrance when he arrived. As she was inquiring about him, Damodar came rushing, and touched his feet with high respect; told his daughter also to touch his feet. He told her that he was a like Nowab in Kolkata he was father-in-law of his late friend Bonomali. Neelabeni just told namoshkar briefly and went inside without caring him. Damodar cordially invited him into his house. He followed him without any greeting. The room was bare, with least furniture. It had only a long bench without back rest and a plastic chair. All the walls were bare except, for a calendar with a picture of God Jagannath with Shubhadra and Balabhadra, hanging on one wall. One side there was an attic full of fire wood and dried cow-dung cakes! The walls were all looking dull without white wash since many years!. The house smelled of cow-dung and hay. Damodar was wearing a blue lungi and a soiled and slightly torn vest. He looked unshaven since three days!. His oily face with protruding thick lips dark with zarda pan looked repulsive!. His daughter was wearing a good Punjabi dress, looked smart and defiant, while Damodar was looking humble but deceptive in his movement!. He offered Tejudden Rehman, the chair and he sat on the bench. He loudly ordered his daughter to bring 'Jolo-khiya' (break-fast in Odiya) and Cha for the guest. As soon she went inside Tezuddeen Rehman handed him the letter from his daughter and told him in a rough way in his booming voice, without any formalities.

"My daughter kept with you ten lakhs, which belong to me . . . . she has written to handover that amount to me. She kept that money with you lest her dirty in laws might snatch them! . . . Hand me that amount now"

Damodar briefly read that letter written in big legible letters in Bengali and respectfully requested him:

"Sir You are becoming my father in-law, I feel honored to receive you to my humble home. I am grateful to you for kindly visiting my house, please take tea and snacks first and discuss other points latter."

"Damodar don't try to disgust me with your false respect, earlier your friend Bonomali Das hidden the fact that he was a cancer patient and married my only daughter who was a fool to love that rogue . . . now you cunningly fooled her now and made her to agree to marry you. I don't approve of this match. But my daughter is an idiot and stubborn. I failed to change her mind, now I don't care for her . . . . so don't waste any more time to return my ten lakhs . . . I will go back to Kolkata."

"But sir that money is hers how can you take it?"

He said in a meek way.

Rehman was furious with him in a threatening way "You are pleading for my daughter even before becoming her husband! . . . don't you see what she wrote . . . do as ordered by her"

"Sir please do not misunderstand me I just tried to tell that as a father you should not take your daughter's money . . . is it not your duty to look for her welfare?"

He retorted with rage "Silly fellow don't tell those nonsensical ideas and waste my time! . . . do as she wrote and never again advice-me"

Cunning Damodar came to him and humbly sat near his feet and with utmost respect he said holding his feet:

"Sir, you are a big man in Kolkata doing business in Crores, this amount is very meager to your property and income . . . why not offer this small amount as dowry to your son in-law . . . it would be a great help to us to set up our family"

Rehman was enraged with those words . . .

"You third class hotel cook! . . . . dirty widower . . . crooked fellow . . . how dare you ask for dowry!"

He violently pushed him on the floor with burning rage. At that time Neelabeni came into the room with tea and snacks. She was shocked to see her father was pushed on the floor, She was enraged beyond control and shouted at the visitor and was about to beat him!

Damodar quickly got up and pacified his daughter and told her calmly that they should not dishonor their esteemed guest. He told her that he was father of Lolita. He told her to go into the house. He informed her that, he just slipped on the floor but not pushed by him. Damodar realized Tezuddeen's hot temper and dangerous attitude. He remembered Lolita's phone warning about him. He decided to handover part money rather face his wrath.

"Sorry sir . . . . for my daughter's bad behavior please excuse me for displeasing you . . . . please have tea I will bring you the money.

"Damodar I am not interested to have tea with you, go and get that money otherwise I will take my daughter with me to Kolkota I will not allow her to marry you . . . also if you do not return the money . . . I know how to extract".

Damodar humbly sad:

"Sir I have to bring that money from the bank locker . . . please wait or come in the afternoon"

"How much time will it take?"

"May be two hours or less"

Rehman reluctantly decided to stay there till he comes. He told roughly:

"You take my Riksha which I kept waiting outside . . . hurry up!" Damodar actually got some lakhs in currency notes in his steel box in the house in a secret place. Damodar never kept major portion of his money in any bank account or locker. He just went out to delay payment to him. Shoilen stayed in the room took tea and started studying a drama dialogues from a book.

Neelu secretly heard their talks. She phoned her right hand man of her rowdy gang silently conveyed that "Listen Guddu today we had an elderly Pathan guest from Kolkata . . . at present he is in our house . . . follow him like a shadow when he leaves our house and tell details where he is staying and when and how he would be going"

She started worrying that her father now bent upon marrying Lolita, she could not reconcile the fact. She heard him threatening his father that he would stop his marriage with Lolita if he does not pay him.

She decided to threaten him when he leaves her house with cash, with her gang and take away that money from him.

Shoilen called for Damodar's daughter Neelobeni, but she did not respond as she was in the back yard. Shoilen went to back yard to ask her about the bath room. When he reached the rear verandah, he saw her taking secretly with a short stubby boy of her age. He came from the back court-yard door. His hair was ruffled and wearing a dark blue T-shirt with white horizontal lines. As they both were seriously discussing; Shoilen came inside stood near the door. He thought that must be girl's lover, secretly meeting her. After few minutes when he left she closed the door and as she turned she found Lolita's father coming out she was a bit worried, lest he had seen her friend Guddu. He asked her, without showing any expression, the location of bath room. She showed him the toilet room located in the back yard. When she came close to him, he observed she looked slightly frightened by her body language. He also seen a thick silver amulet shaped like a coiled snake on her right arm. She had a fleshy oval face with round cheeks, and thick lips. She was tall and looked strong with developed young female body. She had unsmiling and distasteful facial expression!.

Damodar came back after some time and went to his bed room. He closed the door and took out thousand rupee bundles amounting to Eight Lakhs, from his steel box located under, in a small chamber below the floor nicely concealed, with an iron cover. His never showed his secret cash box even to his daughter also. He came to Shoilen and handed him the cash bundles in a cloth bag and pleadingly told him that his daughter latter phoned him to buy Gold ornaments worth two lakhs. As such balance amount he was handing over. Shoilen knew that bluff but still was enraged, and said she had no right to buy from his cash, as such he must return the full amount. Damodar bowed in a most pitiable way and said that he already placed order and two lakhs paid. Shoilen knew he will be wasting his time as cunning Damodar would not give that two lakhs that easily!. He was happy that he would extract at least he could extract eight lakhs, from him.

He showed his displeasure cursing his daughter. He quickly put that amount in his leather bag, even without counting. Damodar heaved a sigh of relief when Tajudden left with the money. He actually put only seven lakhs and kept one lakh aside to give that amount, after some more haggling. He thought to plead with him to keep at least one lakh to his daughter. If refused he decided to give that also latter. He thanked God that he could save three lakhs. He decided to tell Lolita that he paid full ten lakhs to her father. He was planning to take that amount from her in some cunning way stating he had to take a loan from a businessman, to pay her father.

Shoilen took the Riksha to the only hotel of that town where he took a room when he arrived. While traveling in that vehicle he found the same young man who was talking with Nilabeni was following him on a cycle. He became a bit alert whether it was a coincidence or Damodar hired a thug, to rob him. He kept his bag with him while having lunch in that hotel. He requested the hotel manager to hire a taxi for him to go to Soro. He took rest in the hotel for an hour and came out after paying the bill. He sat in the taxi arranged by the hotel and started his journey back, as taxi left some distance at the out skirts the engine suddenly stopped, in an isolated road. In spite of his attempts that old Ambassador refused to start. The driver went out and opened the bonnet was seeing the Engine as if to check the problem. There was hardly any traffic on that road at that time. Suddenly a gang of six youngish ruffians all reached there, without the knowledge of the driver as he was bent and checking the engine. They covered a big towel on his face and threatened him that they will kill him if he shouted or tried to run. Poor driver with his face covered was silent and shivering with fear. Two persons held him tightly. Other four came to the back door of the car and threatened Shoilen with a knives to hand over his bag. Shoilen was also shaken at that unexpected attack. He knew it would be useless to fight or refuse them. As it was still day time he could see the faces of the four thugs. All painted black color to their faces and had black turbans on their heads. Suddenly he found the leader was wearing a silver armlet with shape of coiled snake. Another was wearing a Blue T-shirt with white horizontal lines. He could easily recognize them. He kept quiet and handed his bag to them. They checked in the car and found no other luggage. They forcibly tied Shoilen's hands and feet put a gag in his mouth. They opened his leather bag and took out the bundles of cash kept in the cloth bag. They told the driver to count hundred and after that to take out the towel over his face. They threatened Shoilen also to lie on the seat till the driver calls him. They quickly mounted their cycles which they kept by the side of the road behind a bush. They all left in a flash. The driver counted up to hundred and removed his towel. By that time the robbers had ran away. He started shouting at the top of his voice with vulgar cursing to vent his anger. Still there was no other traffic on the road. He found his passenger lying on the seat with hands feet and eyes tied and mouth gagged with a cloth. As the driver untied him removed his gag, he told him as soon the car is repaired he wanted him to go back to the town from where he started. The driver was still very angry for being robbed; he was continuously cursing the thugs. He thanked God that no harm was done to his passenger. After tinkering for five minutes the car again started. Shoilen sat seriously and not answering any questions put by the driver; who wanted to know how much was his loss. He told him to take the car back to the town to the police station.

When they reached the destination, Shoilen asked him to stop the car much before the police station. He found the driver was very nervous. Shoilen asked the driver in a point blank in a calm way:

"I know you were part of the robbery, as you made a show of car break down exactly where the six robbers were waiting. If I report this robbery and tell the police that you assisted to them, they would arrest you and whip you whole night till you tell the truth, even after telling the truth they would cancel your driving license and put you in jail".

The driver was really frightened to hear his words. He touched his feet with utmost humble way and requested not to involve him in that robbery. He started crying profusely with fear and insisting he doesn't know them. He started taking oaths on his father, mother and God Jagannath to prove his innocence.

"You express your innocence to the police and count your luck if they believe you. I am convinced that you were involved. Come start the car and take to that police Chouki"

Without starting he continued to pressurize him to believe his innocence.

After five minutes Shoilen asked him in a low voice:

"OK, if you say you were not part of that gang but you must be knowing them. They must have threatened you to co-operate with their plan. I can understand your problem, so please tell me who were that gang and I will not report against you. If you deny you will suffer"

The driver was silent for a few minutes and finally uttered in a whispering way "Sir, please don't tell the police that I told you whom I think are behind this robbery . . . . that gang is notorious as they would take revenge on me and put me into misery".

"Bhai! (brother) . . . don't worry! . . . . I promise you. I will not tell the police whatever you tell me".

Once more he saw around and told in whispering way:

"Sir . . . I suspect it is the work of 'Neelo Sena' gang which is notorious in this small town. Its leader is one young woman by name 'Neelobeni'. Sir please believe me I sincerely tell you I have no sympathy with that gang. I strongly suspect them only. Please save me and please do not involve me"

Shoilen suddenly became alert he understood the rogue behind this robbery drama. He told the taxi driver to take him to his friend's place first and later he would decide. He told him his friend's address directed him to take him there.

By the time he reached, he found Damodar sitting in a plastic chair in the front verandah. He told the driver to have some tea and come back. Damodar startled to see Tejuddeen again visiting his house. He feared he must have counted the money and came back to collect that amount. He went and touched his feet in a very humble way and started telling how lucky he was that he came once more to his house.

Tejuddeen curtly told him he has to talk to him in the house. As he entered he bolted both doors and asked him to sit and he also sat.

Shoilen asked him whether his daughter was in the house.

"No sir she had gone for tuition she is expected any time. Poor girl she is so studious"

Shoilen laughed within himself at that remark. He suddenly raised his voice to angry tone:

"Damodar! . . . I didn't know you were a such a dirty rogue to rob me my daughter's cash which you gave . . . . I knew you sent the gang to rob me on the way! . . . . I am taking this very seriously the dangerous game you played with me . . . return that money immediately or I will have to complain to the police"

Damodar could not understand his accusation or able to understand about robbery. He thought he was playing another game to extract more money.

"Nowab saab I am not able to understand your suspicion . . . I never in my life committed any crime like robbing! ask any one in this town. Im an honest gentleman . . . sir please tell me what happened I will help you"

"Don't try to fool me! Did you not send your daughter Neelabeni along with five hooligans to rob me at knife point on way at out-skirts, well they took all the cash and ran away . . . . I immediately recognized your daughter and her friend with whom she talked in your back yard, of this house when you went to the bank. That fellow was following me, when I left your house. Latter they all joined and robbed my money. I don't believe your innocence. If you do not return back my money. I am going to the police and report this crime committed by you with help of your daughter and her friends"

Damodar was stunned to hear his accusation and also involving his daughter.

"Believe me sir there seemed to be some mistake . . . my daughter is not a bad girl. She never gets involved with bad company . . . I will call her right now by phone . . . to clear your doubt! . . . It is unthinkable my sweet daughter never behaves badly or goes with bad company . . . please sir believe me honestly I am telling"

"OK Damodar I will believe you after talking with your daughter . . . I promise you I will not show any anger but only coax her to hear the truth . . . call her to come the house urgently . . . don't tell anything about the robbery or about me visiting you . . . Just pretend that you are having little pain in your chest she must come immediately. Also you lie on the long bench and pretend some uneasiness".

Damodar agreed and made a call to her mobile to come urgently due to little pain he developed has in the chest.

She came rushing within five minutes on cycle worried about her father. Her friends also followed her and stayed outside to help her if needed. She came running to the front door and knocked calling:

"Baba . . . it is me . . . please open"

When the door was opened she was shocked to see tall Pathan opened the door. She rushed to her father lying on the long bench with a towel tied to head. "Baba . . . how are you ? why you are sleeping are you having chest pain?"

She was in tears.

"Neelu Im slightly better now"

Shoilen with drama experience of make-up, found traces of black color still on her face even after getting cleaned. She in fact returned home after robbing Shoilen. She came inside through the back door compound wall. She and her friends quickly washed their faces, and left. She carefully hidden, Tejudden's money, in her bed room. She changed her dress went out telling her father that she was going to tuition class. They sat at their normal secret meeting place. Before leaving she kept one lakh rupees separately for personal use. She told her friends that one notorious goonda from Kolkata harassing her father by black mail to pay him large amount of cash. She told her poor father had no option but pay. She told her gang to help her to recover the money.

They hatched the plan. They also threatened the driver to help them.

Shoilen calmly addressed her:

"Neelu! Your father first fainted when I told him that I was robbed by a gang called Neelo Sena!"

She was suddenly enraged hearing the stranger accusing the 'Neelo-Sena'.

"You imagined some silly gossip in town and believed them . . . You must have been robbed by some bad persons. On road while you were going in a taxi to Soro . . . Neelo Sena group only helps the needy it is a good group doing social service"

"But how did you know I was robbed on the road while traveling by taxi to Soro?. You were busy with your studies and I did not discuss with anyone except your father?"

Neelabeni was realized her mistake and looked for words to say.

"Oh I just thought it that way as you went from house with the money"

"You were not in the room when we talked about money, he did not tell you that he would be going to bank to get money because he left the house in front of me without a word with you . . . you never saw your father giving money to me . . . now tell me how you presumed that I am carrying money unless you secretly watched . . . is it not?"

"I am against my father getting married to your daughter I heard your talk secretly about the wedding!"

She replied with real anger. Her father was hearing with distaste his daughter's hot reply.

Shoilen without retaliation to her angry outburst he calmly said "So you sent your friend, who came to meet you in the morning when your father went out. You secretly met him at the back door. You were instructing to follow me to know where I was staying and my travel plan to Soro?"

"That is a lie . . . he came to borrow some books"

"No it is not a lie . . . I heard you clearly giving instructions to him to follow me when I leave the house"

"You are bluffing . . . I never spoke to him to follow you"

Shoilen slightly raised his voice to give her some shock.

"Then why did he follow me from your house to the hotel . . . . Latter he made a deal with the taxi driver to help your Neelo Sena friends to rob me . . . is it not!"

"That Taxi driver is a dirty rogue I will see how he will live in this town after telling false accusations about Neelo Sena group?"

She could not control her anger . . . especially on the driver she burst in a violent way. Her father was becoming restless with his daughter's behavior.

"You are the leader of Neelo Sena group is it not?"

"So what . . . they made me leader"

"Then you are directly responsible for the robbery. Return my Money . . . otherwise I will go to Police you and your father may be arrested as there are enough evidences"

She was stunned hearing his threat. She shouted "How do you prove I took the money?"

"Neelobeni you are still a child in committing crime. See your face in the mirror you still did not got rid of the black color you applied on your face . . . I recognized you with your silver snake armlet and also your friend who came to meet you in the morning. Even though all of you painted black to your faces, your friend was in same dress till now as I saw him waiting outside. The driver has already informed me that he agreed to help you due to threat. It is strong evidence you cannot defend. He is prepared to inform the police about you and your gang. They will put all of you in lockup and latter send you to the juvenile jail . . . . If you want to save yourself . . . please handover the money I would not want to report against you as my daughter is about to marry your father . . . Don't tell any more bluffs . . . You have no experience and many persons will testify against you for your misdeeds"

Neelabeni was flabbergasted beyond belief to see her well planned plot completely became a flop!. She realized the danger. Yet she tried to be defiant and shouted. Damodar was boiling inside hearing all the evidence; He got convinced at her daughter's dangerous exposure. He shuddered at his daughter was connected with the robbery! He was convinced that his daughter foolishly wanted to help him. He got up suddenly with blind anger and gave a hard slap on her face. She fell on the ground at that unexpected act of her father.

He told her angrily that he was in the dark about her notoriety. It was unthinkable that his daughter committed a crime by robbing seven lakhs rupees!.

He was always god fearing and afraid of police cases and courts. He realized due to his stay in Kolkota his daughter became grown in the house without any proper guidance. His mother never realized that her granddaughter was behaving very irresponsibly outside the home. He also never found his daughter's mischievous deeds because nobody complained.

He shouted at her to go and get all that money immediately otherwise he would not allow her to stay in the house.

Neelobeni was stunned at her father's outburst. She never seen him in such anger and he never beat her till then. She knew she was badly caught and case was against her. Crying loudly she went into the house and brought the notes bundles in a cloth bag and returned back to her room crying hysterically.

Shoilen saw the bundles and remarked it looked less. Damodar hurriedly went in and brought one lakh bundle, uttering apologies,. and put them in Tejuddeen's bag.

"Sir I feel ashamed at my daughter's bad deed. I never knew what type of company she was influenced. You really opened my eyes . . . . I don't know how to express my gratitude to you for not reporting the police and coming to me to inform my daughter's most dangerous attempt. Sir, I really feel it is important to have a woman in the house to take the responsibility of my daughter. Thank you sir, I am very grateful to your help."

Shoilen wanted to return to Soro as early as possible after experiencing a dangerous attempt of robbery. He took leave of him and went to the gate. By that time the Neelo Sena gang had surrounded the taxi driver and trying to get information. He warned them that he may go to police to give a complaint.

When Shoilen and Damodar reached there, they quickly went away from the car and asked Damodar with sincere sympathy about his health. He saw them with angry look and shouted:

"I must thrash all of you for bringing a very bad name to me and my daughter. I am warning you if I see any one of you again near my house I will not hesitate even to kill you . . . . get away from this place . . . you bastards"

They were all stunned at his outburst. To their horror the Pathan from Kolkota took him aside and warned him pointing to their friend Guddu. They all immediately ran helter-skelter and vanished on their bikes without looking back. They could immediately understand their venture failed, and were nervous that they were in danger of being taken by the police.

Shoilen sat in the car after parting Damodar. He told the driver to go to Soro. The driver was also happy that he decided not to give complaint to the police. He decided not to question him about the incident again. Shoilen paid the driver as he got down at a distance from his hotel at Soro. When he found car departed in another direction, he went to his hotel. As soon he reached the room he bolted the door and counted the cash he was surprised to find only Seven lakhs Rupees were there, instead of Eight. He could understand Damodar must have paid seven lakhs only as he did not count. He rushed to his room get that one lakh. As the amount was still shorter by one lakh he suspected Neelobeni might have kept that amount. He decided not to question him again, as that amount of Seven Lakhs was an unexpected bonus from Damodar after getting Thirty lakhs without much serious effort from Bishwonadh!. He rang Lolit and narrated his gain as well his dangerous experience. He cautioned him to be careful from Damodar's daughter Neelobeni.

*   *   *

CHAPTER 7

Sunonda shocked to know Lolita's secret!

Whole of Das's family were in real happy mood in the evening as Lolita whom they all hated, found to be good at heart. They never expected her to be so broad minded and gave costly gifts to all the members of the family, from elders to children, without forgetting any one. They were really sympathetic towards her as she was in dark about her newly married husband, who was seriously ill and died in native town Soro, without contacting his loved wife even once!. He did not tell her whereabouts of his family. All that had become a bad old chapter in her life, now they were happy she would be leading a new life in Odisha. They made all preparations for her second marriage to be conducted in the temple next day.

After a nice dinner all the ladies surrounded her and continued to chitchat for a long time. Only Sunonda and Lolita were restless to go to bed. Sunonda became closest friend to Lolita!; she was treating her like a queen always ready to help even for minor service. She was over joyful for all the costly gifts she got from Lolita. She was eagerly waiting for her last day's gift. She was also sad that next day she would go away with her husband. Only solace was she would not be very far away.

When they returned to Lolita's bedroom, as soon she bolted the door both hugged each other with deep affection. Sunonda found Lolita only likes her and enjoys in her company only and happy to hold her close to her and always felt happy to hold her hand.

Lolita went to the dressing table brought a new lady's hand bag and presented her. Even though she was a bit disappointed, that on the last day she gave only a hand bag instead of Gold ornament. But she did not show her true feeling but praised her with expression joyful smile. Lolita asked her to open the bag to see the contents.

When Sunonda opened the new big hand bag, to her utter surprise two thick bundles of Five hundred rupees notes, a nice gem studded gold ring and a new cute mobile phone. She was awe struck with her new gifts. She fell on Lolita's feet and bowed her with high respect. Lolita sat by her side on the bed and fitted the new gold ring with love. She took out the bundles of 500 rupee notes and kept in her hand stating the one lakh rupees for her to purchase anything or put in fixed deposit in bank for future use. When she kept the cute mobile in her hand; she was overjoyed at owning a cell phone which was her cherished desire. She dialed a number, when it was ringing she handed to Sunonda to hear and talk. She was joyful to hear her husband talking. Happily she told him about the cash of one lakh, the Gold ring and also a nice cell phone. Her husband also felt very happy to hear her. He also talked to thank her and promised to help her for any assistance.

He gave her the sweets as it was getting late. Sunonda ate one sweet only as she was full with many sweets in the dinner.

When she removed her sari and blouse to wear the night dress, Lolita told her that new dress was not available as all the dresses were given. She went to her with happy feeling and brought her to bed with least covers!. she requested to sleep like that only. In spite her request not to, Lolita lightly massaged her body with love, stating that she would feel very relaxed after a massage. Sunonda felt rely relaxed and felt more sleepy due to the drugged sweet.

Lolit became uncontrollably passionate with her uncovered body. He felt very happy to massage her entire body. It gave him hot satisfaction to feel her well-shaped body. Even though Sunonda was feeling shy to get massaged by her, yet seeing her loving attitude she accepted it to please her whims. She could not control her happy giggles when she pressed her body at different parts!.

As she became unconscious he took her very closely. Day by day he was feeling new thrills enjoying her. In day time he used to feel happy remembering the night's joys.

Latter in the night Lolit became exhausted with his escapades. He also fell into sound sleep.

On that day Sunonda got up in the night feeling thirsty. She opened her eyes and shocked to find that she was lying over her Lolita!. She was tightly holding her as if in tight embrace!. With much effort she was able to slide by her side. In the dim night lamp she was surprised to find that Lolita was wearing a hair wig, which came out showing her a cropped male hair!. With further curiosity when she found his body: she was shocked to learn that Lolita was a man in woman's dress!.

She became aware what happened in the night. She was shaken with horror! . . . She shuddered and was about to shriek! . . . when she suddenly she realized that she spent with him all the six days and till today she never had suspected or felt a male presence whole night. She put a hand on the mouth and looking at him with wide eyed anguish unable to decide her next step!. She was frightened and sat as how to expose him. She became angry and nervous for being cheated. She decided to go out of the room and wake the other members and expose the man in the guise of woman as their daughter in-law!.

When she tried to stand still he was holding her hand even in the sleep. She found she was almost nude! She realized that she cannot go out like that. She had to wear her sari. In the mirror she saw her nicely made up face with a nice hair style also her face still glowing with creams, rosy cheeks with Rouge lips with lipstick!. She realized it will take long time to get properly dressed to go out from the bed room!. She started to fear that he may get up and will not allow her to reveal about him. He might even threaten her that she was aware all the days and tonight she was annoyed for not getting a gift she demanded.

She sat again as tears started and trembling with fear. Suddenly the man in Lolita's dress started to talk in the sleep. He was smiling and calling her with love, praising her beautiful body and sweet smile. She was suddenly could not control her smile as he went on talking in sleep, praising her beauty.

Suddenly she realized how much he loved her and cared for her. He gave very costly gifts only to show his love. All these days she was respecting him and showered all her affection. She found some how she was also bodily drawn to him without her knowledge. She only requested him to allow her to sleep on the same bed all the week. She realized if he exposes him he would expose her. He may run away but her life would become miserable and every one would suspect her only. She also realized previous all the earlier days he got up in the morning. If she woke up like that way she never could found his real identity, even this day. She could never have found this secret. She could not understand why he accepted to marry a man! Suddenly she remembered that Lolita had a twin brother. This might be her brother.

She finally determined to keep the secret within her. She decided not to expose him and get herself into troubles.

Gradually she started liking him again. He was always nice to her and presented costly gifts to her, She never asked but he was lovingly treating her and generously gave costly gifts only to her. She realized that she herself was really longing to go after him attracted by his charm. He was always a well behaved nice person respecting as well keeping her in good humor even when he behaved with bad manners with all others!.

She decided firmly to forget what she discovered but behave as if nothing happened this night also. Unknowingly she felt a soft corner for him. No one ever gave her so many costly gifts and showed loving deep affection. If he was only after her body he could have enjoyed ruthlessly and left her with least caring!. She found that he was good hearted and sincere person, only took advantage due her initiative and behaved with loving care. She liked him and decided to keep the same relationship as before.

She felt happy at her decision. She gently went back to sleep by his side. She lovingly adjusted his wig and sari. She felt a happy feeling. She embraced him and kissed him with some urge. But she could not sleep. She realized that she also liked him in her heart. After an hour Lolit got up and found she was embracing him tightly. He became very passionate and started to enjoy her with uncontrollable lust. She was awake but pretended to be in deep sleep. She also enjoyed his love. Lolit found even in her deep sleep she was responding to him positively making more enjoyable night. He even had mild suspicion that she may be awake but he found she was snoring and in deep sleep. She made his last night more memorable!.

*   *   *

Suddenly Lolit woke up on Saturday, with touch of wet lips on his face. He forgot to put alarm in the night. Sunonda's face was close to his face and looking at him with a sexy way and kissing him happily!. For a moment he forgot to be careful forgetting his role. He took her very tight and kissed her to his heart's content. Sunonda got up and in a sweet way "Lolita Deedee I also wish that night should have been more longer, unfortunately morning came earlier!. now please get up get ready as you are the bride today!."

She told with a giggling laugh.

As Sunondo was about to wear her Sari, Lolit went to her to embrace tightly and kissed on her lips as if both were lovers!. She also held him putting her head on his shoulders and weeping profusely. Finally she whispered in his ear:

"Lolita please don't forget me when you go back to Kolkota please talk to me sometimes . . . on the phone"

Lolit laughed

"Sunonda dear you are forgetting that I will stay in Rupsa in Odisha very close to Soro! . . . I will never forget you in my entire life . . . You are really sweetest and prettiest girl I ever met . . . . If I were a man I would have kidnapped you and taken to Kolkota!"

Sunonda giggled in an uncontrollable way as if it was a big joke!. She shyly moved as Lolit was passionately caressing her lovingly and kissing her body unable to control his passion.

"Lolita let me go . . . or somebody may call me . . . it is already late!"

She dressed and left the room happily remembering her night experiences. Lolit became aware that he forgot his role and he exceeded his limits and holding her as if she was his close lover!. He grinned thinking that poor girl never suspected him that he was a man. He was remembering the nice experiences of the previous night.

They all went to the temple at eight in the morning. Damodar phoned him earlier day as well that day morning. He engaged a taxi for whole day to return by evening. As it was no longer a secret he told his daughter Neelobeni about his decision to marry Lolita on Saturday. She was still was not talking freely with him. She was hardly responding to him since the day he slapped her. She told in a serious way that she would not come to Soro. Damodar was worried how his daughter would re act seeing Lolita as her step mother. He thought she would gradually change and accept her.

The wedding took place in a simple way. It was conducted by a Pandit engaged by Das's family. One of Das's uncles did Kanya-Daan as per the marriage ritual.

After the wedding was over, Lolita asked him secretly whether he purchased Gold ornaments as told to her father. He held her hand and sheepishly told that since his earlier wife's ornaments were there, they would be hers only once they reach their home. She immediately pushed his hand and expressed her anger. She told him with almost tears that she was unlucky in both of her marriages that she never got present of new ornaments from her husbands, except garland at the wedding time. She took out her garland and threw it on the floor. Damodar was shocked at his new wife's angry reaction immediately after the wedding!. Luckily there were no other person were in the vicinity. He pleaded that he would give his first wife's ornaments as well as money to buy new ornaments. As she was still unconvinced he took an oath that he will abide by the promise, that he would give the money in his house. To Damodar, it looked like an inauspicious to start a married life as his new wife threw the garland which they exchanged in the wedding time. He started to feel whether he took the right decision to marry Lolita in a hurry!. He started to worry whether he would have a happy married life with her.

After the wedding was over before mid-day, Das's family invited the bride and groom to have lunch in their house. Almost every one expressed that they would miss Lolita after she leaves with her husband. All were impressed by her costly gifts which she gave previous evening. Damodar gave a cheap quality clothes to Das's father and mother. However he presented a very costly silk sari to his bride.

The marriage was over within an hour. Lolit was annoyed at seeing a photographer requesting for a photo of the bride and groom. Bishwanadh quietly informed him, her father Tejuddeen sent the photographer, as he did not wish to enter the temple. Lolit relented as Dada was trying to keep a record of the wedding, for some different reason!. He just smiled at his foresight!.

After the Wedding completed, all reached Bishwanadh's house for lunch. Lolit brought, from Shoilen, a heavy old type of sheet metal clothes box earlier. He had his valuable travelling suit case and a bag. He filled all his sarees, dresses, accessories and makeup articles in his suite case. He even kept the expensive saree which Damodar gave to him, in that suit case.

Before leaving, Lolit took Sunonda to his room bolting the door. He embraced her with a real feeling of pain of separation with her. He really started falling in love with her. He was touched by her nice attitude of transparent affection. He was most impressed with her out-standing beautiful figure. He really loved the happy nights he spent with her. He felt a pang of painful feeling of losing her for ever after that day.

Surprisingly she accepted his deep kisses on her lips and face, as well his lustful fondling her body unashamedly. She also responded with a wild show of love!. Both of them shed real tears with separation.

Sunonda also felt curious how he would manage to live as a wife with Damodar!. She knew he would run away to Kolkata, may be secretly. She controlled her amusement with difficulty when she was seeing the marriage being performed seriously between two men!. One male dressed as a bride and seriously following the rituals with a shy bearing! Whenever Lolit saw Sunonda, both exchanged happy smiles. Lolit was surprised to see sunoda was secretly laughing putting her sari to cover her laugh, seeing Damodar as the groom!. He could not understand why that simple lady exhibiting suppressed laughter!.

He felt she might have found out truth about him while sharing bed and decided to keep the secret within her!. He put aside the suspicion but respected her wisdom; that even after knowing his secret yet she kept that discovery within her!. He told Sunonda to take his suitcase as a gift. She happily accepted with a joyful expression.

He came out and requested Damodar to bring the heavy metal box to the taxi. **He** whispered that all his cash, gold and clothes are all in that box for safety. Damodar most happily struggled to carry that box to the taxi. Lolit held his bag in his hand. Everyone were in tears when as she started her journey with her husband by Taxi. All blessed her heartily when she bowed every one and took leave from them.

They both sat in the car. Lolita took out her dark glasses and wore them during travel. Damodar felt happy to see his well-dressed modern wife. Damodar was satisfied his wife had brought a metal box with her cash and valuables. On way he was boasting about his property and his desire to open a restaurant, his nice life at Kolkota etc. She lovingly asked him in a seductive way that he must give at least three lakhs rupees as they reach, to buy new gold ornaments and clothes for her and their daughter. He was happy to hear that his wife cared for his daughter. He readily accepted holding her hand and promised to hand over her wish as soon they reach the house. Lolit was showing false affection, to keep him in good humor. She lovingly spoke in a soft voice to him, requesting never to send her to her father's house, even if he tells, as she cannot think of living without him even for a day. As they were on the high way she told him in his ears that all the young ladies were envious of her luck to get such nice handsome groom, requested never go after other women!. He felt happy at her wife's fear!. He laughed and said in her ears why he would prefer another lady when so beautiful lady like a sculpture of Konark became his wife!. He added that he would guard her like precious diamond, and worship her feet!. Both openly laughed at each other love thoughts. Lolit demurely whispered that she wished to see Konark. Puri and Bhubaneshwar, as it was her lifelong desire. He happily promised to take her within that month.

He felt very delighted to hear how much she already started loving him as a good wife. Lolita said she was feeling sleepy as she could not get good sleep, due to her anxiety before the marriage. Lolit rested his head on one side, lifted his both feet and rested them on his lap to relax within that narrow space, and fell into sleep. Damodar was very happy to see his beloved wife resting his legs on him!. He continued to hold Lolita's feet with loving care and joyful feeling. As the taxi was nearing his town he started worrying as to how his daughter would receive them. He kept an old lady in the house to escort her in his absence.

Neelobeni was much annoyed at her father's ill treatment to her while she tried to save his cash being taken away by that Pathan. She was horrified to learn his bad choice to marry Lolita and bring her home on Saturday. She felt she would not be able to live in the house with a step mother. Four days before she decided to run away from home and join the Circus Company. She was in constant touch with them over the phone. She came to know the Circus Company had come to Brahmapur of Odisha. She determined to join the Circus, whether her father approves or not. She forged his signature stating his no objection of his daughter joining the circus company on three years contract. She spoke on the phone with the manager that she would like to join them at Brahmapur. She said she would bring the no objection letter from father. Manager readily accepted and asked her to come immediately; as a local girl of Odisha would be helpful for canvassing purpose. Latter he decided to train her in some department. He was impressed with her tall healthy personality.

She kept forty thousand to take with her and hidden the rest Sixty; as she was to deposit Thirty thousand with that company. Being a bold girl from childhood she did not feel any fear of going away from home to join the Circus. She knew she has to work hard for some months. She decided run away in her father's absence. She took Guddu, her right hand person, to escort her and to return after she joins the company. She got her train tickets through another friend from Baleshwar to Brahmapur of Ganjam district. She did her marketing and packed her bag secretly beforehand. On Saturday early hour her father went away by taxi giving instructions to her how she should behave and keep the house well etcetra.

She nodded all quietly without any argument. An old lady came before to give company. At eight she was well dressed and ready. She handed her suitcase to her friend at the back door. She told the old lady that she has to go to school, and left from the front door not even hearing her questions. She told her to bolt the door till she comes for lunch. While leaving she handed a letter in a cover. She told her to hand over that letter to her father. She informed the letter was from his friend.

By late evening Damodar arrived with his wife Lolita in a jolly mood. The house was quiet. He called loudly for Neelu, but there was no response. He went to front door and knocked, calling Neelu. The old lady slowly opened the door with a happy smile seeing him and his beautiful new bride. She told that Neelu went to School in the morning and so far not yet returned. He was worried at that information. He feared she must have gone with her friends in some bad errand. But he kept quiet lest wife gets worried. Lolit entered the house with his traveling bag. He was taken aback by the dirty interior of the house. He inspected the two bed rooms, front sitting room and back dining room and the kitchen. All the rooms were small and equally badly maintained. Only the girl's room was better with posters and decent furniture and a T.V. Lolit found the bath and toilet were located in the back yard. As Shoilen informed there was a back door in the compound. It was getting darker. Lolita sat in the front room, and reminded him of his oath that he would give three lakhs rupees and his late wife's ornaments after reaching home.

When he tried to tell that he would do it in the morning, Lolita got up angrily and said that she would sit in the front verandah only and not enter the house till he kept his promise. As she rose hurriedly tried to open and go out, he tenderly held his bride's hand and said he would give that amount and ornaments immediately; he requested her to wait. He went to his bed room and bolted the door and took out the cash and his first wife's ornaments. He came to front room where Lolita was standing. With a smile he handed the cash and ornaments to her. She was joyful to receive them she hugged him with affection, to express her happiness. She held him close as they went to his bed room. She happily lied on the bed as a satisfied wife.

He sat on the bed near his bride's feet. As Lolita asked him to get a cup of tea, he went in, prepared the tea himself and brought to her with some snacks. The old lady was in the kitchen. Lolit kept the cash and ornaments in his bag and took his drugged sweets from his bag within that time.

When Damodar came with tea Lolit asked him with a happy smile to sit on the bed to enjoy tea with him. He hugged him with a loving care and said how happy he was to be married to a nice man with a sweet daughter.

Damodar felt very happy at his caring wife. When the bride told him tenderly, that In Bengal there is a custom that bride must first give sweets with her hand to husband and others in the house to bring a cordial relationship, he happily accepted gleefully. Lolit took a sweet and put in his mouth tenderly. As he happily eaten it, Lolit took another sweet again put in his mouth. She bent and touched his feet with reverence.

Lolita asked when his daughter would come.

"Don't worry she may come at any time."

She took another two sweets to give to the old lady who was the only guest. When Lolita put two sweets in her mouth she was very happy. Then she bent and touched her feet also. The old lady suddenly remembered about the cover which Neelobeni gave to hand over to Damodar. She gave that to Sunanda telling whatever his daughter told. Lolit opened the letter with curiosity but found it was written in Odiya script. He decided to put that letter near him before leaving.

Lolit took his bag and said he would have a bath and change his clothes in his daughter's bed room. She requested to rest in the bed till then. He went to the back yard and gave a ring to Shoilen who followed them in another car. He changed his makeup to an old respectful man. He told with a grin.

"Dada this is Charulota alias Fairooza alias Lolita alias Lolit speaking . . . In another half hour I will come out from the back door. I will reach railway station and sit in the waiting room. I feel suffocated in this silly Damodar's dirty house . . . I don't know how he prefers to live in such surroundings after staying in Kolkota for so many years!"

Shoilen laughingly taunted:

"Lolita! . . . you should not criticize your legally married second husband! Who knows you may get some part of his property as his wife! . . . I hope Damodar presented you the Jewelry"

Lolit laughed and said "Oh God!. Dadaa you really think of future also . . . I knew why you sent a photographer to take pictures during wedding time . . . you had planned it before?!"

"No CharuLota . . . . it was a last minute's thought, I did not have time to inform you . . . thank god as the bride first you objected . . . but latter you relented . . . . with a sentiment that Tejudden would not enter a temple as such he sent a photographer . . . to see his daughter's wedding photos with Damodar Sahu . . . OK how about ornaments gift?"

"Dada he presented his first wife's ornaments and two lakhs cash for purchasing new jewelry!"

He told with a little laugh. He did not tell three lakhs as he wanted to replace the one lakh, which he gave to Sunonda a lakh from their common kitty.

"Crook Damodar cheated us one lakh! . . . we have to accept minor losses! . . . I will also reach the Railway station"

He said in his usual style of jocular remark.

"Ok Dada I will start as soon that silly stupid goes to sleep. He would happily dream of a happy life with his loved new wife!".

Both laughed.

After finishing his talk Lolit bolted the front door and put off the light, lest his daughter returns. He saw Damodar was unconscious, lying on the bed snoring. He found the old lady was also in deep sleep in the dining room. He quickly changed his dress to his normal men's dress. He left sari and Lady's under garments near the well in the back court yard. He carried only his traveling bag with him, leaving the locked heavy metal box in Damodar's room. If he greedily gets it open, he would find it filled with some bricks and old newspapers!.

After opening the back door, he found no one in the vicinity. Lolit managed to find his way to the road. He took a cycle Riksha to the Rupsa railway station, for his onward journey to Howrah station of Kolkota, along with his friend Shoilen. He looked in his normal way as a smart young man wearing a nice T-shirt. He had a only a small French beard extra without moustache. He was carrying small travelling bag with him; he had his sandals as before. (Not of Ladies type with small high Heels).

*   *   *

LIST OF CHARACTERS
AND IMPORTANT NAMES
MENTIONED IN THE NOVEL

1. Shoilen Dutta: A veteran stage actor of Kolkata.
2. Lolit Sen: Handsome Actor and all-rounder in Theater and Dramas, close friend of Shoilen Dutta.
3. Charulota: Name of a heroine in a play.
4. Rashbehari Avenue: A prominent road of South Kolkata.
5. Maniktala: A locality of Kolkata.
6. Chenchal Reddy: A film producer from Hyderabad.
7. Shyam-Bazar: A prominent Road and locality of North Kolkata.
8. Manjulota Mojumdar—A fictitious name of a lady actor. (Publicity name of a lady actor done by Lolit.)
9. Baijoyonti: Ficticious bride's name (Lolit's disguise)
10. Madhuwonti: name of the pregnant lady passenger (Lolit's Disguise)
11. Kalichron Kundu: A document Writer of Medinipur.
12. Medinipur.: (a large Town of West Bengal.)
13. Jogesh Maity—a document writer of Medinipur, under whom Kalicharon worked.
14. Gobindo Laha—a false name of Kalichron Kundu.

15. Gadhador Kar—another false name of Kalicharon.
16. Romakanto Choudhari—a rich business man of Medinipur.
17. Chandramoni Debi—Mistress (Concubine) of Ramakanto Choudhari.
18. 'Kedargowri'—an old mansion in Medinipur, owned by Ramakantho Choudhari, Chandramoni Debi resides in that building with her mother.
19. Mohunbagan team: A renowned Football club of Kolkata.
20. 'Kenilworth Hotel': A popular five star hotel near park street of Kolkata.
21. Durjoy Basak—A person with nefarious activities. He is the mentor to Chandramoni Debi,(calls himself as her uncle.)
22. Sona-Gachi: A large Red-light area of Kolkata.
23. Brindavan: A piligrimage city in U.P.India (Brindavan-Mathra)
24. 'Sonar Bangla': A famous hotel in Kolkata.
25. Benugopal Sur—a building contractor.
26. Pramod Chandro Ghosal.—A rich propertied person of Medinipur.
27. Malothi Debi—wife of Pramod Chandro Ghosal.
28. Ruma—Second daughter of Pramod Chandro Ghosal.
29. Chandon—Husband of Ruma.
30. Panihati ferry ghat.—A mooring jetty platform for boats in river Hooghly in Kolkata.
31. Debjani: A resdent of Jyotsna Bhawan.
32. 'Help Bank': A fictitious name of a Bank
33. Nilesh Sanyal—an officer of 'Help bank' in Kolkata.
34. Jnanedra Guha.—owner of an old two storied building in Beadon Street area.
35. Beniprosad—(Fictitious name of Shoilen Dutta)

36. Notta Ronjito Bongo Kala Manch—Fictitious name of Bengali theatrical group.

37. Ujwolita—Fictitious name of Lolit in a woman's disguise.

38. Manonmoni Debi—Chandramoni Debi's second name, after shifting to Allahabad.

39. 42, Jyotsna Bhawan, Gaurav Sanyal lane off Dhani Ghosh Sarani (part Beadon steet), Kolkata. (His phone No is 01221012210. (All imaginary addresses)

40. Deepankar Chaterjee: Name of a Police officer (shoilen's disguise)

41. 'Sundor-Bonita': A fictitious Beauty parlor, of Park street.

42. Rupali: fictitious name which Lolit used as a lady from 'Sundor Bonita' beauty parlor.

43. 'Zen' and 'Park Plaza': Two famous restaurants of Ballyganj of Kolkata'

44. 'Mocambo' and 'Bluzz': Popular restaurants in Park street Kolkata.

45. Dhananjoy Roye: A registered Stock exchange broker (Real name of Durjoy).

46. Flury's: A famous bakery in Park Street of Kolkata.

47. 'Yatadura mane pare: Rajanaitika atmakathana': a book written by Late Shri Jyothi Basu.

48. Suchitra: Fictitious name of a Lady. (Latter the police used as 'Operation-Suchitra'

49. Bichitra: a Lady police officer.

50. Mohammad Fateh Khan: Durjoy escapes with that false name.

51. Raheela Begam: an occupant of Jyotsna Bhawan.

52. Jyotsna Bhavan: A fictitious old building near Beadon street.

53. Debjani: a resident of Jyotsana bhavan.

54. Bonomali Das—a friend of Shoilen and Lolit in theater group.

55. Soro: A small town in Baleswar district of Odisha, home town of Bonomali Das.

56. Biswanadh Das: Bonamali das's father.

57. Damodar Sahu: Friend of Bonamali Das, used to work in Kolkata and returned to his Rupsa.

58. Neelobeni alias Neelu: Daughter of Damodar Sahu.

59. Rupsa: A small town of Baleswar district of Odisha, home town of Damodar Sahu.

60. Lolita: Lolit disguises as a fictitious woman.

61. Tejuddreen Rehman: Shoilen's disguised role as father of Lolita.

62. Fairooza: Lolit's disguiseas Tezuddeen's daughter who changes to Lolita.

63. Hotel Manorama: hotel in Soro town, where Tejuddeen stays.

64. Fairooza: another fictitious false name of Lolit as a muslim girl before Lolita name.

65. Sunonda: Bonomali's cousin brother's wife.

66. Pijush Mukherji—a young lawyer of Soro town.

67. Mayadhar: Husband of Sunonda, cousin of Bonomali.

About the Author

The Author of 'Transparent Shadows'—M.V.S.Rao, is from Hyderabad. His first English novel 'The Fork' (ISBN 9781449037949) published in UK/US (Dec 2009). Earlier Two Telugu novels were published. M.V.S.Rao, is an Architect by profession now turned to writing. He visited different cities and various countries. He is a senior citizen.

Books by the same author

*The Fork
(English Fiction)

*Rathnamabaa Muthyamabaa
(Telugu Fiction)

*Sammohini
(Telugu Fiction)

AUTHOR'S NOTE

I have created the next part of this book as 'Transparent Shadows 2' as sequel to this novel. The main anchors of this novel's stories, Shoilen Datta and Lolit Sen, will come forward with some more of their hilarious frolics to entertain you in more episodes!. You may also see what might haunt them if they get into slippery circumstances or might lose transparency of their shadows by their own misdeeds!.

I sincerely wish to convey my apologies if there some grammatical mistakes or other erroritcal language expressions, which might have come out unknowingly!. I wrote the way I could express, to convey my stories to entertain my readers. I wrote this novel with Kolkata as background, out of deep respect for the Bengali Culture and Theatre.

M.V.S.Rao, (Author)